The Gospel of Now

The Gospel of Now

Brandon Pitts writing as
Simon Occulis

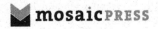 mosaicPRESS

Library and Archives Canada Cataloguing in Publication

Title: The Gospel of Now / Brandon Pitts writing as Simon Occulis.

Names: Occulis, Simon, 1967- author.

Identifiers: Canadiana (print) 20220173672 |
            Canadiana (ebook) 20220173702 |
ISBN 9781771616249 (softcover) | ISBN 9781771616256 (PDF) |
ISBN 9781771616263 (EPUB) | ISBN 9781771616270 (Kindle)

Classification: LCC PS8631.I882 G67 2022 | DDC C813/.6—dc23

Published by Mosaic Press, Oakville, Ontario, Canada, 2022.

MOSAIC PRESS, Publishers
www.Mosaic-Press.com

Copyright © Brandon Pitts 2022

MOSAIC PRESS
1252 Speers Road, Units 1 & 2, Oakville, Ontario, L6L 5N9
(905) 825-2130 • info@mosaic-press.com • www.mosaic-press.com

BOOKS BY BRANDON PITTS

Pressure to Sing
Tender in the Age of Fury
In the Company of Crows

CRITICAL ACCLAIM

The Gospel of Now:

"...it's excellent. An original, fast-moving narrative. Terrific writing."

Joyce Wayne — former editor, *Quill & Quire,*
author, Last Night of the World

A great punk rock coming-of-age story set in Eastern Washington in the 1980s – then emerging as a satellite to the nascent Seattle music scene hub. Hormonal teenage angst meets radioactive rabbit shit as wayward youth contemplate life, jobs, and the future — and escaping the drudgery of their nuclear-bomb-producing factory town.

Wez Lundry — *Thrasher Magazine*

The Gospel of Now is a book our turbulent, mutating world needs right now, and in the peculiar days to come. **Occulis** conjures a riveting story with timeless themes, and places it in a historic time and place in the mid to late 80's, during the first stirrings of the movement that became known as "Grunge." The Gospel of Now is a rare, addictive book you won't be able to read just once. Prepare yourself for an unforgettable journey.

Stedmond Pardy — author, *The Pleasures of*
This Planet Aren't Enough

Occulis:

Simon Occulis writes a vision of words in the same way that stars compose constellations. The work is not of his time. His writing is both a thousand years past and well into the future, even though he's writing of you and me today. That's what great writers do. Is he a great writer? Find out for yourself, but don't bother to tell me cause I already know.

> **Norman Cristofoli** — publisher, *Labour of Love poetry journal*, author, *Relinquishing the Past and The Pub*

Occulis sees the world through a different lens. He translates these feelings and interpretations by utilizing language that is both familiar, yet not. He builds his own world, in the same way David Mamet and Sam Shepard create habitats for their subjects, then allows the reader to experience the world through fresh eyes.

> **Duane Kirby Jensen** — curator of *Everett Poetry Night*, artist, poet, and publisher

The way in which **Occulis** engages multiple facets of the arts brings a vivid energy to his work. His proficiency in spoken word creates a living, conversational energy in his writing; his honed writing creates a particular depth in his spoken word. Further, his work with visual art enhances the imagery in both his printed work and verbal recitations, making them especially transportational. His awareness of political and social issues creates a satiric wit in his words that allows him to directly engage a wide range of topics in our culture. This work in multiple mediums gives the art of **Simon Occulis** such a dynamic and vibrant quality.

> **Paul Edward Costa** — Poet Laureate for the City of Mississauga, 2019-2021

Poetry, written as Brandon Pitts:
Pressure to Sing:

(Pressure to Sing) raises the bar to a level that we haven't seen in decades. A bar that should inspire other poets and writers to reach for.

Carolina Smart — *Lipstik Indie*

A collection of poems written with that undone spirituality you can only get from an irreverent wizard… or a genuinely enlightened hitchhiker.

Origo Books

Tender in the Age of Fury:

Pitts' work is visceral, political, irreverent, historical, biblical, romantic, vulgar, and lyrical. You really need to hear those words and rhythms.

Blogger **Cathy McKim** — *Life With More Cowbell*

Here is that rarest of things in poetry these days: a unique voice.

Jim Christy — author of *The Long Slow Death of Jack Kerouac*

Pitts displays a Frostian command of the American vernacular.

Benjamin Schmitt — *At The Inkwell*

In the Company of Crows:

An ingenious poet who interrogates the oracles.

James Dewer — *Piquant Press*

For my father, Gerald Pitts (1937-2021)
who told me crazy stories about the Hanford Site and was
looking forward to seeing this book published.

CONTENTS

Our town was made famous by making the plutonium for that "Fat Man" they dumped on Nagasaki back in 1945. If it weren't for Hanford, we'd be a small farming community with a single traffic light, or an out-of-the-way place where congress might've put an Indian reservation.

CHAPTER 1

VITAMIN R

The day I quit taking Ritalin, I realized I was fucked.

Eighteen, uneducated, and dependent on a drug I couldn't afford without my father's health insurance—I was already a loser.

Could've tried harder, but what was the point? It was 1986, and my generation was the first in a century that wouldn't do as well as their parents. The music sucked, the clothes were shitty, and everything people valued seemed ridiculous. This is what happens when you elect a movie star as president.

Life used to be different. I was a happy kid and felt good about myself. I was cool with Christ and enjoyed going to church until I was old enough to be called upon to read from the bible. That's when trouble began.

My father sat like a despot, surrounded by darkness, one light over the table to save electricity, watching.

"Mathew 5:5," he said.

"Blee-ed ar te mek, fer the inhart to ert."

This was not the first time he whipped me.

There was school, and teachers who wanted to fix me. Evaluations with psychologists and spirit sucking tutoring sessions while the rest of the kids were outside playing.

I would look out the window, ignoring my hideous reflection to see kids hanging from the jungle gym, kicking balls, and throwing sand. "Focus, Deacon."

Even the church got involved, our pastor presiding over counseling sessions with elders who had watch over my soul. Strangers, placing hands on my body with their eyes closed. "Heavenly Father, we pray that Your spirit moves though Deacon. We ask that You heal his mind of sin so that he can focus and read."

I would squirm when an elder's touch felt too intimate, only to be pinched by my parents. "Be still."

Tutors and teachers made me feel bad about myself too. "Okay, Deacon, try and sound out each letter."

"Si Jeen ra... nnn."

I did my best, only to have them correct me for the millionth time. It confirmed the obvious: that I would never be able to read phonetically, spell, or be successful in school. How could I? Letters always move, my brain corrupts them, making words jumbled.

These well-intentioned teachers merely confirmed that I was worthless.

Each session, each evaluation, and each prayer pushed me further down until I started lashing out at anyone foolish enough to help me. I was unhinged, interrupting the classroom while making every adult's life hell.

Distracting classmates, kicking chairs, violent meltdowns, destroying textbooks, innovating new and exciting ways to disrupt—aggravate—and take control of my defeat. I would choose to fail, rather than be born disabled from dyslexia.

I'd cruised like this until the fifth grade, out of control, until I found myself lying in a doctor's office, EEG electrodes pasted to my head, a nurse with a clipboard taking notes, and then the psychiatrist's diagnosis—accompanied by a bottle full of buffered tablets engraved with CIBA/34.

This will help Deacon concentrate.

This will help him to spell.

See him read from the bible.

He can now show his work in math.

The medication did its job. I got through the school day in a haze, doing what I was told. It only took a week to accept the fact that I was stupid and that this was how it was going to be. I can't recall being happy much since.

The idea to quit the meds came during family prayer. I was baked and realized Ritalin was more potent than pot, and not in a good way. It was controlling me. I had my eyes closed when it entered my brain like a message from Jesus.

Or possibly Satan, prodding me to go out and spread evil.

I opened my eyes to a bowl of bright-colored loops, piled high like an island surrounded by a milky moat. Next to the cereal was a diarrhea-brown bottle with an officious label, obliterating the authority I had over my body.

I slipped the pill into my pocket while Jesus watched, and my father prayed. "Through Christ, our Lord, we humbly offer thanks for this nutritious food that You have bestowed."

Before I quit the meds, I was too stoned on Ritalin to realize I lacked the freedoms other people had. I'd never been on a date, never been laid, never broken the law. I wasn't allowed to watch TV because it was rampant with loose morals and pre-marital sex. I was never allowed to listen to music, except white gospel. Anything with a beat was the mark of the devil. They even excused me from reading John Steinbeck's "Of Mice and Men" at school because it used words like "bastard." Not that I could get through it anyway.

It took less than one Ritalin-free week for all that to change. I owe my rebellion to the best friend I ever had, Douglas "Bone" Reinhold.

Bone was the most stylish guy in school. No one recognized this, not even the school's self-proclaimed fashion diva, Adonai Garcia. But I knew it was true. Bone's approach was new and untested. Permed hair, pencil mustache like Clark Gable, silk scarf, and a leather jacket he had come across at the Salvation Army. He was as decadent as he was genius.

His hip philosophical stoner style owed much to his contempt for his father. Bone had come from a low brow Marine family bloated with patriotism. His dad, a retired Major, lorded over the house as if it were a barrack. Bone's sexually dubious clothes and smell of pot drove the old man insane. His parents were convinced, joining the military was Bone's only salvation. Their pressure was intense.

Bone's grandparents on his mother's side wanted him to go to college. Bone seemed unsure which option was worse. Growing up hadn't entered his mind. That was Bone. It was how he did things.

I was facing a similar predicament. With graduation in a week, I felt a suffocating pressure to pick a course in life. I didn't have any ambitions, and the options fate placed before me looked drab and unacceptable; a slow torture until you die.

There wasn't much future beyond the nuclear industry in our part of the world. We lived in Richland, Washington, surrounded by miles of desert and sagebrush, a four-hour drive from Seattle, and home to the Hanford Site, the world's largest radioactive waste heap.

Our town was made famous by making the plutonium for that "Fat Man" they dumped on Nagasaki back in 1945. If it weren't for Hanford, we'd be a small farming community with a single traffic light, or an out-of-the-way place where congress might've put an Indian reservation. But glowing tanks and split atoms have made us important.

It was a Sunday afternoon when Bone drove up on his Triumph Thunderbird. He'd spent his first two years of auto-shop restoring the motorcycle to its original glory. Bought the frame, rusted and wrecked, at a junkyard for thirty bucks—cash he'd stolen from his grandfather. It was so twisted that the shop teacher told him he'd wasted his money—it'd never run. But after much bending and welding through his sophomore and junior years, Bone finally rode the motorcycle off-campus. By the time we'd reached our senior year, it looked practically new.

I was pulling weeds in the front yard of our military-style house when Bone drove up. Since our freshman year, I hadn't been allowed to hang out with him. My folks considered him a sinner, so he would come by when they were at bible study.

He got off the bike with the confidence he always seemed to exude, his swagger radiating superior genetics out to the universe, calling all would-be mothers to scheme of ways to make him theirs. But this conflicted with Bone's core philosophy; no woman would ever get him into their clutches. He was incapable of commitment to anything but life—full tilt.

"Sup?" he said, the sun reflecting off his mirrored shades. He looked like a radioactive angel.

"Not much," I said, standing up, seeing how different we'd become over the years. We used to be the kids nobody wanted to hang with but were too busy playing GI-Joe to notice. Now he was this sex god, and I was a medicated bomb, dormant, about to explode.

He walked towards me, taking me in as if examining my aura. He arched his eyebrows over his sunglasses and frowned. "You look sick."

"I quit taking my meds Friday night," I said, laboring to push out the words. I was starting to feel queasy.

"Do your parents know?"

"What are they going to do, ram it down my throat?"

"Tell 'em Ritalin keeps you from Jesus," he smirked.

5

"Fuck that. I'm eighteen; I can do whatever I want." I threw down the hand shovel. "All this shit does is make my brains spin. Everybody can fuck off, especially the school."

"I don't know why they ever put you on that crap in the first place," Bone said, reaching into his jacket and pulling out a joint. "If you're going to alter your mental state, do it au natural." He inhaled then offered it to me. It felt like I was looking down on the scene from another dimension.

"No thanks," I said, pulling off my gloves and letting them drop to the grass. "I've spent the past ten years stoned."

He coughed and took another hit, talking while holding it in. "I always say, give the hyper kids pot to mellow them out, it's a lot safer than Ritalin. Reese Whitaker uses marijuana as a study aid, and he's gonna be valedictorian."

"No, I'm good. I just want my brain out of the mire." I put my hands into my pockets and kicked the shovel.

"Since when has a Ritalin kid ever achieved good grades? Never, so take a hit."

I watched Bone holding the joint.

Fuck it. I hit it, burning my lungs.

"Slow down," he said, laughing while I hacked. He grabbed the joint and drew it deep.

I took it back. "Ritalin is as strong pot," I said, already feeling the effects, "though it's a little different. You can concentrate better on Ritalin, but you get some crazy thoughts, and they come at you fast, more like that low-grade half-hit of crank we did."

"You mean the shit Reese cooked in the Chemistry Lab?"

"Exactly, but it's different. Doesn't give you the horrors."

"I had a bad trip on that shit too." Bone shook his head. "He's fuckin' lucky he didn't get caught."

"No one suspects him of anything. Pays to be smart."

"Well, he may be a genius, but he can't cook crank." Bone laughed. "If your parents knew you were getting high on Ritalin, I bet they'd never have put you on it."

"You know I have clear memories from when I was a kid, but the past ten years are a little foggy. I want that clarity back. It's like they've stolen something from me."

"They have, half your fucking life," said Bone, flicking the spent joint onto the asphalt. "And for what? So you can go to school, sit still, chew on what they serve? School is just a training ground for a sheepish workforce, teaching you to show up on time and work hard for nothing." He wiped his sweat and unzipped his leather jacket. "It's like coaxing a donkey with a carrot."

He looked down at the bag of picked weeds. "Hurry up and get done. You and I are going to a party."

I dropped to my knees and picked up the hand-shovel. Bunch of redneck jocks lurching about, looking to prey on the vulnerable, partying to Van Halen. Not my scene. "Who the fuck has a party on a Sunday afternoon?" I said, wrestling with a thistle.

"Carson."

Now I was intrigued. I'd always wanted to meet this guy. He published a zine and was notorious around town for bad behavior. "I thought you hated Carson?"

"I do," he said, getting on the bike, "but this is business. Carson is going to buy a keg off us."

"Where are we going to get a keg?"

Bone smirked and patted the gas tank. "Get on; we have to meet Fenix."

CHAPTER 2

THE OL' STALAG

Held back a grade, Bone's cousin, Collin Fenix, was older than us by a year. Since he was on his second run of twelfth grade, he only had half days. He spent the remainder of his time training to be a guard for weapons-grade plutonium. His real ambition was to be a cop, but his redneck personality and shit grades made him a better candidate for a career in security.

He was typical Richland: Bud Light in the twelve-pack. If the conversation favored Republican Conservatism and Reagan's Moral Majority, he loved discussing politics.

A fan of killing things, Fenix had a near-pornographic fetish with firearms and somehow equated gun violence with jingo patriotism. He would often say that the right to bear arms was what God used to separate His chosen people from Jews and those of color. According to Fenix, white male America is Jesus' anointed flock.

We met as kids in church. Back then, I thought he was pretty neat, but eventually understood he was a racist piece of shit. Through Fenix, I met Bone.

I didn't like Fenix, but he was somehow part of my world.

We found Fenix in the parking lot of a bar called The Ol' Stalag. Crusty nuclear waste workers lubed up there before the morning shift, then came to decompress and fill up with beer to pee out any rads their system might've collected on the job. The bar sat at the mouth of the desert highway that led to the Hanford Site. Why they called this bar the Ol' Stalag, I'll never know. Maybe it was because this town, surrounded by nuclear power plants and desert, was a fucking fascist prison.

Fenix was standing there, leaning up against his father's dirty old white Ford pickup. He wore a flannel shirt, Levi's with a faded chewing-tobacco-can ring on the right ass pocket, and a baseball cap that he never washed.

As we pulled into the parking lot, Fenix took out the can of Skoal and put a pinch between his lip and gums. "You fuckers are late. The lunch rush is almost over. If the cooks start cleaning up, we're fucked."

"Deacon had to pick weeds," said Bone.

"Wait," I said, "what are we doing here?"

"Stealing a keg," said Bone.

"You two are going in the back," said Fenix. "You just walk in and grab one as I drive up. They're stacked right next to the door."

Fenix and Bone moved into action. I just stood there, frozen.

"What's up?" said Bone.

"You didn't tell me we were stealing a keg," I said.

"Deacon, are you gonna be a loser forever?" Fenix slapped me on the chest with the back of his hand. "Let's go. Carson's waiting."

"What if we get caught? "I said. "It'll fuck up our future."

Bone turned to me, a strange look in his eye as if he was all-knowing. "We don't have a future. All we've got is now."

It was like Bone and Fenix were voodoo puppeteers. Even my friends controlled me. Would I ever have free will?

Bone was getting impatient. "Are you gonna do this, or do I have to lift that keg by myself?"

I hesitated. Every morning before I left the house, my mother would say, "Be sure, because your sin will find you out." Even if I didn't get caught, Jesus would know. Jesus was more omnipresent than Santa.

Then the evil ideas returned: Santa wasn't real. He was some bullshit designed to keep kids in line. Maybe Jesus was bullshit too? If thoughts were as sinful as deeds, I was already burning. "Alright," I said, "let's go."

Light, the color of vat oil, poured out of the back door. Bone and I strolled right in, the hum of hood fans drowning out our steps. I could feel punishing heat coming off the stove.

The cooks were so busy they didn't even notice us. They seemed overwhelmed and falling behind. Orders covered every inch of the long ticket holder above the vat.

My father always told me that low wage employees were lazy, that's why they work shitty jobs, but these two were sweaty and miserable. I'd never seen anyone work so hard.

Was this my future? Was this where the uneducated go, slaving for some fuck who collects the money, screaming at me because I couldn't read the tickets fast enough?

Bone slapped me on the arm, motioning towards a stack of kegs resting against the sidewall. He grabbed the top keg and tilted it for me to hold the bottom. My muscles ripped, lifting the barrel as I glanced back at the cooks preparing greasy dishes.

We waddled towards the door with the beer, my anxiety turning to adrenaline, flooding me with ecstasy I'd never felt before.

Was this what it was like to be alive?

Fenix pulled up, and we dropped the keg into the pickup with a loud clunk that I was sure the cooks would hear.

Bone jumped in. "Come on!" he said, helping me up.

Fenix drove straight to the entrance of the parking lot, where Bone had left his motorcycle. He jumped on, kicking the starter and popped a wheelie as he tore past us.

My heart raced as I lay in the back of the truck. Pure joy poured through, and I began to laugh. If this is what it was like being a criminal, I'd steal beer every day. I never felt this good in church or school.

I lay on my back, watching magpies fly overhead, dreaming of a life of crime: slinging dope or robbing banks. I could be like Scarface, sniffing blow off a gilded table.

By the time we reached Carson's neighborhood, I was calm and sitting up, looking at all the newer homes with a stoned eye. Ritalin dulled my senses, forcing me to focus on what was in front of me. But weed brought out the details.

I watched these houses with envy. If your father wore a radiation suit and risked his life, you lived in one of the military-style homes in the older part of Richland. These houses resembled a base, built by the Army Corps of Engineers to house the workers of the Manhattan Project. They were dull, simple Army designs without garages, each variation named with a different letter: A, B, C, etc. But the houses in Carson's neighborhood were newer and built with money, Hanford money, and custom-designed by an architect. They had stuccoed arched columns and long driveways. Some even had swimming pools.

If your parent was a Ph.D. like Carson's mother, you could afford a bit of swank. Maybe this explained why Carson was such an asshole.

Carson went to a different school. It was called Hanford, named after the nuclear site, which was named after some shitty village they'd bulldozed over, displacing its citizens so they could build the Bomb.

Despite being a prick, Carson was a leader in the DIY movement. He held punk gigs and happenings in his mother's basement. Since his father was an absent sperm donor, Carson's single mom seldom denied him anything. She was an executive with the Department of Energy and indulged her emotionally damaged son out of guilt. If Carson wanted to run a gilded palace of punk ethos and sin out of his busy mother's basement, it would tear her up inside to tell him no.

He was insulting and judgmental. Rumor had it that Henry Rollins, singer of the punk band Black Flag, had kicked his ass during their gig at the VFW Hall. Carson was acting like a dick in the mosh-pit, so Rollins beat him with the microphone. The sounds of cracking bones, bruising flesh, and Carson's pain-filled cries boomed through the PA at full volume as the mosh-pit raged on.

When we pulled up, Carson was standing on his manicured lawn with his hands on his hips. His torn clothes matched his fashionable disdain for the white middle-class privilege that comprised his DNA. His Mohawk haircut was long and hung over the right half of the shaved part of his head. He walked up to the back of the truck. "You assholes are late."

Bone ignored him and turned his back, lighting a cigarette, blowing out smoke as he admired the trees.

Carson smacked his gum." You guys got any coke?"

"No," said Bone, looking over his shoulder, giving him a dirty look.

"I thought you stoners were loaded with drugs. Loaded... Get it?" He slapped Bone on the arm.

Bone glared at him, tensing up.

"Deacon has Ritalin," said Fenix, ready to make money off my medication.

Carson's eyes grew wide. "I fuckin' love that shit. How much?"

I was astonished. It never dawned on me that anyone would want to buy Ritalin. Sure it got you high, but it always made me feel like shit.

"I left it at home," I mumbled.

"What's your name?"

"Deacon."

"Well, Deek," he said, walking to the back of the truck, "any time you want to sell some of your meds, you know where I live." He reached out and touched the keg. "Hey! It's warm. What is this? Budweiser?" He turned towards Fenix. "I told you we wanted Heineken."

"What do you think this is?" said Fenix. "You're getting a keg of beer for thirty bucks."

"You assholes," said Carson, "this isn't some stoner party. We want cold Heineken. I'll give you twenty-five."

Bone's shoulders tensed up, and he threw down his cigarette, turning to face him, smoke blowing out his nostrils like a dragon. "Bullshit! It's thirty bucks, now pay up."

Carson smiled at him. "I'm not paying thirty bucks for warm Bud. Take it or leave it."

Fenix stepped between them, putting his hand on Bone's chest. "Take it easy, cuz. Let's take twenty-five."

"Then it's comin' out of your share," said Bone, gritting his teeth.

Fenix turned to me. "Deacon, you don't mind takin' a little less, do you?"

"Uh, I guess." I hadn't realized I was getting paid for this venture.

"Bullshit," said Bone, "Deacon gets a full share."

Fenix ignored him and turned to Carson. "It's a deal."

"Fucking rich punk," Bone said under his breath.

"If you guys are getting full shares," said Fenix, "then you two can carry the damn thing down the steps."

We labored with the keg on the staircase as loud, furious hardcore punk assaulted us. It ripped my eardrums, and I felt the euphoria of music consuming my body for the first time. It made me want to throw myself into oblivion.

Bone looked disgusted. Punk Rock was not his scene. Slam dancing kids kept bumping into us, and he almost dropped the keg.

We put it down, and Bone started shoving the kids on the outer edge of the human whirlpool in an aggressive manner. Though the mosh-pit was violent, it wasn't threatening or an invitation to fight.

Bone couldn't understand this and took each person who moved into his space as a physical threat. When Bone shoved, the kids shoved back.

I was enthralled. I'd heard this type of music coming from car stereos in the parking lot at school. I never got it until this moment— until I'd heard it live. It was aggression and exposed all my turmoil. Every time my father beat me for being a failed Christian who brought my learning disabilities onto myself through sin. Being spit on and bullied, the tests I failed. It all came out, every painful, angry thought that goddam pill suppressed.

Into the pit, I raged, giving myself over to the will of the vortex.

The band in the basement wore torn clothes, combat boots, and spiky hair. Their singer was unlike anyone I'd ever seen. He had hair like a punk Elvis, wore eyeliner like a girl, but was brooding and masculine like Jim Morrison. His jeans were tight, and his shirt was loose and unbuttoned. A sheet with the band's logo hung behind the drum kit in uneven font, dripping like blood and spelling out, "Moral Crux."

I listened to the lyrics:

> *"Is there life before death?*
> *Is there life... Before... You die?"*

These lyrics described my life. Was he singing to me? I felt he was.

I'd never heard live music before, except for the praise team at church and the school band at pep rallies. My parents considered it sinful, and I could see why; its power was addicting. I wanted to swallow it whole and make it part of my being. I wanted to create it, use it to tell my story.

In front of the band was a raging mosh-pit of kids thrashing about in a cyclone. It was like an ancient ritual dance from a culture that valued human sacrifice. A tribe ruled by men who tried to subjugate hardened women who beat them back with sheer attitude. I could feel their rage and wanted to join.

Moral Crux's singer was whipping around and jumping, screaming his guts out:

"Law...
And...
Order... DISORDER!!!!!!"

Strutting and shouting, he pushed anyone who would come near him back into the mosh-pit.

The song finished, and the band stood there, catching their breath, having given more, pushing themselves to the limit. As the group was trying to decide among themselves which song to play next, I looked around the room.

Carson had plastered his basement with Xeroxed posters. They were collages of various adverts, twisted into anti-establishment calls to rally around this white suburban rage fest taking place in his basement. I looked to my right and saw a poster for a gig with a band called "Diddly Squat."

It was a drawing of a punk barfing on a cowboy. I reached up and touched the poster like it was a relic. Rednecks had made my life miserable. There was nothing cool about them; their whole way of being deserved vomit. They were simple folk who imposed their values upon others. I was often the shit that they preferred to kick.

I glanced to my right; a girl with bleached, tricolor hair caught my attention. She had haunting eyes, accentuated by a thick blur of black eyeliner. A skin-tight wife-beater, glued to braless breasts that was tucked into frayed denim shorts, showed off her legs. Her hard-worn look and baby-smooth complexion cast the most tantalizing juxtaposition between naughty and pure.

She glanced at me and smiled. I would have kept standing there, staring like a creep, if it weren't for a loud commotion at the top of the stairs.

"Fuck you!" I heard Bone shout, followed by scuffling and banging.

"Hey, there's a fight," someone hollered, running up the steps.

"Get the fuck outta here, you fucking stoner!"

I joined the flood of bodies scrambling up the stairs.

The Triumph started with a crack. I pushed through the crowd to see Bone spraying sod in a circle.

He gripped the handlebars with a stern look of no compromise. Bone was in his element, destroying the Carson family lawn. The punks were too afraid to get close and pull him down, but still trying to make a show of doing something, jumping out of the way of the spinning wheel and spewing grass.

It was beautiful chaos. Bone was the only one calm as if it were his last earthly command.

For the first time in my life, I understood the no-compromise stance. This was the hidden gem within Bone that made him attractive. He never swayed. Others lived their lives in perpetual compromise, waking up early, commuting to jobs they hated, and other indignities. It made me want to be him, to be something more than a Ritalin kid.

I was startled by a siren screech. Out of nowhere, from opposite ends of the street, two cop cars skidded up to the yard, flashing red and blue lights. All chaos stopped. The moment slowed as the officers stepped out and looked at the kids standing around the yard. Bone shut off the motorcycle and sat there, staring straight at the police.

"Nobody moves until I find out what's going on here," said the cop.

"Just a party," said Carson.

"Whose house is this?"

"Mine."

"We've got reports of fighting and loud music." He pointed to Fenix's truck. "We also got a report of a stolen keg in a white Ford pickup." He slapped the hood. "Rick, run the plates on this piece of shit."

Terror shot through me, causing my heart to hit my chest. I began to gasp, imagining the reaction of my fundamentalist parents. A minor infraction got me a whipping that left welts, followed by weeks of extra chores, bible study, and prayer. How would they react to this? My father would rival Pilate whipping Christ.

A cop walked towards me.

I had to escape. Getting arrested was not an option. For the first time since I started taking Ritalin, I was impulsive.

Desperate, I shoved him to the ground and started to run.

The mall's 1950s sci-fi architecture was some bright person's idea of the future. Even its logo looked like it was out of the Jetsons. Once upon a time, this faded strip of shops was a symbol of the Atomic Age. But walking through this economically stagnant heap of concrete, I knew the future science fiction had predicted would never exist.

CHAPTER 3

WITHDRAWAL

Fear propelled me over prickly shrubs and six-foot fences. Arms and legs pumping, I dodged swimming pools and lawn furniture, shocking people in their gardens.

I hit the street, running towards the river. Sirens were coming at me from behind, a screaming cacophony mixed with red and blue light.

Bone shot past me, the Triumph's engine screaming. He jumped the curb and flew over a berm, heading for a park bench. Braking hard, spinning tires, tearing grass—it was no use. He hit the bench with a loud crack and was catapulted towards the river.

Panicked, I dropped to the pavement and crawled beneath the nearest car.

The cops skidded to a stop, inches from my face. I could see their boots as they ran down the hill. Knowing I had a chance to escape, I pushed myself aside to get out from under the car.

I peeked over the hood. The cops were kicking the shit out of Bone as he lay in a fetal position, protecting his head. They were rabid, beating him as if he'd fucked their wives. If it weren't for a group of stroller-pushing moms watching, they might have shot him.

It was horrible, but there was nothing I could do. Feeling guilty, I ran up the street until my sides hurt, slowing to a walk.

Down the road was a place to hide, a large outdoor shopping mall called the Uptown. I blended with the people, pretending to be a shopper.

The mall's 1950s sci-fi architecture was some bright person's idea of the future. Even its logo looked like it was out of the Jetsons. Once upon a time, this faded strip of shops was a symbol of the Atomic Age. But walking through this economically stagnant heap of concrete, I knew the future science fiction had predicted would never exist.

There were courtyards with benches in between the buildings. I sat to catch my breath. The distinct pungent aroma of a clove cigarette fell over me. It was the girl from Carson's party, hair a mess with sweat on her shoulders. Her flannel shirt was tied around her waist, leaving her arms naked and her nipples hard under the cotton wife beater.

She greeted me in a single upward nod, squinting with suspicion, resting one foot on her skateboard. She threw down her spent clove and skated towards me, blowing the smoke into a deliberate haze to screen her features. She was marvelous looking, black nail polish, red lipstick, a quarter inch of kohl eyeliner around wild eyes. She would've stood out anywhere. Her sexiness was combustible.

Just cowering in her shadow would change me forever, make me a man who loves hellfire.

I found myself staring at the creamy cleavage. Her gothic, bad-girl style seemed to be pulled together by a black studded leather belt.

She held out a clove that I didn't take, shrugged, then lit up. I glanced down at her arm; there were scars all over. She'd been cutting herself. Most cutters kept their arms hidden, but she seemed to flaunt them with brazen attitude.

"Hi," I said. "My name's Deacon."

"I know who you are," she said in a gruff voice, lips holding the cigarette. "You hang out with Bone Reinhold."

I recalled Bone acting like a dick and started to get embarrassed. How did she know me? I'd never seen her before in my life.

"You're dirty," she said, glancing down at my clothes.

I pinched my white shirt, pulling it out to inspect the fabric. "I had to hide from the cops under a car."

"There's grease on your face too."

I reached up to wipe it.

"You're just smearing it," she said, then laughed without smiling as if her dark nature absorbed the humor of the moment.

I shrugged.

"That was pretty gutsy, the way you ran from the police," she said.

"No telling what cops will do if they catch you. They were kicking the shit out of Bone down by the river."

"They were rough on your friend Fenix before I split," she said.

"Fenix isn't my friend. He's Bone's cousin. I run into him from time to time."

"So, you just steal kegs with him?" Her smirk was overshadowed by the cigarette dangling from the corner of her mouth.

"Yeah," I motioned to the bench next to me. "You can have a seat if you'd like."

She reluctantly sat, and kept the skateboard between her smooth legs, refusing to look me in the eye.

"I guess you ran?"

She glanced at me, then averted her gaze. "Richland pigs aren't in the habit of letting people go. Besides, my dad's a cop. He'd beat the shit out of me if I got arrested."

"Mine too."

She shook her head and inhaled, deep in thought. "Dads are such assholes."

"Did anyone else get away?"

"Nah," she said. "The rest stood there like sheep. Lucky I had my skateboard with me."

"What's your name?"

She hesitated, then held out her hand in some semblance of etiquette. "Cher."

Where had I seen her? She seemed familiar. Then it dawned on me; Cher... Cher Hanson... Yes, I knew this girl. She used to look different; long mousey brown hair, clothes that hid her body, no makeup, didn't bathe much. She was the invisible type, forgettable if it weren't for all the stories.

They said she'd run away to live with a man in his forties and had sex with a gang of sailors—despite our town being landlocked by a desert. Fenix's friend Dany Lau claimed she'd given him a blow job in the back of the bus on a band trip. The whole school considered her the town slut, though I'm not sure anyone had ever seen her with a boy.

I don't know what happened to her or why she disappeared, but she had transformed into something unusual, complex, exciting. Girl next door types and popular girls would no longer do. They all seemed commonplace next to her. She was the epitome of rebellion, someone my parents wouldn't approve of, someone the elders would throw out of our church.

The kids at school were a bunch of damned fuckers for what they'd said. She was golden.

I sat silent for a moment, making her feel uncomfortable, so I decided to speak. "You go to Richland High, don't you?" It was all I could think to say.

She spat on the concrete. "I used to. I haven't been there for a while."

"Where've you been?"

"Places," she said, slouching back and hugging herself. "Portland, California... around."

"I can't believe you actually left Richland."

She straightened her posture as if conveying a sense of pride. "I've left this shit-hole more than once."

"You can't be old enough to go off and live on your own. How old are you?"

"I'll be eighteen this August. I'm going to celebrate by leaving again. This time, I won't be back. Legally, they can't force me home like before."

"How many times have you ran away?" I asked.

"A few. The first time I made it all the way to Milwaukee."

"Do you have family there?"

"No," she said, "I just liked the beer, so I thought it might be a nice place."

"Was it?"

"Anything is better than here."

I couldn't believe what I was hearing. If she could leave, maybe I could too? I never thought such a thing possible.

"How did you survive?"

"It's easy. Shakedown guys for money." She aggressively flicked her cigarette towards a yarn shop. "What's a matter, never met a whore?"

I sat on my hands. "No, I was just wondering how I could survive if I left, so I thought I'd ask."

She gave me a dirty glance. "Get a job, turn a trick. You'd do just about anything to get away from a house like mine." Cher stood up. "I'll see you around."

"Wait," I said, "don't go."

She turned and folded her arms, looking away from me.

"I'm sorry. I wasn't judging you." I gazed up to the sky, not sure what to say. "My old man's pretty rough on me. So don't think I'm down on you for whatever you did on the road. I admire that you've got the guts to leave."

Cher looked at me, making eye contact for the first time. I couldn't tell if she was mad, disinterested, or both. "I gotta go," she said.

I watched her rudely weave her board through pedestrians until she rounded the corner. I wanted to run after her and make her my girlfriend, but there was no use.

"Fuck!" I kicked the park bench and sat, burying my head in my hands. She was trouble. Maybe I should just let it go?

I hit the back of the bench, relishing the pain until I started to feel something worse. A creeping headache was getting stronger by the minute, pushing on my frontal lobes. I never got headaches. My whole body felt nauseous, pain piercing my head.

I lay down on the bench, too spent to move.

It had arrived: Ritalin withdrawal.

CHAPTER 4

THE ATOMIC MARBLE

I t was coming on fast. I ran to the nearest garbage can to puke. Everyone stared at me hacking, speeding up as they passed. Not wanting to draw attention, I swallowed my bile and forced myself to walk home.

After several minutes I came upon the Federal Government Building. At seven-stories, this concrete box dominated the landscape of Richland. Built in 1965, it was a shining example of modern architecture that clashed with the town's army base charm.

Why would a small town in the middle of nowhere need such a large Federal Building? Because we were the center of the Cold War.

We made plutonium for the nukes.

I had bad memories of this building from the night of Reese's crank. It was the first time I'd ever taken that drug, and it gave me horrors. My heart was beating so fast I thought it was cardiac arrest. Everything was an emergency without a solution. I became paranoid that my father would murder me. And if I went to the hospital, they would arrest me for hitting crank.

It had fucked me up so bad, I ended up crawling out my window at three in the morning to skateboard and burn the shit off. I ended up in the back of the Federal Building, grinding parking curbs. I'd been there for ten minutes when two men in black suits came around the corner. They reached into their sport coats and pulled out guns.

"Federal Agents," one of them said. "Put your hands up."

"Oh, God, shit!" I fell off my board, clutching my heart.

"I said, hands up." He aimed his piece. "You shouldn't be here; this is government property. See the sign? No skateboarding."

I was about to piss my pants. "Don't arrest me, please. I'll go home—promise."

"Don't let us see you here again," said the other.

Skating off, I turned back and saw a glowing green sphere, levitating mid-air. I may have failed science, but I knew this was impossible. I must've been hallucinating from the crank.

The orb shot off into the night as my board hit a bit of raised sidewalk. I went flying, concrete scraping my skin.

I had heard talk of floating balls of light. No one who saw them thought they were UFOs. When you live in the shadow of Hanford, you assume it's some top-secret weapon.

The next day, I told Reese Whitaker the story as he burned a joint before his trig class. Unimpressed, he puffed and listened. "I've seen those spheres," he said, "they're advanced reconnaissance drones."

"No, they're not, the drones they're testing look like little airplanes. This was a ball of light."

"No, really," said Reese. "New technology. They're at least thirty years ahead of anything you've seen flying around in the daytime. They use these things to locate contamination. They have Geiger counters inside. My father blabbed about it last Christmas after too much eggnog."

"Yeah, then why would the thing be floating around the Federal Building?"

"Because there was radiation there."

"Bullshit," I said.

"Okay, smarty pants; why did those men in suits tell you to leave?"

"Because I was scuffing up the curbs with my trucks."

"Right." He smirked.

"Whatever… What did you put in that crank?"

"I bet those guys were CIA," he said, handing me the joint, "put there to keep civilians away from contamination. Sort of like the Men in Black."

"What, the comic book?" I said, taking a puff.

"Haha," he said, annoyed. "Give me back my joint."

"Sounds like bullshit," I said, coughing from his shitty weed.

"You're the one with the bullshit story." He looked at me with his rat-like eyes and mortician's pallor, holding the joint like an elegant Hollywood starlet.

"Whatever; you're the one with the bullshit crank. What the fuck did you put in it?"

I never told that story to anyone again.

Still creeped out, and not wanting to walk by the building, I turned to cross the street. There was a cop car heading straight for me. Panicked, I looked for a place to hide. I had no choice; I would have to enter the Federal Building.

The Post Office was closed, but the Science Center was open.

The Hanford Science Center was an exhibit dedicated to the Manhattan Project and our nuclear heritage.

Everything glowed from the fluorescent lights reflecting off the asbestos floor and vinyl paneling, making me feel exposed. Worse, I was the only one in the museum.

The curator wore '50s-era horn-rimmed glasses and had her hair up in a bun. "We close in ten minutes," she said, standing from her desk in an uninviting stance.

"I just want a quick look around," I said, ignoring her as she turned off some fluorescents, thankful to be in low light.

She followed me, subtly letting me know I wasn't welcome. I saw my reflection in a glass display, covered in grease, looking like a bum.

Pretending to be interested, I walked up to an old atomic fuel rod in the children's "touch & feel" section. I rubbed it, trying to sense if it was still radioactive. The curator was watching me, glancing at her watch.

"Do you go to Richland High?" she asked, her eyes narrowed in suspicion.

"Yes," I said, walking past her towards the back of the exhibit.

"You must be a Senior." Her words echoed in my head, making me feel angry about my situation. I wasn't sure I was going to graduate, nor what I'd do with the diploma if I did.

"Yeah, I'm a Senior." I sounded testy from the headache and nausea.

"After you graduate, you can come back when you have more time," she said. "You won't be able to see much of the exhibit today."

"That's okay." I approached a large, Plexiglas case. Inside was a balsawood model of the B-Reactor, the one that fueled the Fat Man and Trinity Test bombs. The replica was complete with silos and water tanks. It even had fake trees from the craft store.

The reactor had an ominous look to it. Even though it was just a cheesy replica, the sight of it filled me with awe and dread. This building had given me nightmares since I was child. It was a real house of horror. Maybe because so many people had died from the weapon it made. Maybe this model represented the fount of our eventual destruction. Or I felt guilty because the Atomic Bomb had paid for my braces and put shoes on my feet.

No, it was because working out there in that radioactive cesspit scared the shit out of me. I was worried that this was my future. When it became evident that my skills in reading the Bible weren't going to earn me a degree in apologetics, my parents changed their plan. I would grow up to be a janitor for my father's company, mopping radioactive floors. It was all they talked about.

The curator looked at her watch again.

Further down was a pair of glove boxes used to make atmosphere argon inert. Bone's grandfather was manning one of these when it exploded in his face and zapped him with so much radiation it should've killed him. But he was a real man, so he survived only to be quarantined. They had to hire specialists in white coats with PhDs in nuclear waste to deal with his urine. Every time he peed, it would set the Geiger counters screaming. They called him the Hanford Man.

I was fascinated with the box and headed right to it. The curator followed me.

"How does it keep the radiation from gettin' at you?" I asked.

"They manufacture the glove boxes out of lead glass," she said, ensuring that I wouldn't take time reading the explanation on the mounted plaque. "The built-in rubber gloves are designed so lab technicians can handle ionized product."

"Is this the same kind the Hanford Man had his hands in when he got zapped?"

"Oh, you mean Harlan Fenix? That poor man was bombarded with a near-lethal dose of americium 241." She put her hand to her mouth.

I slid my arms into the gloves and looked through the glass. Inside were wooden blocks and toys so the kids could pretend to be their parents, baking themselves for the benefit of human progress. I started to play with the blocks, building a castle with my gloved hands. I fantasized that I was the Hanford Man, and every time I had to take a leak, I was a danger to others.

"Aren't you a little old for this?" said the curator.

Embarrassed, I pulled out my hands.

"I'm sorry, but we're closing," she said. "You'll have to go."

29

I shrugged and turned toward the exit. Against the wall were three gum-ball dispensers attached to a tubular stand. The first dispensed Bazooka bubblegum. The middle offered black pellets—plastic replicas of the uranium slugs they used to fuel the reactors. The third had a label that read, "Atomic Marbles."

My father had given me some of these when I was a kid. The marbles were dunked in the sludge tanks down at the Hanford cribs, exposing them to Cobalt-60 source gamma rays. This shifted the marble's electrons from their original positions, giving a coffee-colored hue to the glass. After they washed off the radioactive waste, they were stuck in this gum-ball machine for kids to buy at the Science Center. They even came with a small manila courtesy envelope so you could protect your sacred souvenir. These weren't the uranium-doped marbles that look good under a black light when you smoke pot. They were safe—they said—a real treasure.

I reached into my pocket. "My last dime," I mumbled.

The curator arched her eyebrows.

I turned the crank, giving it a slight wiggle in the hopes I could finagle two for the price of one. The old lady cleared her throat in disapproval. No luck, just one coffee-colored radioactive marble dropped out. I placed it in the courtesy envelope and put it in my pocket to radiate.

On the way out, I stopped to look at a large black-and-white photograph of pre-war Richland. An old toothless geezer manned an ox plow in front of a dilapidated barn. Hard to imagine that before the Manhattan Project, Richland had been a couple of wheat fields and an apple orchard.

Next to this picture was a photograph of a construction worker laying concrete for the B-reactor core. The photo arrested me like I was gazing at my future, a future of back-breaking manual labor in a dangerous industry. Was this the fate of a Ritalin kid?

Spooked at the prospect of working at Hanford, I stormed out of the building, knowing I was fucked. When you are as learning disabled as me, you're lucky to have any job.

I wanted to have guts like Cher and get the fuck out before this black hole sucked me in permanently.

My headache had reached a pounding pitch and was peeling me raw.

The curator locked the door behind me.

By the time I got home, my parents were still at bible study. I could finish picking weeds, throw my stained shirt into the neighbor's trash, and they'd be none the wiser.

My headache was killing me. Weeding this garden seemed an insurmountable task. I reached down to grab the hand shovel.

Looking at the paper bag sitting on the lawn, half full of thistles, I knew something was different. I'd been off Ritalin since Friday night, and its absence had somehow changed me. I had defied God, the law, and my parents. The results were fantastic! How could I go back to the way things were?

I thought of Cher Hanson and how impressed she seemed to be that I had the balls to steal a keg and run from the cops. Balls had nothing to do with it, but I felt emboldened—new and improved.

Defiance was great; it even had good music. But what about Jesus? Just thirty hours off Ritalin, and I could feel the church's control slipping. With my new clear thought, I knew in my heart that church sucked—and everything the devil held sacred was awesome!

I reached down to dig out a dandelion and felt bile growling in my gut.

"Fuck this!" I picked up the bag and shovel and threw them in the shed, vowing never to pull weeds again. And for the first time in a long while, despite an aching brain, I was looking forward to tomorrow.

Everyone called our logo "The Bomb." Or maybe it was just an explosion? I don't know. It looked like an explosion to me, a mushroom cloud, Japanese killing blast. I couldn't figure out why everyone called it the Bomb.

CHAPTER 5

THE BOMB

My alarm went off, reminding me it was Monday. My father and I had a meeting with the school counselor. I knew what the outcome of this ordeal would be. He would tell us that I had failed a crucial exam and wouldn't be graduating, casting me into a fiery pit like Lucifer.

Visions entered my head of being hauled into the church basement, fluorescent lights exposing my sin, hands on me as they prayed. Then I would be taken home and stripped of all dignity after being whipped by my father.

I knew it was coming. I had fallen so far behind that I needed at least a C minus on every final. I went into it, knowing I would fail. But knowing and accepting are two different things.

By the time I got off the school bus, the withdrawal was so bad it felt like the world pushing down. I was collapsing. It had fucked up my sleep. I wanted to run from the burning sun but could barely walk into that building.

Once inside, I stood, like a boulder against a river, the rush of humanity passing. Ritalin was supposed to help me learn, but instead, it called my name, picking at my bones, leaving me uneducated.

I began to journey down the school's dark hallway, paranoid of the deep green lockers and my fellow students who loitered around them. Sunlight from the glass doors on either end of the hall gave off a hazy illumination, making the late 1940s architecture and asbestos decor feel like an eerie prison. I had to take each of my steps with consideration, my dopamine receptors throbbing in desperate suck for the Ritalin that was no longer there.

Bone was inspecting a black eye in the mirror that hung in the faux tiger-fur-lined locker we shared. There was a dark bruise on the side of his face. His appearance was upsetting and added to the surreal space I'd entered. I was surprised to see him. I half expected him to be in jail.

He saw me approach and turned, shaking his head. "You're lucky you got away. Look what they did." He winced, touching his cheek. "Though I got to be honest, I'm not sure if the black eye came from the cops or my dad."

"Jesus," I said.

"Yeah, and the old man keeps it real—still got his Navy Seal chops. I think he broke a rib." He touched his side and flinched from the pain, then turned back to the mirror, posing like Jim Morrison. "Guess I'm all beat up for graduation."

"At least you'll graduate," I said, laboring to push out the words. Nausea started to erupt in my belly, and I let myself fall against the wall.

He stepped back and studied me as I lifted myself up to put my skateboard into our locker. "What do you mean?" he said.

"I took too long with my math final. I didn't answer enough questions to pass." I tossed a textbook into the locker with contempt. "I've got a meeting in a few minutes with Mr. Ryers, and my father's going to be there."

He smiled and patted me on the shoulder. "Don't worry, they'll let you slide, they always do. You might have to do summer school."

"They didn't let Fenix slide." My head rested on the wall like a dense blob. "I'm afraid they'll put me on the five-year plan." I cinched my brow and squinted. The headache had crept through every inch of my brain.

"Fenix survived, and so will you," said Bone, primping in the mirror.

Easy for him to say. He was about to graduate.

"Speaking of Fenix," I said. "Did he narc on me?"

"No," said Bone. "He knows I'd kill him."

I tilted my head back, smiling through the pain. "Thank God."

"Fenix is a motherfucker. The dickhead went along like a pussy. Nothing's going to happen to him. His mother will quit buying him chew, and his father won't lend him the truck till August. It's bullshit." His voice came out in an emotional quiver: "I'm the one who's fucked." He paused and glanced around, lowering his voice. "After he got done beating the fuck out of me, my dad told me to pack my shit and go. Says he doesn't want a criminal in the house."

"He kicked you out?"

"Sort of; my mom intervened. She knows I've got no place to go, so they're letting me graduate and stay over the weekend. Come Monday, I either go to the recruiter or get the fuck out. Either way, I have to leave."

I was stunned. "You're not going to join the military, are you?"

"Do I have a choice?" he said, slamming the locker. "I can't afford to move out. Even if I worked, $3.35 an hour isn't going to set me up. Besides, where am I gonna stay while I look for a job? I'd sling dope, but there's no money in it unless you do a grow-op."

He kicked the locker in frustration. "Maybe being a soldier won't be so bad. I'll get to see Asia and Europe."

"Hey!" yelled a teacher, walking by. "No kicking lockers."

Bone ignored him and turned to face me, his eyes bloodshot and twitching. "That's not all; the cops impounded my bike." He blurted out the words as if saying it fast would ease the pain.

This revelation hit me in the abdomen. I knew what the motorcycle meant to him. "How much to get it out?"

"Two-hundred bucks."

"Shit," I said. "How are you going to scrape that?"

"Maybe Grandpa will give me the money?" He grinned, burying his stress under a fake smile. "He's rich. He got a $275,000 settlement from the Army Corps of Engineers. Gets free medical too."

"That's something," I said

In Bone's point of view, he could either become a wage slave or a mercenary. For him, these options meant death. He wasn't going to sacrifice his life and freedom for a country that opposed his pursuit of happiness with their draconian drug laws.

Bone would pull through. He got away with everything. He lived outside the unspoken law, that socioeconomic code that dictated whether you were gonna make it or not. Why should this situation be any different? It didn't matter what he did; his charm always got him through.

He sensed me watching him. "You okay? You look a little rough."

"Ritalin withdrawal," I mumbled.

Bone sighed and shook his head. "Aren't we a pair. I thought we'd have it made by the time we finished school. Now I'm looking at the future and I don't like what I see. We should've turned eighteen in 1967 instead of being born in the Summer of Love."

He glanced at his watch and shook his head. "Look, I gotta go. I'll keep an eye out for you at the assembly. Maybe we can get the fuck out of here?"

This was the first time I'd seen him stress about the future. It wasn't his thing; Bone was always into the present.

I felt alone in the world, watching him walk into class. If it weren't for the rows of students that stared at me through the open classroom door with lifeless eyes, sitting in arm desks like bovine in a cattle transport, I could've been the last person on earth.

The bell struck a death knell, jolting me like a twenty-volt shock. I slowly made my way to the foyer, about to begin adult life branded a loser.

How did this happen? Why was I born into this? I closed my eyes to visions of jumbled words and numbers, drowning in a pool of dyslexic failure.

Random sounds, terrorizing sensations. Teachers giving lectures, and other activity drifting out from classrooms. How was I going to get through this? The withdrawal only made it worse.

I sat down on a bench, trying to calm down, forcing myself to face the office while staring at our school's logo embossed on the tiled floor.

Everyone called our logo "The Bomb." Or maybe it was just an explosion? I don't know. It looked like an explosion to me, a mushroom cloud, Japanese killing blast. I couldn't figure out why everyone called it the Bomb.

This mushroom cloud was our school's logo and mascot, a stylized, R—for Richland High, emerging from the fiery sun that leveled Nagasaki, with the billow of radioactivity rising above it. It was a thing to behold. Our fathers had made the plutonium for the Nagasaki bomb. Damn proud of it too. This logo was a source of civic honor and adorned the uniforms of the Richland Bombers— the best AAA football team in the State.

The school's builders had embossed this mushroom cloud logo onto the floor of the campus foyer in a mosaic. It gave members of the varsity football team an excuse to beat any freshman who walked on it. They did it to Reese Whittaker, and he was a senior. Reese had done more than walk on our school's mascot; he'd stepped on our parent's livelihood.

Our logo of death radiated up from the floor, three feet from where I sat waiting for my future to blow into particles.

I looked up. My father was hovering over me, clenching his fist, digging his fingernails into his palm.

CHAPTER 6

THE BC CRIB

I avoided looking my father in the eye and focused on the dosimeter ID badge hanging over his wide-styled tie.

"We're early." He glanced at his watch.

I didn't want to engage him, so I remained silent.

"This better not be what I think it's about."

I shrugged my shoulders. "I had trouble with my math final."

Resting his hands on the hips of his blue-gray polyester suit, he bit his lower lip, and gazed up at the ceiling tiles. "Lord Jesus, spare me this trial." He took a long, pained moment, pondering what he was about to say. He had suffered for years from my education and was being cheated the promised relief. "Deacon, you'd better be graduating."

"I might have to go to summer school," I mumbled.

He turned in anger. "The Lord has given you the gift of an education, and you're squandering it." He looked around to see if anyone had witnessed his outburst. Taking the seat next to me, he closed in, index finger leveled like an accusation. "Things are crucial at work right now. I can't be dealing with this."

"What's wrong?" I said.

"I guess you don't read the Washington Post. We're in trouble with the EPA. They're all over us about the BC Crib and a spill. Our CEO is testifying before Congress, and it's up to my team to see that he's got all the answers." He leaned forward, elbows on his knees, wringing his hands "We could lose our contract if things don't go well."

"What's the BC Crib?"

"Waste storage. Well, I wouldn't call it storage; it's more of a dump." He sulked into his suit and appeared small for a moment. "Back in the days of the B-Reactor, they ran out of tank space for a sizable batch of nuclear waste. So they dug a few trenches with a backhoe, and when no one was looking, poured the sludge in and covered it up—called it the BC Crib."

Listening to this story, I couldn't fathom why he would want his own flesh and blood to work in such a place. "That sounds pretty stupid," I said.

"Stupid?" My dad looked at me, anger in his eyes, lingering on the word. It was if he were directing it at me, lacing it with contempt for how I'd turned out. "It was stupid," he said, breaking the tense moment, "but that's how they did it back then."

He loosened his tie. "But as stupid as that was, what they did after was worse. They fenced off the pit with chain-link, topped it with razor wire, and left it to radiate."

"So what's so bad about that?"

"It turns out," continued my dad, holding out his hand to animate his story, "that they paved a lot not far from the chain link and I've been parking my car there for the past three years."

"Didn't your radiation badge pick it up?"

He ignored the question.

"So if this happened so long ago, how did the EPA find out about it?" I said, wanting to distract him from my poor performance in school.

He shot me a dirty look. "Deacon, it's all over the news. There's a liberal senator from the westside who was up in arms over Hanford's environmental record. So he forms a senate investigation committee with people from the EPA, and they charter a bus to tour the Site. Just before they arrive, there's a nuclear waste spill on the road. Hoping they won't notice, the Hanford Patrol lets them drive right through it, tires trailing contamination everywhere. A total disaster.

"To make matters worse, this fool running the tour pulls up alongside the BC Crib, pointing it out to every tree-hugging liberal from Washington DC, as if it's local flavor. Now the Chief has to go before this committee to defend our handling of hot product. If we lose our contract, we'll all be laid off."

I hung my head, trying to process what I'd learned. "Bone told me that his grandfather has to live out there, quarantined for years because he's so full of radiation, and technicians have to dispose of his pee. I wouldn't work out there for any amount of money."

"Well, you'll do a lot worse if you don't start taking your schooling a little more seriously." The anger in his statement amplified my defeat. "Do you have any clue how I put food on the table?" My dad sat back with his hands on his knees and tried to slow his breathing. "Look, Deacon, you've only got a few days left. You knew you had to pass that test to graduate."

My hand started to shake. "Yeah, I know. It takes me longer to finish. I didn't have enough time to answer all the questions."

He looked down at me. "What's the matter with you?"

"I don't know."

"Why's your hand trembling?"

"It's nothing." I shoved it into my pocket. I didn't want him to know I was going through withdrawal.

He stood up and started to pace. "I can't believe this. Come here," he said, reaching for my hands.

I rolled my eyes. Was he going to do this in the school's foyer? The embarrassment was mortifying. He pulled me up and closed his eyes while tightening the grip on my fingers. I looked around, hoping no one was watching.

"Dear Heavenly Father," he said, "I lift up before You my only begotten son and ask that You heal his mind and cure him of his perverse and deviant nature..."

As he prayed, a Ritalin free thought hit me: Was I so perverse? Was I so deviant? I'd spent my whole life trying to please my parents. All I ever wanted was to be accepted and loved.

"Lord help us be more effective in our witness and example before Deacon."

Listening to his prayer, my future didn't matter. School, church, a job—I began to grasp Bone's fuck it all attitude. All we have is now. If I were such a shitty son, going to hell, then why not own it? I wanted music, loud and fast, and the love of a girl that my parents and their god wouldn't approve of.

The office door opened, and Mr. Ryers stepped out, wearing his usual brown polyester slacks, and an off-white shirt with pink and brown stripes. His dishwater hair was greasy, parted on the side with a mustache that was too big. His look was the sort that had fallen out of fashion along with disco.

Any normal person would've cut their prayer short, but not my dad. He didn't care; he was covered in the blood of Christ. Nothing and no one was going to keep him from getting to "Amen."

Mr. Ryers turned away as he waited for us to finish. Then, as if there was nothing weird about it, my father opened his eyes, turned, and shook Mr. Ryer's hand.

I stared past them into the office. Books on shelves, diplomas on walls—the room seemed to mock me, speaking in subliminal whispers, telling me that I could never succeed on this path of academics and exciting careers.

My father tugged my arm, leading me into the prick's office. Though this meeting was ominous, it was just one of many stops in my slow-motion decline into defeat.

41

I shook Mr. Ryer's hand and slumped in the chair. The counselor sat down in front of a mural portraying a football victory. "Go, Bombers!" was painted above it. An aerial photograph of a nuclear reactor hung on the wall.

"I've asked you to come in today to discuss Deacon's eligibility for graduation..." I already knew what he was going to say.

The counselor and my father were talking over me about my bleak future. It was more than I could take. I tuned them out like I was tuning out a sermon from the pastor. I sat there dreaming about a parallel universe where I was good looking and smart, where people approached with respect and trusted me with things that needed to get done. I'd sit on a fern-lined veranda with Cher and pay for her to get tattoos—maybe I'd be famous like Sid Vicious?

I began to daydream that I was in a band, a raging sort of group that thrashed and was too loud. Dickheads like the jocks at school would pay money to hear me scream and shout angry lyrics at them from the stage. I imagined the captain of the Bomber football team, Steve Hannity, his brute mug staring up at me from the mosh-pit. I would stage-dive and smash his face with my microphone, the way Henry Rollins had beaten Carson.

Over and over, I played out the scene, and each time Steve was more afraid... Afraid... "I'm afraid Deacon doesn't have enough credits to graduate," Mr. Ryer's voice crashed through my daydream.

My father's face seemed to be losing color.

"Test scores in Math and English just came in and Deacon fared worse than usual. As you are aware, his grades depended on at least a C minus."

"Can he retake the tests?" My father was desperate.

"It's not that simple," said Mr. Ryers. "He's failing Home Economics, and Civics as well. We can excuse Home-Ec and Civics, but State Law mandates that Deacon needs to meet the most basic requirements in Math and English. He has two finals left, and even if he passes those, he still won't graduate."

I sat up straight, my daydreams crashing to a halt—foolish ambitions anyway. I had no musical talent. I wasn't even allowed to sing Silent Night at the Christmas pageant because the quality of my voice was an insult to the Baby Jesus. I couldn't learn guitar because my parents believed it the devil's lyre.

"So Deacon's not going to graduate?"

"Yes, Mr. Jones," said the counselor, "I'm afraid he's going to have to do another year."

There it was, the five-year plan, just like Fenix. I began to drown in a sea of despair. Another year of hell, failure, prayer, and bullies, living with my parents while my classmates went on with their lives.

Fuck no! This was not an option.

"I don't understand why he can't retake these tests?" said my father, upset, sitting forward in his chair. "He has a week left."

"I'm sorry," said Mr. Ryers. "Deacon is an adult and these are real-world consequences. We've given him every accommodation. He's been allowed extra time to complete his finals; it's in his Individual Education Plan. We are willing to work with students but considering his attitude…"

Here they were, discussing my life like I was an object. This is always how it's been: psychiatrists, teachers, the pastor; everyone poking and probing, wondering why I didn't get good grades.

Not everyone can be great at everything—but what was I good at? Where were my hidden talents? Did I have any passions? I'd been beaten down for so long I was almost afraid to dream.

"Frankly, Mr. Jones, I don't think Deacon is willing to put in the effort."

If they only realized how hard I'd tried over the years—twice as hard for a lot of Ds and Fs.

My father elbowed my arm to get my attention. I was so deep in self-loathing that I hadn't noticed they'd stopped talking and were standing. Panicked I was missing something, I jumped up and glanced around, trying to see if one of them was waiting for me to respond.

"It was nice meeting you," Mr. Ryers said to my father. "I have another appointment, so you'll have to excuse me. Deacon, I'll see you next year." He smiled in a way meant to be positive, but I took as mocking.

My dad slumped over, deflated. I didn't know what to say; I wasn't rebelling against him or my mom. Hell, I didn't even feel like I was rebelling. In the past, I had done everything to please them. But each assignment was like smacking my head against a concrete wall.

"Deacon," my dad said once out of the office, "this is unacceptable. You need to answer to the Lord for your sin."

What this might entail filled my heart with terror. Small offenses brought beatings and condemnation for my sinful deficiencies. But not graduating; this was huge!

"Your problem," said my dad, "is that you have no ambition. Sloth is one of the most craven sins. If you're not going to work out at Hanford as a janitor, then you need a trade."

I held my breath and stared at the Bomb, imagining myself hunched over a hot grill like those two cooks at the Ol' Stalag. "I don't know. I guess I've got another year to figure it out."

"A trade, why don't you think about that?" said my father, pointing at me. "You can tell me what you've come up with when I see you tonight."

He walked down the hall in his crazy 70s-era suit. His closet was full of them. I wondered if I would ever have a job where I would have to wear a business suit. You need to be a decent reader, or do math without jumbling numbers out of sequence, to have a job where you wear a suit.

The large metal doors closed behind him, and I was alone again in the foyer. I glanced down at my trembling hands when I realized I'd stepped on the Bomb.

"Fuck this school!" I said, stomping my foot on the mushroom cloud mosaic. If I wasn't going to graduate, I certainly wasn't going to the year-end rally, nor was I going to finish the day. It was time to drop out!

I hacked up a wad of phlegm and spat on the Bomb, smearing it with my foot until it mixed with dirt from the floor, soiling their precious monument to Japanese annihilation.

The bell rang. I looked around to see if anyone had witnessed what I'd done. There was Steve Hannity, captain of the Bomber football team, smiling with a mixture of glee and outrage.

This mushroom cloud was our school's logo and mascot, a stylized, R—for Richland High, emerging from the fiery sun that leveled Nagasaki, with the billow of radioactivity rising above it. It was a thing to behold. Our fathers had made the plutonium for the Nagasaki bomb. Damn proud of it too. This logo was a source of civic honor and adorned the uniforms of the Richland Bombers—the best AAA football team in the State.

CHAPTER 7

RICHLAND BOMBERS

These moments are the worst, knowing the pain that you are about to endure, humiliation, and everyone thinking you're weak. Any resistance would prolong and increase suffering. And if I were to fight off Steve, an endless supply of goons would emerge from the shadows to defeat me. The status quo's power depends on it. These people will crush all dignity to the degree that you'll never be able to enjoy looking in the mirror. And any success you manage to achieve will feel undeserving. Better to let them beat you because they'll never kill you, just destroy you. You'll have to end it yourself in private if things get that bad.

And of course, the school faculty won't come to your aid. Steve and his friends play for the champion team which brings pride and a sense of identity to the community. Their status is firm. Victory is everything. People depend on it to make themselves feel good about their place in the world.

According to the charter, if the school decided to punish them, they would be ineligible to play for the team. The victim's wellbeing would let down the entire community, everyone hating this poor beaten sap for the victory that could've been.

Steve needed to trash me. On a subliminal level, he understood I was a threat to order.

We didn't move. Steve stood against the river of students filtering out of class. Despite his ugly face, Steve's confidence and chiseled body made him glow like an Adonis from an ancient fable.

A couple of football players joined him. These two had a reputation for going around school inflicting misery on anyone exhibiting a hint of weakness: shoving into lockers, tripping, physical and mental intimidation. They were star quarterback, Mack Freewater, and front lineman, Dick Jameson. All three were wearing their Bomber jerseys. They made their way towards me.

"I saw what you did." Steve stepped in front of me, mixing my dread with a feeling of worthlessness. "Remember what happened to your pal Gandhi?"

"You mean Reese?"

"Of course, I mean Reese, you fucking idiot." Steve grabbed me by the back of the neck and shoved me. I stumbled and recovered.

Dick Jameson pushed me from behind. I stumbled again, and he kicked me in the back of my thigh, causing me to fall onto the Bomb. Pain shot through my leg. They all laughed as I began to hyperventilate.

"You made a mess, now clean it."

I glanced up and saw a group of students gathered to watch the entertainment. They were all laughing. It was a nervous reaction to the guilt they felt rejoicing that they weren't the one getting bullied.

Agony moved through my body. If I could've willed myself into death, I would've ended it right then.

Steve knelt and grabbed me by the back of the neck, forcing my face into the tiled mosaic. "I said, clean it!"

"How?" I shouted into the mushroom cloud.

"Lick it."

The smear of muddy spit had already dried. I could feel Steve's grip tighten on the back of my neck. "Lick it like you're giving it head."

Steve pushed my face into the hard floor with all his athletic might. He kept pushing harder. I held on until the pain became unbearable. Knowing my cheekbones would give out long before Steve, I touched my tongue to the base of the mushroom cloud. Ground zero. Nagasaki.

It was forced worship of my own destruction.

I worked my way up the stem of the blast as Steve pretended to moan. "Oh baby, lick it some more," he said as the others laughed.

The texture was gritty, and it tasted sour.

"Get up!" Jameson kicked me on the side of my leg.

Mack Freewater reached down, pulled me up by the hair, and punched me in the eye. My brains rattled. White sparks fired as the back of my head hit the floor.

"We heard what you did to that cop," he said. "Only an asshole assaults an officer of the law."

Somebody hacked, and I felt phlegm spray across my face. "That'll teach you to spit on the Bomb and disrespect the police."

"Now stand up," shouted Steve. "You better show some school spirit by getting your ass into the year-end-rally. And watch your back; we'll be waiting with a razor."

Total defeat. My body and soul ached as I walked, being forced to attend an assembly to celebrate the achievement I failed to reach. This school was an inferno that I couldn't escape.

I had no choice, so I made my way to the gym, passing the classrooms that held every torment put before me for the last four years.

It didn't seem fair. I wanted that diploma; my future depended on it. Steve didn't give a shit about the degree. For him, it was a minor step towards success. To me, it was everything.

I entered the gym and stood at the top bleacher, looking down the staircase. Row upon row of long green banners hung from the ceiling, each embroidered with our school logo. Order and might floated in the balance, beckoning me to join or be crushed. The marching band was playing our school anthem, the Green and Gold. Bass drums pounded with felt mallets as students milled down, taking their place on the bleachers. I sat in the first empty seat I could see, cold aluminum causing a sensation to stab through my pants, aggravating my bruised flesh.

The entire gym sang along. I just licked the sleeve of my shirt to get the foul dirt out my mouth, glancing at the invisible hand shaping humanity—this pecking order that we are all conditioned to accept through school sports.

You could see it when you looked at the school's population. Only one percent would make the team, and they would be boys. As for the girls, the best ones would go to the elite members of the team. The bleachers were filled with the rest of us, celebrating the team's accomplishments as if we were blessed by being part of their success.

Some of these kids would serve in the military, risking their lives to further global economic agendas, while yearning for the same honor and victory that these ballplayers received. Most of this crowd would be average, working ordinary jobs—two weeks vacation on a credit card. Some of the kids would grow up to be alcoholics, some drug addicts, some go to jail; most would slave for decades to pay off a mortgage and student loan, making it to old age to retire with dignity. Only a slight few would share in the dream.

It was like the bullshit my mother repeated: work as a virtuous slave for less, and you shall reap vast rewards upon death.

I looked down upon the scene; the graduating class was oblivious to our place in society. From my years of Ritalin, I thought it all normal. Now that I can recall this event with clear thought—remembering the sports uniforms, the Richland High T-shirts and sweaters, the mushroom cloud logo on the banners, backed by the choral cries of the school song, I believed that I had been paying witness to the rekindling of the Hitler Youth.

Then came the Führer, Coach J.C. Warrington. The crowd became emotional and started chanting "Nuke 'em till they glow... Nuke 'em till they glow!"

He raised his hand. Everyone was awed into silence.

The Coach closed his eyes, gripping the podium, savoring a slow intake of Jesus-blessed oxygen interlaced with a dash of radionuclides. It was so quiet that his breath resonated.

Then he spoke: "We have been bruised and hurt in the arena of war. This school year, more than any other, has seen countless physical sacrifices: Jameson, number thirty-three, a broken shoulder. Hannity, number seventy-two, a sprained knee. Freewater broke his nose. It's been tough, but we've grown strong; for it's in the off-season time of peace that we grow fat and die. But in this school year," cried Coach Warrington, "we have waged war on a battlefield 100-yards long! So it's my pleasure to present to you the Washington State AAA Champions, the Richland Bomber football team!"

Everyone went nuts as they walked onto the riser.

"Before you," the coach motioned to the row of uniformed players standing at attention, "before you are the noblest of soldiers. These boys know there's no virtue in defense but bone-crushing attack. Victory in football is the earthly judge between right and wrong, and God loves a winner. God loves the Richland Bombers. Now fight with me. Fight with me!"

Every student stood, cheering, except me.

I felt a tap on my shoulder. It was Bone, pushing a stick of gum into his mouth. "What the fuck happened to you?"

"Those fuckers kicked my ass for spitting on the bomb."

Bone smiled. "Someone should've spit on it a long time ago, fucking repulsive mascot. Sorry you got beat but I'm glad it was you who had the guts to do it. Let's get out of here."

"Where are we going?"

"Atomic Lanes."

CHAPTER 8

ATOMIC LANES

Atomic Lanes was a bowling alley with a video arcade. It was close to school, and the burgers were cheap. We opened the doors, greeted by the resonant crack of bowling balls hitting pins. They had painted the place like the hull of a battleship, musty and dark.

A guy with a thick mustache and mullet was the only one using the lanes. You could tell by his posture that he took the game seriously. He sent his ball into the alley with the grace of a ballet dancer.

The arcade was back in a darkened room. Reese Whitaker was playing Ms. Pac Man, his body caved under the trench coat that he always wore despite the heat. Phosphorus lights from the console's screen reflected off his shaved scalp, dampened by the occasional scab. He had the remnants of a black eye.

I recalled the struggle, how they pinned him down, screaming—the electric razor and everyone refusing to help.

He was Richland High's future valedictorian, a guy who made the whole school look good. He broke academic records and secured the bursary. To pay him back, they made his life resemble a trip through Dante's Inferno.

Bullies accosted guys like Reese and me on an hourly basis. Me? Okay, I can dig it—who the fuck am I? But Reese? He was the academic star. It just wasn't enough. They were going to break him and melt him like a golden Hathor on the slopes of Mount Sinai.

In addition to being the smartest kid in school, Reese was the type you'd expect to hide an ingeniously crafted pipe bomb in his locker or shoot up the campus.

Bone shook his head. "Pretty fucked up what happened to him. That could've been us."

"I'm next," I said, bothered by Reese's intensity. "All he did was step on the bomb. I spit on it. He's the valedictorian, something to be proud of, and they treat him like this? What are they gonna do to me?"

"Shit," shouted Reese, hitting the joystick as if his life depended on the game.

A guy with Barry Gibb hair and a clear visor greeted us at the lunch counter. He wore a light grey Izod shirt with the Atomic Lanes logo embroidered on the breast, a couple of bowling pins surrounded by rotating electrons.

"Two burgers," said Bone, dropping a ten-spot on the counter. "Make'em with tater-tots to go. I've got class in forty minutes. I better eat in the arcade... Fucking test is half my grade."

We took our drinks and sat down to wait on the burgers.

"What happened with the counselor?" he asked.

"Five-year plan," I mumbled.

He shook his head, feeling my pain. "Things could be worse. You could be in my shoes. I'd give anything to be on the five-year plan. Think of it this way; for one year, you don't have to make a choice. Anyone graduating on Saturday has nothing but choices: what school to attend, what career path to follow."

I heard Reese shouting at the screen in the distance and thought of his bald head. "I'd rather die than do another year," I shot back.

"I guess we all have problems." Bone was nervously pulling and pushing on his straw to make the Styrofoam cup honk.

I glanced back to get another look at Reese when I saw Cher Hanson walking towards the bowling alley. I could barely make her out through the glass doors, but the attitude was unmistakable. I sat up, my pulse rising.

Cher flicked her cigarette against the wall and entered the building, blowing smoke throughout the foyer. The guy behind the counter ran to apprehend her as she made her way to the arcade.

"Excuse me, miss; you know you're not supposed to be in here."

Cher pretended not to hear him.

"Miss, our manager has banned you for smoking in the arcade. You need to leave."

"Look, I won't do it again," she said, facing the Donkey Kong tower, prying her hand into her tight cutoffs to find a quarter.

"Miss…" He grabbed her arm and pulled her towards the exit.

"Fuck you!" she pulled away and kicked open the door.

"Hey, that was Cher Hanson," said Bone. "She sure has gotten hot. I'd love to hit that, but I'd be afraid of catching gonorrhea."

"Whatever," I said, standing up. "That's a horrible thing to say."

"What?"

"Nothing; I got to go."

"What about your burger?"

I ran outside to catch her, but she was gone. I thought she might have walked into the greenbelt. When I got there, she was nowhere in sight.

"Fuck!" I kicked the dirt path.

When I got back to Atomic Lanes, Bone was waiting out front with my burger. "What's up?"

"Sorry, man, I'm a little uptight—Ritalin withdrawal and not graduating."

He handed me the burger. "Look… I'm sorry."

"Don't worry about it." I unwrapped it and took a bite. "We're cool."

"You like her, don't you?"

"Yeah," I said, ravenously swallowing the half-chewed meat.

He nodded. "She's better than Mikultra Skala."

"Like I've got a chance with her."

"Don't sell yourself short." He patted me on the back. "You could probably have them both. Let's go. I've got a final in Humanities."

Depressed, I returned to school to clear out our locker. The assembly was still going, and I could hear the band playing "Thriller" by Michael Jackson. There were lipstick kisses all over our locker, and someone had written the words, "I love Bone" in blue eyeliner. I stared at this monument to his sexual prowess as I shoved each demonic book into my backpack, wondering if people would ever love me the way they loved him.

When I got to the last book, I lifted it out, uncovering a pile of assignments that I had finished but never turned in.

I remember the first time I hid an assignment. I couldn't take the negative criticism anymore. I crumbled up the paper, made ugly by my muddled brain, and stuffed it into the depths of my desk, only to glance at it months later as I cleaned out my belongings at the end of the term with my failed grade. It was like a stillborn baby, causing me to relive my original shame as I gazed down at the illegible misspelled crap. Writing, unrecognizable as human thought, polluting the page with moronic scribbling, failing to reach even the lowest standards of communication. I was incapable of displaying intelligence. Hello—anyone in there? Jesus, he's breathing.

Better to not hand it in than face them telling me of how shitty my work was.

It was always, "Deacon is extremely intelligent but doesn't apply himself. When you talk to him, it's clear he knows the material; he just refuses to prove it. He never finishes his work or tests."

How can I? Dyslexia is the time thief. It stands as my ultimate obstacle, keeping me from participating in a society based on written words or math.

I walked the halls, kicking the sea of strewn papers on the floor. They were graded assignments, all of them with better marks than I'd ever achieved in my life. I reached down to pick up some: Bs, Cs, or better.

"Oh, this person got an A-minus. Must be nice." I flung it against the wall and picked up another to torture myself.

Feeding through the stack, I saw a crude xeroxed DIY skateboarder zine. This was it, Carson's zine! I knew I was holding the Holy Grail in my hands. I ran to find a bench to read it and sat, excited. Then the specter of dyslexia killed my joy. When had I ever read for pleasure? Never. Reading was torture, and my ego could only take so much.

Discouraged, I threw the zine on the ground.

I looked at its grainy photocopied cover laying on the floor. Why couldn't I just read it? Something so simple could bring such happiness.

The zine called to me. I wanted it, even if reading it would make me feel stupid. I can read, just not fast enough to keep up with society's demands. I had two hours to kill, so why not try?

The bell rang, and students bustled in all directions. Some freshmen saw the zine and went to pick it up. I lunged at it. "Sorry, that's mine," I said, "must've dropped it."

I thumbed through the pages. It was simple, crude, and, best of all, interesting. Then it dawned on me, I could use this and other zines, like Thrasher and Maximum Rock' n' Roll, to practice reading. Maybe punk rock would give me what I lacked after all?

The zine seemed to vibrate in my hand, like a magic talisman. For the first time since elementary school had crushed my spirit, I wanted to be a better reader. Not for my parents or Jesus, but for me.

There wasn't much text, mostly photocopies of Polaroid pictures. It was called "Milk-Bone," its name and logo ripped off from the dog treats. The cover had Ronald Reagan's face pasted over the Pope's, with one of his quotes: If You Can't Make 'Em See The Light—Make 'Em Feel The Heat!

I had heard about this punk zine for months. It was notorious. How it made its way onto the floor of our school was a mystery.

Milk Bone's reputation was flawless. All the punks read it to keep up with things. Even the heshers dare not talk shit. Carson was a shepherd, and his zine provided our small town with a gateway to the future that lay on the other side of the mountains.

I opened it slowly and took my time, figuring out each word.

Articles about new bands filled the pages. These groups were doing the unthinkable, mixing punk and heavy metal, slowing it all down. The bands had names like Skin Yard and The Melvins. There were pictures of them dressed in strange fashions—hippy meets lumberjack. I'd never heard these bands, but the whole spirit enthralled me.

From what I could tell from my spotty reading, Carson had discovered this new type of music during an unsupervised trip to Seattle that his mother financed. He had seen the Melvins at a place called Gorilla Gardens. This was an all-ages club that had two rooms: one for punk and the other, metal. As usual, the punk and metal crowds didn't mix. There were fights in the lobby, but things cooled, and one group started to influence the other. Carson predicted that this was the future of music.

"The whole world will bow to Seattle in five years," wrote Carson. "This music and fashion will dominate the 90s. This is the next thing."

I believed him and wanted to be a part of this future. But how? I wasn't skilled at anything. Maybe I could be a roadie?

There was something about this zine, and how I was able to struggle through it. It made me feel that I might have a future.

There were other articles. Milk-Bone also bridged the gap between queer and straight, two groups who, before the early eighties, in small towns like Richland, did not mix.

Carson wrote about a Seattle all-ages club called the Monastery, located in an old church. The place was filled with a dark gothic post-punk attitude. Rumor had it that the middle-aged fuck who ran the club gave MDMA to the kids for free in exchange for sexual favors. He allowed street kids to live there too. It was a regular commune of sin and scene, gay kids hanging out with their straight friends. Carson had even spent the night there, blowing the money his mother gave him for a hotel on drugs. Feeding through the pages, I could see that his indulgences knew no end.

This crudely laid out handmade magazine showed me a world where I might fit in. I started to dream about taking in a gig at Gorilla Gardens and sleeping on the floor of the Monastery with the street kids. Maybe even play in a band. Carson's do it yourself magazine filled me with longing for freedoms I'd never known, and a group of kids who would accept me.

I was so fascinated by Milk-Bone that I hardly noticed the bell ring. It was 2 pm. Two hours had passed. The end of this torture had finally arrived.

CHAPTER 9

RITALIN KID

No one wanted to let me sit next to them on the bus. There were rows of students, facing forward, refusing to make eye contact or scoot over. I decided to find somebody lower on the pecking order and force my way into the seat. That person was my next-door neighbor: self-proclaimed fashion diva, Adonai Garcia.

I stood over him. I wasn't sure, but I suspected he was wearing girl's pants. They had a high cut waist, and a thin belt with triangular metal enforced ends. He matched them with a white dress shirt and bolo tie. His hair stood stiff in an amazing pompadour, often imitated but seldom replicated. His black hair was bleached and teased on top, locks growing down over one of his eyes—sort of like Prince—and gelled over the ears. If I had stared at him any longer, I might have noticed a smidgen of eyeliner.

Adonai moved his upper body towards the edge of the seat to block me. When I wouldn't leave, he looked up and growled, "Oh, it's you."

"Nice to see you too. Mind if I have a seat?"

He faked a smile and turned to look out the window without scooting over.

Adonai thought he was a supermodel. He had the strut, the presence, the confident eye toward the coming trends, but the school hallways were as close as he could get to a catwalk.

His family emigrated from the Philippines when his father took a job at Hanford. Our families shared an A-duplex on Abbott Street, where the whole neighborhood knew he was gay. My parents often prayed that Jesus would "deliver this poor child from homosexual perversion."

As usual, I was forbidden to talk to him. Because of my imposed unfriendliness, Adonai told everyone that he hated me as a neighbor, said my presence never matched his attire. It was bad enough for him that I lived next door, with our houses joined, but we were forced to sit next to each other in Home-Ec class too. He would frown at me every time I showed up to take my seat.

His best friend was Christy Gadget, girl next door par excellence, and every mother's dream for a daughter-in-law. He always had a group of girls hanging around him; all of them beautiful creatures, each asking him for makeup tips and fashion advice. Fenix called them fag hags and considered feigning homosexuality after observing Adonai in action with his platonic harem.

"May I sit here?" I asked, poking him in the arm with the tip of my skateboard.

He overreacted and yelped, "Ouch," sliding over, disgruntled.

I sat down and leaned back, closing my eyes, hands resting on the nose of the skateboard positioned between my legs.

If only I could be numb. Maybe taking Ritalin was the right thing to do? I thought about residing in a world of darkened silence, trying to imagine a life where I could escape this town. The stress of the day caused me to let out an involuntary "Ugh."

Adonai turned to me and crossed his arms over his chest. I opened my eyes to his scowl. "Look, if you are going to sit here, you can't make disgusting noises."

"You don't have to worry," I said, "this will be the last time I ride this stinkin' bus."

He moved his head in to inspect my black eye. I pulled back.

"Look, I'm going to say this once," he said, "only a loser steals a keg of beer and beats up a police officer."

"I only shoved him."

"Really? I suppose that shiner just happened. Who do you think you're talking to?"

Is this what people thought; that I beat my way free from the police? Who was spreading this story? "Does the whole school know about this?"

"Just about. Fenix is telling everyone who'll listen." Adonai tilted his head back as if posing for a camera. "Most of them think it's pretty neat, but I know the truth. If you're going to continue to go on crime sprees with Neanderthals like Bone Reinhold and Fenix, you'll end up in prison or working at the Tastee Freeze." He turned away from me. "Trash can only drag you down."

"Fuck you."

"I would never fuck you," he said, shaking his hair to the left and right. "I only do men who are gorgeous."

I ignored him until the bus stopped where Mikultra Skala got off.

Mikultra went to our church. Every Sunday, I watched her walk down the aisle to her pew in form-fitting clothes. It was the only thing that got me through the service.

During the school year, I looked forward to this stop every day. It was such a pleasure to see her walk past and fantasize that I was her boyfriend.

This time, instead of ignoring me, she said, "Hello, Deacon."

I blushed as she walked towards the front of the bus. It was a dream come true. I never had attention from girls before, especially ones as stunning as Mikultra or Cher. What was different?

Adonai caught me staring at her. "Ew," he said. "You don't like her, do you?"

"She's hot enough to make you straight," I said.

"One of Andy Warhol's muses, maybe; Joan Collins for sure, only because Alexis Carrington is so much like me. But Mikultra Skala would never make me straight. Her only redeeming feature is her youthful chest."

"You mean her ass."

"Ew… you are disgusting, and she's a tramp, full of herself— like she's some muff stud. The only reason she's saying hi to you is because she's heard you're some badass who beats up police. You two deserve each other."

I was beginning to discover the benefits of having a lawless reputation. Just as optimism began to fill my soul, I felt something gooey running down the back of my head. I reached around, and whatever it was had stuck to my hand.

"It's glue," said the person behind me. "Now you'll have to get a haircut, and this faggot here can give you a bald head makeover."

I turned around. It was Dick Jameson. All his minions started laughing and cheering him on. It wasn't my stop, but I got off anyway, jumping out with about five other students.

Dick got off behind me with two of his friends. "Hey loser," he said to my back, "you fucking spit on the Bomb."

Anger shot through me. I took my skateboard and swung it, hitting him square on the side of his cheek.

"Fuck you," I shouted.

He fell back and dodged the board as I went in for a second smack. The two minions who got off with him started throwing dirt and garbage at me from a nearby can. One of them threw the metal lid like it was a frisbee. I blocked it with the board, and it rolled down the street into some bushes.

Seeing that I was rabid and raw, they backed away.

"You're a dead man, Jones," Dick shouted, holding his jaw. "I'll beat your ass at graduation if I have to."

"I'm not going to graduation, fucker." I looked around fuming. There was Mikultra; she'd been watching the whole altercation.

Embarrassment, anger, and sorrow; my emotions were boiling over. I never had outbursts like this on Ritalin. I would always take the sucker punch. But now I was cut loose and would never turn back.

Faced with looking like an idiot in front of Mikultra, I decided to own it. "Bring it on you fuckers. I'll beat you like I did that cop."

They could see it in my eyes. I was out of control, and every one of them believed the story that I was so intense I was capable of anything. They all backed away.

"Get the fuck outta here," I said.

"We won't forget this, Jones," Dick said, motioning for his friends to retreat.

I looked over at Mikultra. She smiled at me and waved, disappearing down a gated driveway.

My heart hurt, and I felt boxed in. I was in this fancy neighborhood and a long way from home. Behind the houses was a green belt that separated the neighborhood from a service road. I ran among the trees to get away, breathing heavy. Once alone, I dropped to my knees, staring at the dirt.

If only I could read, I wouldn't have these problems. No one would single me out as weak.

Why was I like this? Why couldn't I just read like everyone else? Just a simple thing. Was it too much to ask? I just wanted to read!

I wrote what I thought was the letter "d" in the dirt with my finger. "If I do one thing in this life," I said to myself, "it will be to master the difference between a 'b' and a 'd.'" I continued writing "d's" with my finger over and over in rows and columns at a furious rate. Again and again:

bbbbbbbbb
bbbbbbbbb
bbbbbbbbb

thinking I was writing "d's."

Then I tossed off my backpack and pulled out a textbook. "US Government be damned." It fell open to page 213, some garbage about the electoral college. I struggled to read the first sentence: "Eeeech State sheall appear int such manner Leej-slater theeev may direct." direct! There it was: "direct." It started with a lower case "d."

I referenced my textbook to compare its "d's" to my "d's." I stared for a while, convinced that I had overcome an unsolvable problem until the letter moved like an insect, my brain orienting it into its proper form.

For a terrible moment, until the letter returned to jumbled type, I could see that its "d" and my "d" were different. I had written "b's" instead of "d's."

Despair came over me, and I screamed in anguish, flinging the textbook at a tree. "Goddammit!!!!!"

I pulled out my Dummy Math book and hurled it to the sky in rage. It came back at me like a savage bird of prey, wings flapping, the corner of the hardcover cutting my cheek, sending me into chaotic abandon and pure hatred for life. I knelt in the dirt, destroying the "b's" I'd written and gripped the soil with my hands. I felt incarcerated in hell, trapped.

"I want to die," I screamed, hands clawing at the clay, tears flowing down my cheeks. "I want to die right now. I hate my life."

I knelt there, still for a moment, staring at the soil between my fingers. I was lower than I'd ever felt. Another year of glue in my hair, school making me feel like a basic form of bug, and my parents and their fucking Jesus Christ; it was more than I could bear. I wanted out, and if I couldn't escape, I'd rather die.

When I got home, I put off going inside. I knew what was waiting for me. Suicide was starting to look like an option. I stood at the front door, its weather-worn wood a mere four inches from my face. I had to be ready to confront them.

"Fuck it," I said, sticking my key into the latch.

CHAPTER 10

COTTONWOOD

I stepped into the house, wanting to die, knowing I'd blown it. Denied last place, stopped two feet from the finish.

"Deacon?" my mother called out from the other room.

The sound of her voice was poison to me.

I walked into the kitchen. She was sitting at the table, pinching her fingers, worry all over her face. She looked like she'd been waiting all day. The whole room was clean, everything in order. She had strategically placed magazines in front of her. It was like she wanted the environment to subdue me because she lacked the guts for confrontation.

She sat silent as I looked about the room, trying to assess the situation. All I could come up with was that desperation had finally driven her to make a feeble stand.

She saw my cut cheek, black eye, glued hair, and stood up. "What's happened?"

"Nothing," I said, trying to get past her.

"Your face."

She tried to touch me. I slapped her hand. "It's nothing."

"Your father told me you have to do another year."

I rolled my eyes and pushed past her.

"Where are you going?"

66

"I'm covered in blood and have glue in my hair. Where do you think?"

"Are you okay?"

"Seriously?" I started to walk upstairs and locked the bathroom door. I turned on the fan to drown out her bullshit.

She tried to open and knocked. "Deacon, I need to speak to you."

"Go to hell," I said, under my breath.

I looked up and saw my reflection in the mirror. My beat-up face shocked me. The blood and shiner were the least of it. What bothered me the most was the glue.

"Fuck this," I said, opening the medicine cabinet and pulling out my razor, removing the blade.

I ran the shower hot and let the water cover me, closing my eyes as my mother beat on the door. Breathing in the steam, I thought about doing another year, the mortifying embarrassment with each assignment and test, getting bullied by underclassmen, surviving the school day only to come home to my parents and their Christian abusive ways.

This was the end of my time. I could not continue. I let my mouth fill up with water, sprayed it upward, and sat down in the tub, feeling the intensity of the water as it rained down.

Thoughts about how everyone would be better off without me swam in my brain. My parents wouldn't have to pray; teachers wouldn't feel like failures.

Maybe I could be reborn fortunate? If I found myself reincarnated, what would I look like? I began to visualize it. I would be handsome and lean, with a girl like Cher Hanson at my side. I would dress and wear my hair the way I wanted, not some conservative look to get a job or please my mother. I would be someone who basked in the freedoms I'd never known.

I imagined myself playing drums or guitar. I had tattoos and looked like that band in Carson's basement. The thoughts filled me with joy until I was interrupted by my mother's banging.

"Shut up," I yelled, picking up the razor. One way or another, I would find peace.

I tilted my head back, slowed my breath, and slit my wrist.

Watching the blood spiral around the drain, I felt control for the first time in my life. It was nice. I could see why Cher cut her skin or people got tattoos. I finally had ownership of my body.

I began to think about Cher. I was sure she liked me. Despite not graduating, maybe in some odd way, things were looking up? Dick Jameson poured glue in my hair, but he was the one with the broken jaw. And Mikultra waived at me. What can one make of that?

I went to slash my other wrist and stopped. I didn't want to die. I just wanted out, to take charge of my destiny. I hadn't cut deep enough anyway. If I could get away from the world I inhabited, everything would be alright.

"Don't die," I said aloud, "just find a way to get the fuck out."

By the time I got dressed, my father was home, sitting on the couch. Despite the warm weather, I wore a long sleeve shirt to hide my wrist. My mother was in the kitchen. "Sit down." She pointed to a chair at the table; my dad got up from the sofa, folding the newspaper. "I'm making a snack for your father. Would you like a ham sandwich?"

"Sure." I was reluctant to be seated. Being at the table with the two of them could only lead to suffering. I lingered before the kitchen table as if it were a trap. My father sat down, glaring.

My mom smeared some Underwood deviled ham on a slice of Wonder Bread. She called it "angel ham," telling everyone she was "reclaiming wholesome food for the Lord."

She set the plate before me, forcing me to sit. I looked at the Underwood sandwich. I was starving, but nobody could touch their plate until my father said grace. The length of this prayer depended on how hungry he was. If he was starving, a few words sufficed. If he'd had a bag of chips on his way home, we were in for a sermon. My mother held our hands,

"Heavenly Father," he began, "we come before you with our son, Deacon, whom you have given us to raise..."

This religious bullshit was more than I could take. My mother must have felt my body language stiffen and gripped my hand tighter, shaking it in silent reprimand.

My father continued, "You have given Deacon a solid mind, and he has used it for frivolity instead of purpose. Please help him recover from wasting his gifts. We ask that you help him see the wickedness in his nature and help him make the most of this extra school year that You have given..."

Anger shot through me. I stood up and slammed my fist on the table, knocking over my chair. "I'm not doing another year!"

My father bolted up. "How dare you disturb grace!"

He was about to lunge at me when my mother put her hand to his chest. She was always trying to negotiate between keeping peace and maintaining their control over me. "Deacon, that was very disrespectful; not only to your father but to the Lord."

My dad sat down. I was beyond hungry from withdrawal and took a bite of the sandwich as I picked up my chair and sat. "I don't want to be prayed over," I mumbled with my mouth full.

"Deacon," said my mother, "I know you're upset about not graduating, but you need to do another year and see this through. It's non-negotiable."

"Why don't you ask me what I want?"

"Do you even know what you want?" said my father.

"No," I said, taking another bite in defiance.

"Every child in this great nation is required to get an education," my mom said. "Another year of school might give you the time you need to figure out what it is you want. I think you need to apologize to your father."

"I'm sorry. I meant no disrespect to you or the Lord." The sheepish way I said these insincere words repulsed me. I just wanted to eat my sandwich and get away from them.

My mother forced a smile as if her white teeth could change our moods. "Who knows, you might bring up your grade point average by going an extra year."

"I don't think I can do another year," I said with a mouth full of food.

"Why not?" She braced her hands on the edge of the table, readying herself for my answer and her husband's reaction.

"I no longer have it in me."

She thought for a moment before speaking. "Deacon, have you considered going back to the higher dose of Ritalin?"

"To tell you the truth," I said, taking another bite of my sandwich, "I've thought about it every second, all day long."

"Then why don't you go back to the old dosage?"

I hesitated before responding. "I quit taking it on Saturday."

"You need to go upstairs and take a pill right now," my father said.

I put down my sandwich and gave him an angry look, clenching my fists.

My mom motioned for him to calm down. "Deacon, you never spoke like this before," she said. "You're missing a few credits, and you're giving up. You used to be happy attending class. Maybe you should reconsider taking the medication."

"Nah," I said disgustedly. "I don't like the way it makes me feel. Like my brains are twirling."

"You don't like the way it makes you feel?" My dad shot forward. "You're not going to like how it feels being a bum either. You need to go back on it."

"Mark," said my mother in desperation.

"The school insists." He pointed at me. "He has no choice."

"I do have a choice." I pushed my chair back from the table. "It's not their decision. What are they going to do, expel me in the final week? They have no jurisdiction over my body. I can fight for our country, vote, but I can't be trusted to sit in class unless I'm sedated with pills?"

"Deacon," said my mom, sensing my defensiveness, "your father and I want what's best for you. God put you on this earth for us to raise and keep safe."

"That's the thing," I said, "I'm not safe at school. I'm in constant fear."

"Are you bullied?" she said with a worried look.

"What do you think?"

"Why didn't you tell us?"

"I just lacked the will to do something about it. This drug you've got me on helps me concentrate because I'm too stoned to notice anything but what's placed in front of me. I've thought about the medication all day, not because I think it will help me, but because I'm addicted, and the withdrawal is leaving me psychologically depressed and suicidal."

"Oh, dear." My mother looked pained and put her hand to her mouth. She reached out and touched the side of my cheek. "We had no idea." She began to cry. "Deacon, you're ruining your life. Just help us understand."

"I've tried," I said. "I view the world differently now. It's like I've been living in a dream. Now that I'm awake, I'm not going back."

"Come here." She pulled me close and wrapped her arms around me, petting my hair. "Lord, I come before You with a heavy heart in regards to our son Deacon. He is struggling so much with everything right now. Please guide him..."

I pushed her away. "Quit praying over me. There's nothing wrong with me. Just leave me alone."

71

"That's it," said my father. He walked around the table and hovered like an immovable giant, the same as he did when I was an infant, denying me my way. I relived the moment. It was like I was three years old all over again, and he was the moored power. "You're coming with me, out to the yard."

My mother cried as he pulled me to the sliding glass door. We both knew what this meant. Even the most minor offenses found me out back by the cottonwood tree. Each time I'd have to go out there, my father would have me cut the branch. The wood would have to be just right, or he'd make me start the whole excruciating process again.

If my dad got to six or seven lashes, and felt the bow too light or flexible, I'd have to go back and pick a sturdier branch. Then he'd start the whipping all over. If the branch broke by the ninth lash, he'd start over from the beginning with a stronger bow, working his way back up to ten.

The Lord would only be satisfied with ten good lashes.

If my father left welts, my mother would write a letter excusing me from wearing shorts during PE on religious grounds.

He stood behind me as I looked up to the tree, the cotton floating down around us like snow or heavenly manna, giving my father the divine right for what he was about to do. I studied the branches until the perfect specimen of cottonwood bow presented itself. Over the years I'd become skilled at whip selection.

My father handed me a pocketknife. I reached up and cut the bow and pulled off the small sprigs before giving him the bare branch.

"Pants," he said.

I undid my jeans and underwear, lowering them to my ankles, standing there, vulnerable, my most private parts exposed.

"Grab your knees," said my father, positioning himself to achieve the best smack.

I bent over and saw my masculinity hanging there, shamed in the open air. My pubic hair reminded me that somewhere inside this depleted shell was a man.

"You're going to take your medication, by God, if I have to give it to you myself," he said, slicing the air with the branch, causing it to whistle as the wood cut into the back of my thigh. I let out a gasp, feeling it more than I did in my drug muddled past.

"I am pained that you've forced me to do this, Deacon." He whipped me a second time, bringing me to my knees.

"Oh God," I cried.

"Get up! You've made me feel the way Abraham felt when the Lord commanded him to kill Isaac." He pulled back to send the branch cracking into my flesh.

I shot up and grabbed the bow as it smacked against my palm, sending pain shooting up through my wrist. I held it with resolve, looking him in the eye as he tried to pull away. I yanked him towards me and towered over him. It was the first time I'd noticed that I was taller than him. "I'm not taking the pills anymore."

He pointed a finger up to my face. "Yes, you will."

I grabbed his wrist with a resolute grip. "Try and force them down my throat." I pulled him closer, gripping him tighter. "And this is the last time you'll ever whip me." I threw the cottonwood bow down on the grass. "I'll not be your lamb."

The realization that I was physically superior spread across his face, and we stood staring at each other, both of us knowing. He changed from a threatening stance to a calm self-preserving posture. "All right," he said. "We'll give it a try and see how it goes. But any behavior problems, and back on the Ritalin you go."

"Whatever," I said, pulling up my pants.

I walked inside, grabbing my sandwich off the plate, and stood over my mother in a dominating stance. "I would like to be excused; I don't feel well."

"Did he whip you too hard?" she said, eyes filled with tears.

"No," I said, pissed off. "I'm experiencing Ritalin withdrawal. I'm going to bed to sleep it off."

CHAPTER 11

STUDY BUDDIES

It was Saturday, Bomber commencement. I would have preferred to disappear, floating off into space, but no, it was going to be worse. After this day, everyone would know that I didn't graduate. There would be no ceremony for me unless I chose to be a spectator.

Other kids were excited about what lay ahead. Why? I don't know.

I had been sleeping and moping since Monday, and the withdrawal was gone. I pictured Bone and Adonai getting ready for the big day, while I refused to leave my bed.

"Get up." My mom tore open the blinds. "It's ten-thirty. If you're not going to school next year, then you're getting a job."

I was shocked. I sat up, eyes stinging. "It's Saturday. No one hires on the weekend."

"That's right," she said. "That's why I've set up a meeting for you today with the youth pastor." She pulled back the sheets.

"Mom!" I pulled the comforter back over my body.

"He's going to help you create a resumé and fill out a job application." She bent down and kissed my cheek. "He's also going to counsel you on what jobs are appropriate for Christians."

Would the control ever end?

She poured on that cheesy *Let's be positive* smile she always conjured in these situations. "You can start applying for jobs on Monday."

Job hunting terrified me, the thought of putting myself out there for them to decide if I was good enough for their shitty job. What kind of a lowlife would I be if a minimum wage employer rejected me?

And the youth pastor, how would he help? I recalled him trying to be cool with his spikey hair: "Hey Deacon, I skateboard too." Yeah right!

"Can't this wait till next week? I haven't had any summer vacation."

"Summer vacations are for those who go to school," she said, pulling back the comforter again. "Adult life is starting today. One who is slack in his work is a brother to one who destroys."

I rolled my eyes. "I don't know who'd hire me," I said, half sarcastic, half-serious.

"A haircut might be a great place to start. Get out there with a nice professional look." She was kicking dirty clothes to one side of the room. "The youth pastor has some ideas. Your appointment with him is at three. Oh, and he wants you to bring an application. You'll need to stop at McDonald's and grab one on the way."

Maybe getting a job wasn't such a bad idea; use the wages to get the fuck out of this festering pit of shit, radioactive Christian hell, move to Seattle.

I waited for her to leave before getting up. I stood, looking in the mirror. My hair was showing some length. "I'm not getting a haircut," I said under my breath, grabbing some clean clothes.

How had it come to this? How could I have mismanaged my life to this degree and in such a short time? I was peaceful; I had gone to church and bought into their control. I didn't steal, well, not before the keg. I hadn't done drugs. Well, I had been smoking a lot of hash, and there was that crank Reese had cooked. Anyway, I didn't do heroin or coke, but I suppose you could count getting high on Ritalin as drugs.

Ritalin!

I rummaged through my dresser, rumpling the clothes, making my mom's handiwork a mess. There it was, a large bottle of Ritalin sticking out from a pile of socks. I remembered Carson offering to buy it. I had this intense desire to be a part of his world. The mosh-pit and the crowd, Milk Bone, it all burned inside. This music seemed to be the only thing that understood me. I could sell my Ritalin to Carson, and maybe we could become friends. I put the bottle of pills in my pocket.

After an English muffin for breakfast, I got up to leave.

"Here's ten dollars for the barber," my mom said, putting down her newspaper. "And don't dawdle. You don't want to leave the youth pastor waiting. Ganzel's is always busy."

"I'm not going to Ganzel's. A bunch of greasers work there, and they put tonic in your hair."

"Then go to Supercuts," she said, smiling as I took the money.

Instead of getting a haircut, I skated to Carson's. I walked right up and rang the bell. His mother answered. I stepped back, floored; Carson's mom was hot! She was brunette, tan, and had taken up bodybuilding. She had chiseled arms like a man. I stared at her grapefruit-size breasts that stretched her shirt, wondering if they were real. She looked like the type of woman you'd imagine Bon Jovi dating. I was about to ask for Carson when I realized I didn't know his first name.

"Are you here to see Chad?" she said, smiling.

Chad?... I nodded. She put her hand on my shoulder, shooting desire into my body. "Come on in; Chad's in the basement."

I walked down the steps, admiring all the Xeroxed fliers that lined the stairwell. Carson sat among a group of punks gathered around a coffee table, sniffing glue. Cher Hanson was with them. We made eye contact, and she blushed.

"Hey," said Carson, standing up to shake my hand, "look who's here, Mister Cop Crusher." He started to sing a punk song by the

Vandals, "Pat Brown... tried to run the cops down. Pat brown... ran 'em to the ground. Pat Brown..." He motioned to the couch, across from where he held court. "Have a seat."

I could've sat anywhere, but I pushed my way between some dude and Cher.

"Man, that was some crazy shit; the way you and your buddy bolted from the cops. So tight I almost want to forgive your pal for ripping up my lawn."

"Yeah, sorry about that," I mumbled.

"No need." He reached across the coffee table to grip my hand again. "The way you guys ditched those cops—worth the hassle just to see. Outta sight. It's all we've been talking about. Besides, no harm done, except for some grass. It'll grow back."

He became serious and sniffed a bit of rubber cement, passing it to the punk on his left.

"My mom was pissed. I can't have parties here till September." He smiled, trying to get back into the moment. "Not to worry," he threw out his arms like a referee in a boxing match, "I found an old house in Pasco where we can have parties. It's practically condemned, owned by this old hesher. Says we can have bands. We just have to let him work the door. He gets to keep the cover. Speaking of which..." He turned and reached for a stack of handbills. "Here." He handed me a flier. "Diddley Squat is going to play the night before the Boat Races."

I looked at the handbill. It was a sketch of a guy, half punk, half rocker, running from the police. The print on the leaflet read:

Carson's Boat Race Mosh—The cops can't touch us!

$5... Corner of 6th & A-Street, Pasco.

The guy on the sketch resembled me, but a fictionalized me; what I would want to be. I looked up at Carson, not understanding.

"Yeah," he laughed, "it's you. I told you that shit was outta sight! That lovely lady next to you bolted too. You oughta get to know her."

Cher moved in her seat, smiling at me with desire, our legs touching as she repositioned herself. I looked back down at the flier and knew I'd reached some axis as if the whole universe was changing and everything would start going my way.

"I hope you can make it," said Carson.

I looked up and smiled. "I wouldn't miss it for the world."

Carson grabbed more fliers. "Here, invite your friends. Even Fenix and the one on the motorcycle. He's a dick, but I can dig him. What's his name, Bone? She-yeah; love it!"

I stuffed the fliers into my pocket.

"So," he said, framing the back of the couch with his arms, "you haven't told me what brings you to the Basement?"

I pulled out the sepia pill bottle and placed it on the table. "You said you wanted Ritalin."

Carson's eyes widened. "Holy shit, that's a three-month supply."

"Yep," I said with certainty, leaning back.

"What do you want for it?"

"You tell me."

He picked up the bottle, examining it. He laughed and slammed it back down on the table. "I'll give you fifty."

"Seventy-five."

"Deal." Carson got up. "Let me go speak to my mom."

I watched him leave and turned to Cher. "It's good to see you again."

"Yeah, you too," she said, almost nervous. "I knew you'd come." She lit a clove and blew smoke out of the corner of her mouth.

"How did you know?" I asked, sensing her nervousness, feeling like I was in control for the first time in my life.

"I'm slightly psychic," she said, holding her cigarette with a delicate hand. "I can predict stuff."

"Really?" I laughed.

"Really," she said, unaware of how crazy she sounded. "I have prophetic dreams. I had one last night about you." She pointed to something invisible with her index and middle finger that held her smoldering cigarette. "I dreamt you were famous."

"Really?" I said, finding her fascinating. "What was I doing?"

"I don't know—you were just famous." She wanted to change the subject as if revealing the dream put her at a disadvantage. "Have you ever been in love?"

"I thought I was, but I guess not."

"What made you think you were in love?"

"Well," I said, leaning back into the couch, "it was the Aurora Borealis."

"The Northern Lights?" she said, moving closer to me.

"Yes. A girl I was friends with was moving. Her father had taken a job in Texas. She was leaving the next day and wanted me to come over on her last night in town. So I snuck out of my house to walk eight miles to see her. I looked up, and there were the Northern Lights."

"So you took it as a sign of love?"

"An omen, I suppose."

"But it was only an omen that you were going to get laid."

"You could say that." I didn't want her to know I'd never had sex or a girlfriend.

Cher laughed bitterly, gazing at the cigarette's cherry; then her whole demeanor changed. "Well you can find love—but I cannot."

"Why not?" I asked.

"Most men are pigs. They want a trophy girl who will build up their status, but that's not me. Funny thing is, these women are bigger whores than I'll ever be. I'd never let a man support me. I'll be a dyke before I cow-tow to some man." She put out her smoke in an ashtray with disgust. "What about you; you want a trophy girl?"

I thought about Mikultra Skala, who I considered the prettiest girl in school, and how I wanted her over the years. Now suddenly, Mikultra was paying attention to me, but I didn't care. She was nothing compared to Cher.

"Just what I thought," Cher said, looking me in the eye. "You'd never date a girl like me."

"Of course, I would," I said, "I'd love to go out with you."

"Yeah?" Cher scribbled her number on an old receipt she pulled out of her pocket. "Then prove it by calling, but don't call after four. That's when my father comes home. To say he's overprotective doesn't describe him."

"I can only call at certain times too," I said. "Will your father be home tomorrow?"

"Not as long as it's before four," she said.

Carson came down the steps, his cocky air deflated. "Hey man," he said, embarrassed, "my mom only has fifty. Can we work something out?"

"Your Boat Race Mosh," I said, pointing to the flier; "admission is five bucks. Put me on the guest list, plus three, and we'll call it even."

"Alright!" Carson slapped my hand. "I knew you were cool."

All the punks started patting me on the back as he handed me a fifty-dollar bill, filling me with confidence. Carson was their shepherd, and for the first time in my life, I felt popular and accepted.

"Want to go with me to the mosh?" I asked Cher.

She squirmed a little and smiled. "Yeah, I'd like that."

Carson pulled a pill-crusher from a nightstand. He dropped in a tab and proceeded to grind. He spread the powdered pill out in a line onto the latest issue of Milk-Bone and snorted my Ritalin up his nose with a short straw.

"Ah, she-yeah!" He tilted his head back and shook it as if to disperse the hit throughout his skull. "God, I fucking love this shit."

He passed the pill crusher to Cher. She smiled at me with brooding sexual desire, looking me in the eye as she ground the pill. I watched her snort my medication, feeling a little odd about it. She whipped her hair as she threw her head back after snorting it all in. I wanted her more than ever.

"This is the first time I've ever snorted Ritalin," she said, wiping her nose with the back of her hand. "It's cool, but heroin is better."

"You do heroin?" I asked.

"I've snorted it before. It's awesome."

It was like she was admitting it to scare me off or test me. Her danger only made me want her more.

"My God, what have we done?"

"Sit down Lewis; you ain't seen nothing yet. Wait 'till Charles spills that Fat Man over Nagasaki. That bomb's from Hanford!"

CHAPTER 12

BOCKSCAR

I left Carson's with a lust for life. The day had just begun, and it was perfect. I didn't know what to do with myself, so out of the habit of obedience, I went to Ganzel's. I looked in the window at all the tattooed greasers rubbing tonic into short hair and shaving heads with razors.

"Fuck this!" I said and called Bone from the nearest payphone. "Hey, what are you doin'?"

"Baked," he said. "Commencement is in four hours. I can't go like this. I'm too stoned."

"Then let's go for coffee."

He fumbled with the phone. "Sure."

"I'm buying. I got fifty bucks off Carson, sold him my Ritalin."

"Fuckin' sweet," he said. "Did he say anything about his lawn?"

"He forgives you. He thinks you're cool 'cause you split from the cops. Put us on the guest-list for his Boat Race Mosh."

"No, shit?" he mumbled. "We'll see; you know I don't dig that scene. I'll meet you at the cafe. Just give me twenty minutes."

The Bockscar Café was something Eastern Washington hadn't seen before, an espresso bar. The place was founded by an overpaid Hanford worker with disposable income that needed to be invested. He had experienced the Seattle Coffee scene while on vacation and thought that selling lattes in a Manhattan Project town, out in the middle of nowhere, was a good idea.

At the grand opening, he told the Tri-City Herald that he modeled Bockscar after a Seattle café called the Last Exit. Carson had mentioned this espresso bar in his zine.

Instead of capturing the cutting-edge chic of the Last Exit, he ended up with a gaudy place and an overly friendly staff. Being clever, he named it after the plane that dropped the bomb on Nagasaki and decorated it with a pastel seaside motif. Out front, it had a large patio with a fountain.

Right when you walked in, you got the feeling from the décor that their target demographic was the upper-middle-class. But instead, the place would fill up with students, freelancers, and deadbeats, pulling down the average ticket. It was Bone and I's favorite place.

The walls were covered with photos of wartime Richland. There were pictures of the Fat Man and Little Boy mushroom cloud detonations. A framed front page of the Daily Herald, dated August 10th, 1945, announcing to everyone at Hanford that they had been working on the Nagasaki Bomb. The article explained how the good folks in Richland had stopped the war, saving many lives. They even had framed autographed photos of Paul Tibbets & Charles Sweeney.

When I was a kid, my pa took me to an air show where Charles Sweeney was diving with a forty-three-second pull away, just like he did over Nagasaki. He and some other World War Two ace were there charging money for autographs. My folks didn't want to pay for the photo, so I went home without a souvenir. They said making money off his patriotic duty was a sin.

Once the drama class put on a play where they reenacted the two bombings of Japan. Out of the student body, it starred Reese Whitaker as Colonel Tibbets, Bone as Dutch Van Kirk, and Collin Fenix as co-pilot Robert A. Lewis. Adonai boycotted the play on moral grounds, stating to the attendance office that he was a conscientious objector. The prominent roles, more relevant to our community, were those of the Nagasaki pilots. These, of course, went to Steve Hannity and his ilk.

The play started with Tibbets recruiting his team and drama with their wives not wanting them to go on such a heroic mission.

"Alright boys," said Reese as Tibbets, voice filling the auditorium. "We got forty-three seconds to pull this baby nine miles back from ground zero, or we'll be toast like those Japs."

"We can do it chief," said Bone, doing his best Van Kirk.

"You can count on us," added Fenix.

"Okay, saddle up. We've got to get this fortress into the sky over Japan. But first, let's autograph the bomb before we load her up."

At this point, they would dim the lights and broadcast a Foley recording of an aircraft engine.

"Alright, open the hatch and let that baby fall… Look at her go."

"Colonel Tibbets, I think it's a dud," said Bone.

"It's no dud, Van Kirk, that bomb's American made. Brace for the jolt!"

A movie projector cast the glowing ball of doom, pulsing like a copulating mushroom onto a screen above the stage, and Fenix jumped up and yelled, "My God, what have we done?"

"Sit down Lewis. You ain't seen nothing yet. Wait till Charles spills that Fat Man over Nagasaki. That bomb's from Hanford!"

And the kids cheered like midnight joy at the turning century.

I waited for Bone, looking at all the photos from the Manhattan Project, praising our ingenuity regarding human destruction. I was checking out a picture of General Douglas McArthur standing in front of a group of humiliated Japanese when Bone walked in. He was still high.

He stumbled up to the counter. A fleshy girl with creamy skin was there to greet us. "Hi, welcome to Bockscar. How may I better serve you?"

"Doppio Macchiato," said Bone.

"What's that caramel drink you guys have?" I asked, not being able to read the menu.

"You mean our Signature Carmel Delizia?" She seemed ecstatic by executing her role as a customer service representative. "Can we make that a Ventizamo size?"

"What's a Ventizamo?"

"A large."

"What do you call a small?"

"A Piccolo."

"I just want a small caramel thing."

"One Piccolo Signature Carmel Delizia and a Doppio Macchiato," she shouted to the barista. Bone and I looked over to the bar, and there was Adonai. He huffed and pouted at our order.

"Did you get that?" shouted the girl, letting down her customer service face.

"Small caramel latte and a double shot with steamed milk," he shouted back.

"Sorry he didn't call your drinks back accurately," she said. "Enjoy your Legendary Bockscar Experience."

"We will," I said, walking over to the drink handoff.

There were five people ahead of us. Adonai was backed up. He wasn't paying attention to what he was doing, spraying milk and sputtering steam, under-filling some of the cups and over-filling others. A Hanford executive in a suit glanced at his watch. "Here's your latte, sir." He handed off the drink, tilting and spilling with contempt. An elderly woman frowned and shook her head. "Help these days."

"Can I have mine in a porcelain cup, for here?" I asked.

Despite the rush, production stopped, and Adonai stood there scowling at me. "Your drink will taste better in a paper cup."

"I'd prefer not to chop down any trees."

"What-ever."

"Hey," said Bone, "shut up and make our drinks."

Adonai slammed a paper cup onto the drink-handoff.

"Is this my drink?" I asked, confused.

"What did you order?"

"I don't know. A caramel something."

Annoyed, he threw up his hand. "No, this is not your drink. This is a Skinny Latte with legs; yours is a Piccolo Signature Carmel Delizia. This is your drink. Thank you, sir."

"Facetious fuck," said Bone. "I'd kick his ass, but every girl in town would hate me."

We sat down on the couch with our drinks. Bone took a sip from his tiny cup, fingers fanning out.

"God, Adonai makes shitty espresso," he said, wincing, and positioned himself to face me. "So, are you still planning to drop out?"

"Yep," I said with resolve. It seemed to be Bone's way of bringing us to the subject that we were pretending not to face—my not graduating and his joining the military.

"What are you going to do with your life without a diploma?" he said.

I was wondering if he was saying it to make himself feel better about his own scene. Flames of emotion shot through me, killing my mood. "I don't know, the same thing you'll do with one, I suppose." I pushed away my coffee and buried my head in my hands. "I can barely read; what can I do?"

"I'm sorry, Deacon. I was asking because you're my friend," he said with an uncertain air that was unbecoming for him. He gyrated his cup, watching his remaining coffee whirl as if he were trying to see his future in the dregs. "I guess this is what I'm trying to say." He looked as though he were in a trance. "Don't be in my situation; do another year. Tonight, I am going to graduate. My folks will take me out to a stilted dinner because it's their last obligation as parents. They will give me a card with a check for a hundred bucks, then I'll go to the kegger down at the delta—drink and drive like all the other graduates. Maybe some will die tonight, weaving on the dark road, smashing through to the other side. Maybe one of them will be me. Don't be me, Deacon. Make different choices. Prepare yourself for the dark times ahead. If you do, you may find yourself the only one in a lifeboat."

I gripped the arms of my chair, not wanting to understand what he was trying to say. This talk horrified me. He was giving up. What did he have to worry about? He got good grades and would do well in life if he applied himself. He just had to figure it out.

"Don't worry." He laughed. "I'm not going to kill myself. I'm not that brave." Bone set his demitasse down. A worried look crept across his features like quick-spreading jaundice. "Monday my father's going to drive me down to the Recruiter."

Even though I knew it was coming, it still shocked me. It would go against everything Bone was and stood for.

"So this is it, you're joining the Army?"

He chuckled, shaking his head, and frowned down at his espresso. "No... the Marines."

I sat there, stunned.

"I'm eighteen," he said, looking pained. "They found pot when they searched me. They're also charging me with theft, supplying alcohol to minors, assault, vandalism, and resisting arrest. My lawyer thinks he can get me off if I join. It's either homelessness when I get out of jail or the Marines."

He downed the last bit of his coffee and smiled, looking me straight in the eye. "Things are so bad at home. They've given me a case of Top Ramen to eat, and I'm not allowed at the table. I've been smoking shake. I'm only welcome in the house as long as it takes for me to ship out. He leaned over and patted me on the shoulder. "You see why I'd trade places with you? You've got a whole year to figure out what your next step is and you're throwing it away. I would've failed a class or two to put it off, but it's not an option. Might as well get it over with."

He didn't understand. I could go to school for twelve more years. I wouldn't learn anything. An extra year would buy me time, but my problems were never going away. No matter what, they would haunt me for the rest of my life. There is no cure for Dyslexia and Dysgraphia. I was born this way. An extra year would only reduce my self-esteem to nothing.

Bone looked at his watch. "I hate to say this Deacon, but I'm due to graduate from Richland High. I'll have to leave you here unless you want to come with me to commencement."

"No, I don't want to go. Fuckin' bums me out. Go ahead without me."

He stood up, wanting to change the subject. "Will you be going to the keg tonight?"

"At the Delta? I don't know. I'd have to sneak out to do it."

"Not sure if I will either. It's one of those things where everyone expects you to go. Well, if I decide, I'll have Fenix call you. See you soon, okay."

"If I don't see you, good luck and congratulations."

"Yeah." He set down the cup and left.

I looked up and saw Adonai staring at me with a wet bar towel in his hand. He had been listening to our conversation. "You aren't graduating?" His voice and manner had lost all semblance of the bitch within.

"Nope." I sighed into my empty cup.

"What are you going to do?"

"People keep asking me that." I sat up tense. "I'm not sure what I'm going to do. I don't even know if I'm capable of filling out a job application. I find the whole process a little scary."

"Don't worry," he said, motherly, "like the phoenix, you will rise again."

"How can I rise again when I've never risen in the first place? What about you? Shouldn't you be off work, getting ready for commencement?"

"I'm not going. Marching down that aisle with all those tacky people isn't my idea of the red carpet."

"But you graduated?"

He wrinkled his nose. "I told them to mail me the diploma. I've got better things to do then go to their peasant celebration. It's no fun being the only queer in town."

We shared this moment without talking, where we both quit looking at each other and became absorbed in our thoughts.

"Okay," I said, breaking the silence, "see you next door."

"You wish," he said, posing in defiance then walking back to his espresso machine.

My encounter with Bone was depressing. I looked up at the clock. I had just enough time to skate to the church for my fucking meeting with that stupid youth pastor. The thought of it depressed me even more. I needed an application. Defeated, I stood up from the couch and went up to the counter.

"Hello again," said the same cheery girl. "It's a great day at the Bockscar Café. How may we better serve you?"

"Could I have a job application, please?"

"Sure," she said with a smile. "We're always hiring. We're a people company that serves coffee."

Adonai pushed his way past her. "Excuse me, I'll handle this." He smiled at me. "Sir, how may I better serve you?" He frowned and tilted his head with a sultry stare.

"If you don't mind," I said, "I'd like a job application."

He took his hand off his hip and held it up; palm titled towards me, rolled his eyes, and said, "What-ever."

"What do you mean, whatever?"

"I mean like you'd ever get hired here, 'whatever.' They only hire beautiful people." He flipped his hair as if to make it flow like the ocean, but it stuck in one place from all the styling products.

"Look, I don't want to work here. I just want an application."

Adonai looked at me with distrust and reached under the counter for a pad. He tore off the app with a slow and graceful motion, handing it to me, held between his thumb and forefinger like it was a soiled napkin.

"Thanks," I said. "The youth pastor at my church is teaching me how to fill out one of these."

He lost his composure and let out a hearty laugh. "What-ever. I've got to get to work."

"You don't have any customers," I said, looking around.

"Then I'll spend my time polishing the counter until someone walks in. It was a pleasure serving you, sir." He wiped the area around the cash register, ignoring me.

"Fuck you then." I marched out of the café.

The Garcias had immigrated to the US when Adonai was a kid. His dad worked on the railroad at the Hanford Site, transporting plutonium warhead slugs. His mom often told my mom about how bad it was back in the Philippines and what a struggle they had gone through to get where they were today. With all that hardship, you'd have thought Adonai would have a better attitude.

He pissed me off. Adonai always seemed to have the air of a disgruntled super model refusing to go out onto the catwalk. I wanted to apply there to spite him. Besides, to get out of this fucking desert, I would need a job.

I turned around and approached the counter. The girl smiled at me. "How may I better serve..."

"Can I borrow a pen?" I smiled at Adonai. To his dismay, I went back to my seat to fill out the application.

CHAPTER 13

SLURPEE

O h, the horror—document of dread. I was now facing the decisive conclusion of one who fails school because of learning disabilities—filling out a job application legibly and without error. What if I reversed some letters or misspelt my name?

I sat down to complete it like a Faustian pact—selling my soul for minimum wage, signing it in blood-red ink. I struggled to fill it out, smearing as I wrote with my left hand.

My father once told me that in his day, lefties got it strapped behind their backs until they no longer favored the Devil's claw.

What if I had been born in another time and place, when the priests scribed from right to left and used hieroglyphics? I might have been king, a Mesopotamian lord with seven wives, one for each day of the week. Men would travel by camel to seek out my wisdom, and the ancestors of those who bullied me in this life would cower before my armies.

But no, I was born in the shadow of Rome, where they write from left to right—so I smear the ink with my southpaw—and the middle of words look jumbled. This makes me a loser.

If I couldn't fill out a job app, how was I going to read things while working the lowest of jobs?

After spending over an hour to complete the simple one-page document, I approached the counter. "Here," I said, handing the job application to the girl. I was so anxious, I was sweating.

"Great, I'll give it to my manager."

Adonai gave me a dirty look.

When I got home, my father stood, looking at his watch and blocking my way to my room. "You missed your appointment with the youth pastor. It's almost five," he said. "What have you been doing?"

"Job hunting."

"The youth pastor was supposed to help you find a job. You should have called him and let him know you weren't going to show up. That was extremely rude." He was standing firm, despite Monday's altercation by the cottonwood tree.

"What does he know about finding a job? He's spent his whole life in the service of the church."

"Maybe that's the point. If you were job hunting, where did you apply?"

"Places." I pushed my way past him.

I could tell he was thinking hard, realizing this altercation wasn't going to be easy. There was no way to prove I was lying. "Okay, where exactly did you apply?"

"Bockscar Café."

"And? You were gone for a long time."

I had to respond fast. "Atomic Lanes, Sgt. Bubs, Zips, and Arctic Circle. I was thinking about applying to Nuclear Fission Pizza on Monday."

"You can apply with my company on Monday," he said. "Some entry-level janitorial positions just opened up."

For a split moment I was tempted. A Hanford paycheck would be the fastest way to leave home. Then that old fear returned of working out at Hanford, being controlled by my father, getting zapped like the Hanford Man; it sounded like a trap.

"Your mother gave you money for a haircut." He stood there, reasserting his position with his fists clenched.

I tossed the ten onto the kitchen counter. He looked at it, navigating his way through the tension, not wanting to relinquish physical control over me, but knowing there was nothing he could do.

"Why didn't you get a haircut?" he said, studying me, looking for a hole in my confidence where he could pounce.

"I'm getting a job; I'll pay for a haircut with my own money," I said.

He stepped up, pushing his chest out, raising his fist. "Listen, in this house we have rules..."

"And what rules have I broken—not letting you beat me?" I moved up close. "You want me to get a job; I job hunt. I don't need the youth pastor's help."

Desperate, my mother came between us. "Deacon... Mark... Please..."

I stared at them. "Look at my face; you think I can't take a beating? I've had enough. Don't pray over me; don't tell me what to do. I understand your rules: go to church, say grace, do chores, and yes, Mother, if I don't go to school, I have to work. I get it, now back off."

You could see it in my father's face—like a tomcat who accidentally wanders into another's territory, he was trying to figure out a way to back down with dignity.

My mother sensed his helplessness and decided to speak and ease the tension. "Deacon, next time, maybe you could bring the applications home before filling them out. We would like you to work somewhere that has Christian values. And you need to call the youth pastor to apologize."

I was about to respond to this bullshit when the phone rang. My father answered. "Hello?" He frowned while looking me in the

95

eye. "Who shall I say is calling?" He handed me the phone. "It's for you."

It was probably that stupid youth pastor. "Hello?"

"Deacon Jones?" It was a woman.

"Yes?"

"Deacon, this is Sharon Richards from the Bockscar Café. I was looking at your job application, and I want to make sure that I'm reading it right. I think it says you're available to work any time. Is that so?"

"Um, sure." Anxiety began to hit me.

"That's what I thought. Your application was a little hard to read."

I became afraid of getting the job. What if I'd have to read or other unknowns?

"Here's my situation," she said, "I'm in a bit of a pinch. I had to let someone go which left us with uncovered shifts. If I were to hire you, would you be able to start tomorrow morning and work this person's schedule?"

"Yeah, sure; whatever you need."

"Then you've got a job. Welcome to the Bockscar team. We're pleased to have you on board. See you at seven tomorrow morning. Oh, and dress in black."

I hung up, feeling strange and doomed.

"Who was that?" asked my mother.

"I've been hired at the Bockscar Café."

My mom looked at me in disbelief, mouth open like she'd had a lobotomy. "Did you hear that, Mark? Deacon has a job."

"They didn't interview you?" said my father.

"Guess not. They sound desperate."

"They must be desperate," said my dad. "A job like that is a poor substitute for a diploma."

"Well, Deacon, I think it's wonderful. You're off to a good start," said my mother.

I was still standing next to the phone when it rang again. Instinctively, I reached to answer it. My father stopped me with a motion of his hand. I was never allowed to answer the telephone. It was forbidden. When I was old enough to be left alone to do chores, my parents would randomly call from bible study to see if I'd answer.

"Hello?" He grunted and handed me the phone. "It's Collin. Make it quick."

Despite Fenix's drinking, cussing, and chewing tobacco, I could receive calls from him because his family went to our church. His mother and my mother were friends. Whenever he called, it was a message from Bone who was off-limits. They considered Bone and his family sinful because they were agnostic.

"Hey man," said Fenix, "no more Richland Bombers!"

"Yeah, whatever."

"Listen, Bone and I will meet you tonight at the 7-11, ten sharp. We're going to the keg."

"I've got to get up early tomorrow. Maybe I'll see you at church on Sunday?"

"Unless you've got plans with pussy, you better be there. You want to be a loser your whole life? Come on, it's graduation!"

"Yeah, graduation," I mumbled. "I got a job and have to work in the morning."

"Fuck that," said Fenix. "We'll pick you up at ten."

Fenix hung up the phone. My parents had just turned on the television. We had recently gotten cable. The 700 Club and other conservative Christian shows now had their own network where you could tune in anytime. Watching Christian programming had become a nightly ritual for them. Pat Robertson was explaining the Moral Majority and praising Ronald Reagan on the TV. Last night, he was carrying on about how feminism leads to socialism and women killing their children. The light from Pat Robertson's head surrounded my mother's like a halo.

"Where are you going?" she asked as I passed by.

"To bed," I said. "I've got to work in the morning."

"I want you to consider applying out at Hanford," mumbled my father, stuffing potato chips into his mouth.

"It's a good living." My mom smiled, reaching into the bag.

I went to my room and lay down, staring at the ceiling until I started to see visions in the popcorn texture. I stayed like this for hours until my parents were asleep. I climbed out my second-story window, jumping to the tree to scale down.

Streetlamps made the whole neighborhood glow in a monochromatic tone. I looked at the tree. It had taken on a sinister shape in the darkness, a black creature from mythological depths. Everything gleamed in the moonlight but the tree. It absorbed the luminosity like a vortex, making it a dark phantom whose branches were used to beat me.

I cut through the green belt. It was dark, and the trees bore shapes of hallucinatory nightmares. Every step of the way heightened my already pensive nerves. I was on the lookout for skunk, smelling them in the distance.

Emerging from the dark, I saw the glowing 7-11. Summer is always time for Slurpee, so I entered, blinking from the bright florescent lights.

The clerk stared at me as I walked past him to the Slurpee fountain. I wondered if he'd graduated from university, and this was the best job he could find. Was this the future of the average person in this great land? I assumed that he had at least graduated high school. The thought caused me to sink lower.

After filling my Slurpee, I moved to the pop fountain and topped it off with Coke. I hated super frozen Slurpee and preferred it watered down. You get more flavor and less brain freeze. He was still watching me as I took a sip and added more cola.

When I got to the counter, I took another sip. "Excuse me, my Slurpee is too dry. I want to top it off with some more fountain pop. I'll be right back."

"You'll have to pay extra if you top it off," he said.

"Bullshit," I said, taking a sip. "I won't buy it then."

"Why should I care if you buy it or not?" he said, sounding drugged. Maybe he was? "I don't even care if you pay me at all. Take it. It's not like 7-11 pays a commission."

"But they pay you."

"Minimum wage, then they act like they own you. This location even has the most Slurpees sold in the country. They should give me a little more if they're gonna have me hawking a million Slurpees a day."

I didn't know what to say; I just examined him like I was inspecting my future.

"Do you know how long I've worked without a smoke break?" he said. "Six hours straight. I can't even stop to take a shit. Keep the fucking Slurpee. Drink it for free."

"Excuse me," said a woman standing behind me. "You're being paid to work, not talk to your friends. I expect some service. Give me a Lotto ticket."

The guy just stared at her for a moment. "Do you want to pick the numbers?"

"Give me random," she said, opening her purse and forcing me out of line with her girth. "I've got some winning scratches too."

I could smell her perfume. It gave me a headache. The clerk punched up the ticket. There were three people behind this woman, and she was holding up the line with Power Ball and scratch tickets. I walked back and refilled my Slurpee. "Fuck it," I said, walking out of the 7-11 without paying.

Bone and Fenix drove up in their grandfather's Plymouth Duster. Bone had borrowed it shortly after they impounded his motorcycle. Once, it might have been red, but weather and time had dulled it to the color of vomit. There was rust underneath the fenders. One of them had a hole large enough to expose the bald tire. Even in the dark, I could see through the window that the upholstery was ripped and had been repaired with silver duct tape.

"Slurpee?" said Fenix, passing me a can of Bud Light through the passenger window. "Fuck that. Let's party!"

"No, thanks." I took a sip of slush, quick and hard, freezing my brain. "It's too hot to drink warm beer. I'll hit the keg."

"Slurpee over American beer? Get the fuck in, Communist," said Fenix. He was still wearing his commencement cap, reminding me that I had nothing to celebrate.

Fenix was lit and tilted his head back to pour beer down his throat. "Tonight is going to be the best night of our lives," he shouted.

There were about a million places I'd rather have been than in the back seat of that car. Why had I even let Bone and Fenix talk me into this?

Bone inserted an 8-track cassette. "Break on Through to the Other Side" by the Doors blared through the speakers.

"Do we have to listen to that Sixties shit?" said Fenix. "How about Motley Crüe?"

Bone turned it up.

"So how was dinner with your folks?" I asked.

"Fucking sucked."

"Bullshit," said Fenix. "They took you to Clink & Dagger, where they serve water in pewter mugs."

"It still sucked," said Bone.

"So what did Uncle get you for graduation?" Fenix took another swig.

Bone rolled his eyes. "You're not going to believe this." He reached over to the glove box and pulled out a gun.

CHAPTER 14

THE DELTA

"Holy shit!" Fenix jumped back, startled.

I stayed put, too shocked to say anything. Bone held it up, finger on the trigger, posing like James Bond, his other hand driving.

"Fuckin' sweet," said Fenix, leaning in with awe, as if the gun was a holy relic. "I wish Uncle would've given me a pistol for graduation. Let me see it."

Bone handed the gun to Fenix who held it in both palms like it was a baby bird. "This is so fucking cool."

"You can have it," said Bone, waving him off. "I don't want it."

"I'd love it," said Fenix, lifting it to his face to ogle it like a jeweled crown, "but I don't want to answer to the Major when the piece goes missing. Uncle can get real."

"What on earth am I going to do with it?" said Bone. "I can't even sell it; the registration is in his name."

"For fuck's sake, you shoot it," said Fenix. "God, who the fuck raised you? Certainly not my uncle."

"You could sell it on the black market," I said.

"And have it traced back to my dad? No thanks." Bone shook his head. "That gun is only good for shooting people. Besides, he forgot to include bullets."

101

"You're a faggot," said Fenix. "The Major gave you this gun as a coming-of-age present. It's your God-given right as an American adult to carry this piece." Fenix took the gun, turned around in his seat and aimed it at me. "Second Amendment, baby!"

"What the fuck," I said, ducking.

Fenix started to laugh.

"Hey," said Bone. "Give me that."

"I'm cool." Fenix lowered it. "Let me just hold it a while longer."

Bone took the gun and placed it on the seat next to him as "Break on Through" played out.

The Delta was a wildlife refuge, upstream from where the Yakima River flowed into the Columbia. Bone pulled into a gravel parking lot. The air smelled of swamp and Russian olive. Next to a Forest Service information board was a metal barrier gate, partitioning off a dirt road that led to the river.

We walked down the path that cut through tall grass and trees, leaving a hole in the dense foliage, making it look like the mouth of a leviathan. Frogs and locusts hummed away. The limbs of the trees were so thick and tangled they reminded me of neurons with axons and dendrites. It was the type of trail where the Headless Horseman might throw a flaming pumpkin. My imagination began to conjure lions and tigers and bears, lurching in the shadows.

Up ahead was an area where the river had cut a bank. Fenix's friend Danny Lau had driven his truck around the barrier and parked it in a clearing. Despite the warm weather, the kids had made a bonfire, cutting silhouettes against the moonlit river. A large group of guys gathered around the back of Danny's pickup, where they kept the keg. The boys were in one group and the girls in another, each holding a red plastic cup in their hands. Motley Crüe's "Shout at the Devil" blared from the truck stereo.

I stood back, looking at these people, knowing I had traded in an evening of sleep just so I could suck up to every jerk I'd attended school with and never wanted to see again. There was Adam Price, lug-head extraordinaire, spilling beer on his hand. Mack Freewater was there too. Danny Lau was manning the keg.

If I stayed in this town, and toed the line, I would end up like these people. I would eventually devolve into something like Fenix. The thought horrified me. Maybe Cher was so intriguing because she was different from them. Maybe it was because she'd left.

Bone walked up to the keg.

"That'll be three bucks," said Danny. He poured Bone some piss warm brew that was mostly head.

"I guess cold is too much to ask," said Bone.

"Shut up and quit being a faggot," said Fenix, punching Bone on the arm, burping. "You're a high school graduate; enter the real world and drink up." He turned to me. "Can you dig this guy? Says he doesn't like warm beer. What the fuck? He's a fucking socialist, picky as fuck. But tonight bro, you and I are going to get laid."

Bone lifted the plastic cup and forced it down. I stepped up to pay Danny, knowing that he had slept with Cher, the woman I wanted more than any other. As he poured the beer into my plastic cup, it felt like I was accepting sacrament from a molesting priest.

"Sup, Deacon?" he said.

"'Not much," I felt like I wanted to hit him but could not. "Thanks for the beer, Danny," was all I could say.

"No prob."

I began to hear whispers as I walked under a low hanging gnarled tree. "Hey, that's Deacon Jones, the guy who punched a cop and stole a keg. And there's Bone Reinhold."

Adam came up to us, wasted. "Is it true what they say?" he said swaying. "You stole a keg and ditched the cops?"

"Yep," said Bone, pouring out his shitty beer and taking a joint out of a cigarette case he kept in his pocket. He lit up

103

without offering any to the jock. "Deacon ditched the cops; they caught me."

"You guys rock," said Adam, spraying spit as he tried to talk.

I looked to my left, and there was Mikultra Skala, standing five feet away, looking right at me. She wore powder blue jeans that gripped her lavish hips. A skintight shirt invited my attention to her cleavage, held futilely by a bra. She had sprayed her hair like a poodle, teased and spritzed everywhere, but flattened bangs in front. Matching blue eyeliner accentuated her eyes in a vain attempt to advertise her sensuality.

What made her so attractive? It might have been her frame, bursting with pubescence, that gave the illusion of eternal spring—but I was Hades and could not keep her. There was a part of me that would not want to, for right here, right now, she was perfect and could only decay. I wouldn't be able to bear one small change in her, whether physical, mental jading or a minor adjustment in fashion. It was because I didn't love her. To me, she was second-rate compared to Cher.

"Hello," she said.

"Hi," I said, trying to think of something to say. "Enjoying the party?"

"I think so." Her words were raspy and sensual, dripping out of her mouth like cloverleaf honey. "It's fun."

"Yeah, I guess."

"You go to my church, don't you?"

"Yeah," I said, embarrassed. Why? I don't know. She went to the damn church, too.

"I heard you stole a keg, then hit a cop to escape." She was looking me up and down.

"Word gets around," I said, taking a sip of beer and not making eye contact, "though it didn't quite go down that way. I didn't hit the cop. I just shoved him, and he fell."

"What was it like running from the police?" she asked.

"You know," I said. "It's a thing."

"It sounds thrilling."

"Well, it's not for everyone. If the police catch you, they kick the crap out of you. Ask Bone."

I had heard some women gravitated towards lawless men, women who married prisoners on Death Row, or fell in love with outlaws. But I'd never seen it. Now here was one of the most sought-after girls in school, talking to me because I'd pushed a cop. She'd never noticed me before. She even had to ask if we went to the same church. Now I was someone she'd never forget.

"It's nice to know you go to my church." She pushed her chin forward while cocking her head in a slow sumptuous manner.

"Yeah," I said, feeling awkward.

She took a sip of beer and looked back at her friends. They were giggling. "Well, I better get back to my girls. It was nice talking to you, Deacon. Maybe I'll see you at church on Sunday?"

"If I don't have to work," I said.

"If not, I'm sure I'll see you around. Take care."

Fenix walked up and put his arm around my shoulder. "Deacon," he said with bad beer and tobacco breath in my face, "what's up with Mikultra Skala?" I could smell the body-odor on his shirt.

"I don't know," I said, ducking out from under his arm.

"Seems to me that she likes you."

"She's fucking hot," said Danny Lau, swaying, spilling his beer over his knuckles.

All the rednecks started patting me on the back, saying things like:

"Fuck her man."

"God, that girl has a nice body."

"I bet she's a virgin."

They were lavishing me with attention, bolstering me with confidence. It felt good.

"Deacon's getting laid," said Fenix, punching me in the arm. "She likes you, bro."

"Whatever."

"Didn't you see the way she looked at you?"

"No."

"Work it, man. Work it," Fenix said. Then he turned around in a circle, arms extended to heaven. "Everyone, get over here. I've got something to say."

All the guys positioned themselves around the bonfire, swatting mosquitoes. The girls ignored us.

Fenix lowered his head like a preacher on Sunday, spat his tobacco into an empty soda can, and said, "Come and gather 'round the fire. Let me tell you the story of me, Bone, and Deacon Jones."

"Jesus, Collin," said Bone.

"The three of us stole a keg and sold it to the punks for thirty bucks. We had to fight 'em cause they didn't want to pay, only gave us twenty-five. When the cops came, Deacon hit the officer so we could all get away. They caught me and Bone, but Deacon and that punk-dyke Cher Hanson were able to run."

"Cher's a slut," said Adam.

"Cher's a special girl," said Fenix. "She gave our friend Danny a blowjob in the back of the school bus on a band trip."

Danny blushed, giggling and looking scared.

"Shut up, Fenix," I said under my breath.

Fenix ignored me and continued. "We can all learn from Deacon and Danny to help keep the dream alive."

"What dream?" asked Danny swaying.

"The dream of freedom—to walk tall, like Alexander Hamilton, Benjamin Franklin, or George Washington."

"I want to be like them," said Danny.

"You are like them," continued Fenix. "Cher imparted Danny with wisdom. If she were with us today, she'd have one thing to say… 'Let's fucking party!'"

Fury boiled within me, and I wanted to punch Fenix in his loud mouth. I pushed him back and poured out my warm beer. He was too drunk to notice. I pulled back and was about to hit him when I heard someone shout, "Hey, loser!" I turned around, and it was Steve Hannity, emerging from the trail. "Yeah, Jones, I'm talkin' to you!"

I stood there, watching the school bully walk right towards me. I had lived in fear of Steve Hannity since we were little kids. He was master of the playground, shoving and dominating.

Now I wasn't afraid; he seemed small. I guess I'd reached the point of nothing to lose.

The entire party stopped, and everyone stood in silence.

"You think just because school's out the rules don't apply?" he said, pointing at me. "You spit on the Bomb. We're not done." Instead of looming large, he was ridiculous.

"I could give a fuck less about your stupid Bomb," I said. "You and your friends can beat me down and shave me, but you better kill me, cause I'll sneak into your house and murder each one of you in your sleep. As you say, I'm a loser. I got nothing to look forward to so I might as well take you down with me." I spit on the dirt, just like I had the Bomb.

Adam Price whispered into Steve's ear. "This guy's crazy. He hit a cop."

Steve twitched and looked at him. "He's a pussy. He won't do anything."

"No, he's for real. The cops chased him for miles. There's two of them; the guy on the motorcycle is over there." Adam pointed to Bone.

Steve stepped forward. "Only an asshole assaults an officer of the law."

"What are you gonna do about it?" I said, unflinching, wishing he would hit me. Bone moved up to stand by my side.

"You should listen to your buddy," said Bone. "If we can take it from the pigs, we can take it from you." Bone reached into his leather jacket and pulled out the handgun, pointing it at Steve.

Everyone jumped back, gasping.

"Unlike my friend here, who plans on murdering you in your sleep, I'm happy to do it right now while your girlfriend watches."

"We're cool," said Steve, putting his hands up. "We don't want trouble."

"Then back the fuck off," I said, staring him down.

"Let's go, Deacon," said Bone, flicking his joint into the river, "this party's lost its charm." He turned to Fenix. "You'll have to get a ride home with Danny, cuz."

Bone and I walked to the car through the passage of trees, confident enough not to look back.

Once inside the Duster, we started to laugh. "We don't want trouble," Bone mocked Steve in a stupid voice.

"He's a fuckin' idiot," I said.

I felt good, but I was shocked to see Bone with a gun. It wasn't like him. I imagined him in fatigues with an assault rifle, betraying everything he believed in.

Bone put the gun back in the glovebox. "Stupid fucking gift."

He put his hands on the wheel without starting the car and just sat there. "My father doesn't know me at all." He turned and smiled. "I know it's early, but do you mind if I take you home?"

CHAPTER 15

R.A.D.D.

Sleep is its own enemy. When you need it most, worry kills it. I woke intermittently in panic, fearing my alarm hadn't gone off.

Six a.m., it jolted me awake.

"God, no!" I shouted to the pitch-black room and hit snooze.

I fell back asleep and had to relive the horror nine minutes later when it went off again. I leaped out of bed and pulled open my blinds—early morning light. If I kept this job, come winter, I'd go to work in darkness and get off work in darkness.

After walking across town, I arrived at my new job. An acne faced teen, two years my junior, was standing behind the counter operating cash. "It's a great day at Bockscar. How may I better serve you?"

"Um… I'm Deacon Jones."

"Oh," said the boy, flattening his beaming smile into a condescending frown, and becoming a different person, "you're the new guy."

I looked over to the espresso machine; there was Adonai, scowling at me.

"Come with me to the back," said the teen, barking it like an order. "You'll enjoy working here. Every day's a great day at Bockscar."

I followed him into the back as he continued his informal orientation. "It's a work environment based on Respect, Dignity, and Diversity. We call it RADD. It's imperative that you comply with the sentiment."

The back room was a mess, stale coffee and smelly bar towels. Metro shelves piled with cups, lids and other supplies lined every wall. A large woman in a black Bockscar t-shirt and black slacks sat at a desk, making a schedule.

She turned and smiled. "Hello, Deacon. I'm Sharon. It's great having you work here. We're all so excited."

I glanced at the teen. He didn't seem excited; he just frowned back at me. His nametag said, Crispin. Dumb name.

Sharon looked down at my feet. Dirty white Converse All-Stars. "Oh my. Your shoes aren't black."

"Is that a problem?"

"As a matter of fact, it is. Black is our dress-code. I thought I made that clear?"

"Sorry. Everything else is black."

"When you walk behind the counter at the Bockscar Café," she said, "you do more than represent the greatest company in the world to work for, you are the most important link in our customer's day. You have the power to make a difference. So when you're not in dress-code, you not only let down the customer, who has come to depend on you, you let down your Collaborators."

"Collaborators?"

"Yes. At Bockscar, we call each other 'Collaborators' because we share in the creation of our company's success."

"You mean if the café makes more, we get paid more?"

"No," she said, "it's the shared success of taking ownership."

I was beginning to see that this job was full of bullshit, and if this feel-good positive crap were real, how did a guy with an attitude like Adonai's get hired?

"Speaking of Collaborators, let's get to know some of them. You've already met Crispin." The teen gave a sarcastic smile and crossed his arms over his chest. "Crispin's only a barista, but we're grooming him for our shift-supervisor position."

The punk began to gloat.

"There's lots of opportunity at Bockscar," she said. "Crispin will show you around and train you."

I followed Crispin to the espresso bar. "Here's our barista all-star, Adonai," he said.

Adonai turned to us with a flip of the hair, "Spare me the stress. Like, he's my next-door neighbor, and now he's my co-worker."

"We don't use the word co-worker, Adonai," said Crispin. "He's your Collaborator. Let's be welcoming to Deacon."

Adonai turned and whispered in my ear, "They can't fire me. I've worked here longer than anybody, and the owner is married to my sister."

"Don't mind Adonai," said Crispin. "He's just PMSing. Let's start you out with Point Of Sale. When you greet a customer, remember your laws of positive attraction, say, 'How can I better serve you?' Then your subconscious will pull your actions into alignment with our trademark, world-famous customer service."

I wasn't sure how they were world-famous with only one location in Richland.

Crispin pointed to the cash register. "This is our Point Of Sale. POS, get it?"

My heart sank. There were at least a hundred buttons, dyslexia jumbling them into an incomprehensible mess.

"The POS is the heart and soul of this business. Without it, we cannot deliver our legendary service to our valued customers. Accurately recording transactions is the most important thing we do. Take a few minutes to familiarize yourself with it."

Anxiety caused me to sweat, my heart racing. I wanted to run but forced myself remain. I needed money to leave home, and this seemed better than the Hanford janitor option.

After several hours of spirit crushing attempts to ring in customers, looking at all the jumbled buttons, Crispin got impatient. "Look, I was supposed to go on break a half-hour ago. It's slow. Just take your time and Adonai will help you."

This is how it always was, nobody wanted to take the extra time that I needed to read and learn. I stared at the sea of multicolored buttons. My dyslexic brain registered it as a challenging word search puzzle that brings you to your knees. How was I going to do this job?

After a few minutes of futile studying, in walked this executive type. Despite being blonde, he had a brown mustache. He carried a briefcase in one hand and a car phone in the other. I stared at the car phone with interest because I'd never seen one before. I'd heard of car phones and expected them to look like a regular phone, not a brick with a thick antenna.

The guy reached into his pocket and pulled out a five-dollar bill, tossing it onto the counter with disrespect, continuing his conversation.

I wasn't sure what to do with the money, so I looked for body language cues. After a few seconds, he noticed that I didn't know his order and interrupted his conversation to say, "Regular," then continued talking.

Assuming "Regular" also denoted size, I grabbed a small cup and poured him a steaming coffee. He looked at it, annoyed.

"Yeah, Ted, hang on. I'm here at the Bockscar, and the kid has screwed up my order." Then to me, "I said, Regular."

"Isn't this Regular?" I asked. "Do you want the bigger size?"

"Regular, MY regular, a grande latte. L-A-T-T-E: my regular. Get it? Sorry, Ted, this guy needs to get to know his customers. Did you finish the report on the Westinghouse account?"

Adonai saw I was struggling and pushed me aside to ring him in, humiliating me with a dirty look.

The next customer was a little different. She was nicer.

"Welcome to the Bockscar Café. How may I better serve you?"

"Oh, I just love the way you greet your customers. It's great."

She looked down at a brown and green ceramic mug on display in front of the espresso machine and rotated it by its handle. "How cute. Not sure that it will go with anything of mine. I decorated my house in a powder blue motif, and this has more of an earthen tone to it. Oh what the heck, I'll take it, and a Grande-no-foam-Skinny-Latte, 100 degrees, for here… But make it with legs and a sleeve. I like the way the paper cup makes it taste."

I wasn't sure what she was talking about, but I repeated the order to Adonai who scowled. I looked at the cash register buttons—there was no use.

She put a five-dollar bill on the counter. "Keep the change."

Unable to ring her in, I put her money in the tip jar and continued to decipher the cash register.

"Here's your latte," said Adonai, placing her drink on the handoff counter.

He watched her sit down with disdain. "That lady's complained for months that we don't serve organic coffee and use Styrofoam cups for our drip. And every day she sits here, drinking a lukewarm latte through a straw poked into a plastic lid. She's all show and wants people to see our logo on the cup. You can tell by what she's wearing, Harve Benard and Covington. If she had real taste, she'd have on Prada or Gabbana. And did you smell her fragrance? Pierre Cardin? I'm so sure. These peasants have no charm."

"And you do?" I said.

"I am the epitome of charm, and you know it. Like Andy Warhol, my fifteen minutes of fame will be based purely on charisma. I am an artist, and this is my art." He spread his fingers and fanned his mortal frame, posing like Venus de Milo. "I shall be famous, just because."

"Yeah, good luck with that," I said, returning to the dreaded cash register.

How was I going to be able to succeed at this minimum wage job? As usual, I couldn't even achieve the lowest mark. And what of it? Working at the Bockscar Café was not RADD. Nor was I feeling dignity or respect from the customers, Adonai, or Crispin.

By the end of my shift, I was exhausted, barely able to punch out. I shouldn't have gone out with Bone and Fenix the night before.

I sat on the curb at the far end of the parking lot, feeling like a loser, that I'd never be independent. Like my parents always said, I was born this way, mired in sin. What they really meant was that I was born to lose.

Adonai emerged a few minutes later, changed into immaculate white jeans. "Sitting on the curb like a bum is bad for business; it's going to chase away customers."

"Fuck you."

"Excuse me?" he said, coming down to face me.

"You heard me. It's my first day, and you and that fucker Crispin acted like dicks. How did they treat you on your first day?"

He stopped and bit his lower lip, then pushed his shoulder out, like he was posing. "You're right. I'm sorry."

He sat next to me on the curb. "You look tired and stressed," he said, trying to be nice.

"I am. I don't read very well, and the cash register is daunting."

"I'll show you some tricks tomorrow," he said, voice filled with compassion. "If you go off the colors, and you know the largest size is to the left, and smallest to the right, then you don't need to read. Just remember, hot drinks and their different sizes are the brown buttons. Cold drinks are blue. Tea, red. The cash button is green. He stood up and began to walk away, strutting to his father's car.

"If you are really sorry about being a dick, you can give me a ride home," I said.

"Ugh, is this going to be a regular thing?" He walked around his car and unlocked the passenger side, opening it for me. "It's bad enough that I have to work with you, live next to you, and now we're commuting?"

"It saves on gas and reduces pollution," I said, walking up to the passenger side.

"So would walking." He tossed his dirty work uniform into the backseat. "Do I look like a taxi service?"

"Yes."

"I doubt you could afford the drop. Get in."

CHAPTER 16

EUPHORIA

Adonai looked at me while starting the car. "You look like you aren't going to make it."

"I might not."

"I tried to tell you this job sucks," he said, twisting as he reversed, "but you applied anyway."

"Oh come on. You just didn't want me working there," I said, sulking in the seat.

"You should've listened. Momma knows."

"If you think this job sucks," I said, "why have you worked there so long?"

"Why do you think? I need money to get out of Richland. It's not the safest place to be if you're gay. The rural peasants do love their fag bashing." He held up his right hand with two crooked fingers. "This is what happens when you're gay in rural America."

"What happened?"

"I broke my fingers defending myself against a group of rednecks in the parking lot of the 7-11. Happened shortly after I came out."

The thought of a bunch of jocks jumping out of their jacked-up truck to kick the shit out of him upset me. I'd often heard them boasting about that sort of thing at school. I always had to worry about the same things but for different reasons.

"That's fucked up, letting everyone know you're gay and then getting beaten up for it," I said.

He laughed. "It was the most wonderful and horrible day of my life."

"I would've just kept it a secret," I said.

"Of course, you would. That is why you're so miserable. It's hard living when you aren't true to yourself. You've got be open and make a stand about who you are. It's all about self-love.

"For years," he continued, "I lived in fear that someone would recognize I was gay, see it in the way I walked or things I said, the way the older fags could see it."

"When I got beaten up, I can't tell you how liberating it was." He smiled and looked as though he were reminiscing. "For the first time, I could stop hiding."

"It's too bad people around here can't just accept you for the way you are," I said.

He shook his head and seemed sad. "It is. I often wonder what sort of a world we live in that would persecute a person for wanting to love another human being. As a Roman Catholic, I struggled for years, believing I was an awful person and unworthy of all the blessings life had bestowed. I grew up with the idea that a man loving another man was an abomination. Finally, I gave in to temptation."

He turned to me at a stoplight and had a dreamy look in his eyes. "I was at the mall, and an older man offered me a ride home. I was scared and exhilarated all at the same time."

Adonai was never usually serious, but his whole demeanor changed and he stopped talking for a second, as if he recalled some warm moment. "He seduced me, giving me a blowjob in his car a few blocks from our house."

"How old was he?" I asked, shocked.

"Thirty—forty; I don't know. It doesn't matter. It was dark, and I never saw him again."

"How old were you?"

"Sixteen."

"You've got to be kidding!" The thought of him and some older man seemed horrible to me. "Isn't that molestation?"

"I considered it consensual. But it's true," said Adonai, thinking hard about what he wanted to say, "he did take advantage of my young age and need for self-realization. He seduced me before I was ready, but I wouldn't trade it for the world. That man freed me."

Adonai breathed deep and accelerated through the intersection. "After that, I began questioning my religious beliefs. How could what I had just experienced be wrong when it felt so good? Who was I hurting? Had this man hurt me?"

It was refreshing to hear someone else questioning their faith. I thought about what my parents would do if I were caught having sex, let alone sex with a man. I was already going to hell for bad grades.

"Do your parents know that you're gay?" I asked, trying to understand him.

"My mom knows. A mother always knows these things. My father..." He paused, looking sad. "Should be obvious, right? The man has such powers of denial. 'How're the girls, Addie?' He imitated a low voice with a Filipino accent then rolled his eyes. "I am so sure... I just say, 'Fine Amá.' It's been apparent to everyone but him since I was three. Even his mother: 'Chiba, do you find Addie a little effeminate?'" He faked a woman's voice when he said this.

His eyes seemed to visualize what he was saying, like a mirage on the road. "I don't want to hurt him, but I have to be who I am. I love him, dearly. He'll probably disown me, and demand the family sever all contact, but every punch I take makes me stronger."

Then Adonai slumped, his energy draining. "He still thinks I'm going to the University of Washington." He turned to me and flashed a grin laced with sorrow. "My parents want me to be a doctor or an engineer. I plan on attending the Art Institute of Seattle for fashion and mingling with the fabulous. I'm saving that bomb for the final second when I'm ready to leave home... Then pow! Go Bombers! Hey, Amá, I'm gay and I'm going be a fashion designer with my own fragrance."

His eyes lit up. "I'm going to call it… Euphoria." He fanned his palm outward as if pushing his statement out to the world, making it reverberate for centuries. Then he whipped his hair like a lion.

"Some guy from Richland, making his own perfume? How're you going to make that happen?" I said.

"Fragrance," he corrected. "It'll be easy. All designers have a signature fragrance. Karl Lagerfeld has his."

"Who's Carl Lagger-field?"

"He's a famous designer of haute couture. That's what I intend to do. I'm not going to design clothes for JC Penney. I'm going for the Paris runway."

"I don't know. It seems impossible, something a big company would do."

"It seems impossible to you because you don't believe in your own dreams."

"That's because I don't have any dreams," I said, gazing out the window so he wouldn't see the disappointment on my face.

"Of course, you do," he said. "You just don't love yourself enough to connect with what you really want. You've been programmed to have limited options. You have to do a bit of soul searching, and develop personal criteria, then you'll be able to see that your options are endless."

"That's easy for you to say; I can barely read. I'm starting to worry that I won't be able to survive. The truth is, there's very little I can do."

"That's because you've let your family decide what your options are. If you don't establish your own criteria, someone else will do it for you."

"Easy for you to say; you're a good reader."

"There's options, even for someone who has trouble reading," he said. "Just like the color-coding on the cash register, there are ways around your disability."

"It's not that easy," I said.

"I didn't say it was. Who do you think you're talking to? I was born gay in a Roman Catholic family, and I live in a small town. If I were like you, I'd be engaged to some Filipina who was waiting for me to get out of med-school before she got pregnant."

Adonai looked at the road before him in contemplation, then continued, "I consider myself a Buddhist. When the Buddha was born, they foresaw that he would either become a great king or a holy man. His father, wanting his son to be king, kept his options limited. They sheltered him, making him believe that he had only one destiny. That's what your parents are doing. Don't let other people convince you that your options are limited. The universe is at your command."

"What's that supposed to mean?"

"Don't ask me; I'm just the messenger. Everyone has a dream. You just need the guts to go for it."

"I do have a silly dream," I admitted.

"And?"

"Sometimes, when I daydream, I picture myself a singer in a band."

"Like David Lee Roth?"

"No; something more gritty and true, with a bit of anger thrown into the mix." My brain started to draw pictures of myself on stage, covered in tattoos like Henry Rollins, screaming my guts out, transferring my anger and pain to a crowd of people, swirling in a grand mosh-pit. I would stage dive, and they would hold me up.

Adonai repositioned himself to face me, ignoring the road, almost excited. "I get it; you want to make music that's a lifestyle."

"Hey, watch where you're going," I said.

"Like 70s disco, lifestyle music."

"Well, I wasn't thinking about disco. But yeah, the way disco embodied a lifestyle. If I were to make music, I would combine the depth of what Bone listens to with the heaviness of metal and the rage of Punk Rock. Maybe slow it down without sacrificing power. It's about lifestyle and authenticity."

I was getting excited. "We were born in the Summer of Love and Sgt. Pepper. We were babies during the first moonwalk, raised to believe in infinite possibility. Instead of a moonwalk, we're coming of age into a world of frivolity and cable TV. I want to do something that mirrors what people our age are going through, that sense of isolation. Our generation doesn't stand for anything, and our future seems uncertain and bleak. We don't have a war to protest. All we can relate to is our own decline. A lot of what's out there seems fake. It's all show. It means nothing. This is why I like Bone's scene. He's stuck in the 70s and 60s, but the music he listens to used to mean something; it started a revolution. When Nixon ordered the Guard to shoot those protesters at Kent State, Crosby, Stills, Nash, and Young had a song about it on the radio, days after it happened. What those old groups did was relevant. I want to make relevant music, but update it, be a mirror for the decline of our society."

"Deacon," he said, as if he were my father, "you need to be true to yourself. You wear clothes your momma bought you. You have crushes on girls who don't suit you, like Mikultra Skala. Instead, you should be learning to play an instrument. Align yourself to the inner you, then jobs like the Bockscar become a means to an end, rather than a future."

"You're right, but I don't have any talent."

"How do you know? You haven't even tried. These people who make music worked hard to develop their talent.

"Look," he said, pulling into the carport on his side of the duplex, "you need to be true to your inner self. And you need to get off your ass and start making some music, even if it's terrible."

We stepped out of the car, and he flipped his hair like a supermodel, returning to the same old Adonai I knew at school.

"Thanks for the ride," I said.

He made a coy pose and squinted his eyes. "What–ever!"

I laughed at his show. "See you tomorrow."

"You wish!" He fanned me away like the Queen of England shooing off an annoying courtier.

"Oh, hey," I called after him.

He turned, crossing his arms, posing.

"I think I've found the girl."

"And?"

"It's nothing," I said.

"Don't 'nothing' me. You can't feed sass to the queen of stress." Adonai gave me a reprimanding look. "Honey, don't be coy, give me the news."

"Her name is Cher Hanson."

Adonai bit his lower lip in contemplation. "I think she's perfect for you. She's got band girlfriend written all over her, real diva potential. I can see it, the two of you. Now get off your ass and make some music."

CHAPTER 17

LESLIE GROVES

I was so tired; I could barely make it to my front door. I looked at the kitchen clock and had just enough time to call Cher before my parents got home from bible study. It rang five times before she answered.

"Hello... Cher? It's me, Deacon Jones."

"I know who you are," she said, as if flatlining. I could hear her chewing gum.

"So... you wanna go out tonight?"

She hesitated, causing my heart to race. "Sure," she said, blowing a bubble and letting it pop. "Meet me at the jungle-gym at Leslie Groves Park, 9:30."

"Can we make it ten?" I had to make sure my parents were asleep.

"Alright." She hung up the phone.

Who cares if I had to be at work at some hateful hour? I was going to be kissing Cher in the dark and feeling her body. I sat there for a whole minute, listening to the ring tone until the phone started to beep.

I hung up just as my parents came home.

"How was your first day?" asked my mom.

"Tiring," I said, wanting to remove myself from their presence. "I think I might just go to bed."

"At four-o'clock?" said my father.

"I had insomnia last night."

"I think going to bed early is a wonderful thing," said my mother, "get a well-rested start to the workday. The soul of the sluggard craves and gets nothing, while the soul of the diligent is richly supplied."

My father frowned, not sharing my mother's sentiment. "Sluggards crave menial vocations; the diligent crave a good Christian education."

"Where were you?" I asked, trying to change the direction of the conversation.

"We went with the pastor to greet a new family into the church," my mother said.

"It's always nice when a family finds their way to the Lord," I said, sucking up just to get the fuck away from them.

She smiled and put her hand in mine. "Deacon, I am so proud of you. You're making an effort. The Lord rewards those true in intention."

I kissed her and went upstairs to take a shower then a nap. I set my alarm for 9:30, keeping it under my pillow so it wouldn't alert my parents.

Leslie Groves Park was named after a Lieutenant General of the Army Corps of Engineers. After overseeing the construction of the Pentagon, Groves was selected to head the Manhattan Project. He chose Hanford, Washington, along with Oak Ridge and Los Alamos, to build the most destructive weapon known to history.

After personally picking Hiroshima and Nagasaki as targets for his mighty bomb, all that would be left for this man to do in life would be to devise a weapon capable of swallowing the universe. Unable to do this, a quaint park in Richland would have to satisfy his legacy.

I climbed out my window and skated down to the river. Moths gathered under the streetlamps and mosquitos bit my ankles.

I reached the edge of the park five minutes late and stepped on the dew moist grass where I could see the jungle gym's silhouette in the distance. As I drew closer, I noticed the slight glow of a cigarette.

Cher sat on the platform, next to the slide, legs dangling over the edge. Her hand was shaking as she drew deliberate drags from her smoke. She was looking out to the water.

"Hello," I said.

"You gonna just stand there or are you gonna come up?" She flicked her cigarette into the sand. I stepped up to the platform and looked down at her.

"Sit," she said. "I don't bite."

Our legs and arms touched from the lack of space when I sat down. "Do you usually hang out by the river?"

"Yeah. I love it down here, especially at night." She smiled, looking out to the moon reflecting off the Columbia. "I can feel the river moving towards the sea, leaving this place, never to return, changing along the way."

Her determined stare morphed into an unfocused haze. She tilted her head as if looking back into her thoughts. "How I am envious of that water." She took a deep breath and refocused on the distant moonlit ripples. "I hate it here. I've got to leave."

"Me too." I imagined the river carrying us to Portland, Oregon. "If you were able to leave, where would you go?" I asked.

"Seattle. I love Seattle."

"I'm thinking of going to Seattle too," I said.

"Really?" Next to her feet was a pole to slide down. She patted it and looked me in the eye to study my reaction. "Would you judge me if I told you I'm planning on being a stripper?"

"No."

She reached up to the pole and slid her hand along it. "I come here at night to practice. It's how I'm going to escape this town forever. Go down, and you can be my guinea pig."

I jumped onto the sand. Cher slid around the pole in a rapid spiral, then turned upside down, spreading her legs. She was amazing.

"I've already got a job lined up," she said, spinning upright and wrapping her legs around my neck, pulling me towards her. "It's in a club called Deja-Vu. If you ever get to Seattle, come and see me; wait for me to get off work."

"I'd like that," I said.

"Yeah, there's lots of opportunity in Seattle for this sort of thing. That town has a strip joint on every corner."

While still gripping the pole, she took one arm and pulled me by the back of the head further into her pelvis. "Do you have any plans when you get to Seattle?"

I opened my mouth, then doubt caused me to pause. I was about to say no, then thought about Adonai's pep talk. "Yeah, I think I'll join a band," I said, feeling stupid as the words left my mouth.

"Really?" Cher abandoned the pole and pushed me towards a park bench. Then she put her arms around my neck and straddled me. "I can see you in a band. What instrument?"

"Lead singer," I said.

"That would be awesome." Cher sat on my lap, facing me, playing with my hair. "You gonna forget me after you're famous?"

"Never," I said. "Maybe you'll be my girlfriend?"

"Shhh." She put her finger on my lips, then bent down to kiss me. "Don't say that." She started giving me a lap dance, gyrating against my groin.

"I mean it," I said. "I'd like you to be my girlfriend."

She got serious and looked away. "I don't know what you see in me."

"You're the most amazing girl I know."

"Yeah, right." She rolled her eyes. "You must not know many girls."

"No, I really like you."

"That's impossible. You don't even know me." She continued to grind in my lap.

"There are things about you that I like," I said. "In fact, I'm envious."

"Bullshit."

"It's true. I love it that you don't care what anyone thinks," I said. "I wish I were like that. You inspired me to start following my own path and gave me the idea to leave town. I never thought of escape before I met you. I want to leave so bad; I'm working a shitty job in hopes of escape. You just ran away without money, and made it happen. I started rethinking my life the day I met you."

She smiled and took my hands, placing them on her breasts. "A girl should give lap dances to her man."

"So does that mean you're my girlfriend?"

"I can't be anyone's girlfriend. But I'll be your lover, and you can do anything you want to me." She danced erotically over my lap. I put my hands on her hips, and she started to grind. My head fell back with a rush of desire as I pulled her down into my kiss.

We made out for about five minutes until she knelt on the grass at my feet, and unzipped my pants, going down. I couldn't believe where this was heading. Her mouth had the warmest feeling, better than anything I'd ever felt in my life. It flowed through me like a shot of dope. I could've stayed in this state forever, numb with ultimate pleasure. I sat there, giving myself over to the spirit of ecstasy.

What just happened? It seemed that all my dreams would now come to pass, as if I were almost human, inching my way into being a man.

She sat down next to me, placing her head on my shoulder. We sat there for a few minutes in silence until she said, "Yesterday, at Carson's, those pills we snorted, I know they're Ritalin, but what were they for?"

"They are the worst thing that's ever happened to me," I said. "I'm so happy right now, I'd almost forgotten I was ever on that shit."

Cher lifted her head and lit another cigarette. "Why were you on it?" Her drag illuminated her face.

"It was supposed to help me learn and keep me from being hyper."

"You seem pretty mellow to me."

I turned my head to look back at the river. "It's because my mind wanders when I read or do math. It wanders because I have trouble deciphering words and the sequence of numbers. It's hard to concentrate on a page when you can only make out the first and last letters of words. That, and I was wild and disruptive. That drug subdued me."

She looked at me. I could tell by her expression that she knew she had stumbled upon my acute sense of failure and all its accompanying sorrow. She put her hand on the side of my face, leaning in for a kiss. "You're sweet," she said before our lips touched. Her mouth pressed into mine, and she held the kiss so we could savor the moment.

We mutually pulled away and sat looking each other in the eyes.

"Thank you," I said.

She laughed. "You don't have to thank me."

"Of course, I do. You've made me happy."

Cher had a huge beaming smile, her face glowing in the moonlight. "I like you," she said after a moment. "I don't know why, but I trust you."

I began to feel giddy. She was the girl of my dreams. I stroked her arm and felt the scars from cutting; they felt good.

"You like my scars?" she said.

"Yes," I whispered. "Why do you cut?"

"Release. It's the only thing that distracts me from all the bullshit. It lets me pretend I'm in control." Her head shot up as if she remembered something she had to do. "What time is it?"

I looked at my watch. "Almost midnight."

"Shit!" Cher stood up. "I have to go. My mom will be back from work soon." She stopped and looked pained. "I'd like to see you again."

"Me too." My response seemed to calm her.

"Can we meet the day after tomorrow?" she said as if taking a chance.

"Sure, I'm off at 1:30."

She smiled and began to walk away. "Perfect. I'll meet you at the Fingernail at two."

I felt weird letting her leave. "Can I walk you home?"

She started to make her way towards the street. "That's okay. I can manage."

"It's dark. Walking you home would be the gentlemanly thing to do."

"You are a gentleman." She stopped and turned, looking as though she were trying to control her emotions.

Cher pulled me towards her. Our tongues met in full passion, my hand reaching behind to her lower back. Her body felt good.

After several minutes she pulled away in a dreamy drunken state. "I do like you, but I have to go. Please trust that I'll be alright."

I nodded and watched her walk off. She got about ten feet away, turned back, and whispered in a voice that I swore was laden with tears, "I'll see you Friday?"

"Yes," I said.

I may have been a loser, but at that moment, I knew I had won. Instead of skating home, I walked. And for the first time in my life, I sang out loud, and in a full voice, making up lyrics to songs I did not know.

If your father wore a radiation suit and risked his life, you lived in one of the military-style homes in the older part of Richland. These houses resembled a base, built by the Army Corps of Engineers to house the workers of the Manhattan Project. They were dull, simple Army designs without garages, each variation named with a different letter: A, B, C, etc.

CHAPTER 18

THE FINGERNAIL

My alarm went off at 4 am on Friday, sending a severe shock to my system. We had closed the cafe at midnight, and now, through some scheduling incompetence, Adonai and I had five hours off between shifts. With this job, I was either up before the sun or getting off after midnight.

The work was fast-paced, hard, and stressful. Each night I kept waking up panicked, thinking my alarm hadn't gone off. When I was asleep, I had coffee nightmares where I couldn't keep up, and customers were complaining. People kept ordering things like "Skinny Delizias with legs" while my dyslexic brain couldn't read the buttons on the cash register.

Just as my dream self was about to explode, I'd wake up, heart racing, checking my alarm: 2:43 am. Shit! Then I'd struggle to go back to sleep. It was my first week at this RADD job, and the wildly varying start and end times were taking its toll. How was I supposed to get used to this?

When I got off work, I walked down to the river to meet Cher at the Fingernail. I was so tired, seeing her was the only thing that kept me going.

The Fingernail was an outdoor amphitheater. Folks called it the Fingernail because it looked like a large fake acrylic nail. To me, it looked more like one of those Preway cone fireplaces everyone had in the 1970s. It used to be an office for a gravel quarry. When the quarry was no longer using the structure, they moved it to the park on the river because its shape made it a natural amphitheater.

Each month they had a local band play. These events were attended by every kid in town but me. I was never allowed to go, but I could hear the muffled music while I pulled weeds, convinced I was missing out on the meaning of life itself.

I would hunch over my mother's flowerbed, imagining the band pushing the kids into a state of rebellion. Even from a distance, I could feel the sheer volume. It made young people understand that they were a sort of tribe who spit on the boundaries that held normal humans back while I pulled weeds.

When I arrived at the Fingernail, Cher was sitting on the stage. She was magnificent, wearing torn fishnets and a miniskirt like Nancy Spungen, with eyeliner a half-inch thick. She stood as I approached and pulled me into her kiss. Passion rose as her essence shot through me. She pushed me away in a flirty manner. "It's good to see you."

"Good to see you too," I said, my hands resting on her hips.

"I wasn't sure you'd show up."

"I wouldn't miss it for the world."

"Well, you wouldn't be the first guy to stand me up." She held me tight and whispered, "My mother got called into work." She reached down and grabbed my crotch with a mischievous smile. "I want to take you home."

"Alright," I said, exhilarated.

I followed her through old Richland neighborhoods where the houses were Army Core of Engineer letter homes, built during the Manhattan Project from 1943 to 1953. Cher lived in a single-story H-house. The driveway was empty.

She unlocked the door and pulled me inside. The living room was small, with an old couch swallowing the space. The side of a spinet piano greeted us as we walked in. It had a lace doily with ceramic animals on top, as if it were a perverse shrine to a non-existent innocence. An old scuffed wooden tube television faced the couch.

Cher led me to her room and threw me down onto her bed. She stood above and studied me as if convincing herself that this was the thing to do. Behind her was a poster of a band. They were four leather-clad punks with tall wild Mohawk haircuts. The group was Charged G.B.H. I stared at them in awe, making a silent determination to own a leather jacket. Above her bed was a poster of the Dead Kennedys' album, *Plastic Surgery Disasters*.

She walked over and put a record onto the turntable. A voice scratched through the speakers, "We got the neutron bomb! We got the neutron... Gonna drop it all over the place..." The music arrested me, causing me to sit up and give it focused attention. The song was glorious.

"Who is this?" I asked, drawn to the speakers.

"The Weirdoes," she said. "They're from L.A."

The music's force burst out of the stereo, taking on a life of its own, resonating outside of the shitty pressboard speakers. This hovering energy was contagious and entered the skin to pollute the blood. It was what my parents considered the antithesis of good; it was menacing evil. How can there be salvation in Jesus when there was music like this?

"When I get in a band, I'm going to play music with this intensity," I said.

"I can see it," she purred. "I told you, I had a dream you'd be famous." She grabbed me by the crotch and started biting my earlobe.

When the song was over, I went to Cher's turntable and stood before it like the record was a holy relic. I glanced back at her and motioned to the 45 with both hands. "Can I see it?"

She chuckled with delight. "Go right ahead."

I lovingly lifted the 45 off the spindle and held it up to the light. The label was yellow, jumping off the dark vinyl. It had repeated black silhouettes of the Little Boy bomb they dropped on Hiroshima, getting smaller as they fell to earth. This record felt magical. Like it was my purpose for living, my destiny. Was this what it was like being a fan? I wouldn't know.

"Great record, huh?" Cher said, walking towards me. "The Weirdoes are my second favorite band."

"Who's your first?" I said, enthralled by the driving song that had come out of her record player.

"The Germs. If you like the Weirdoes, you'll love them. They were in that movie, *The Decline of Western Civilization.*" She held her bare forearm up for me to see. Below her cutting was a round burn scar on her wrist, made by pressing a lit cigarette into her skin. "It's my Germs Burn."

I looked at it with reverence.

"Their singer's the best," she said. "His name is Darby Crash. The band's disciples burn circles into their wrists as a sign of devotion."

I couldn't believe it. Even Bone's music didn't command such reverence.

"I want to make music that's powerful enough to inspire people to burn circles into their arms."

"Why don't you?" she said, leaning back on the bed.

"Because I suck."

"So? It's not about that. You just have to get the message out. This music has something to say. If you can't sing, learn to play guitar. If you can't play guitar, just be a fan—spread the message."

At that moment, being a fan became my sole purpose.

Cher walked over and pulled a black album from the shelf with a round fluorescent-blue circle on it. She put it on the turntable. "Darby Crash can't sing."

She put the needle to the vein. The drums punched through the speakers. Cher mouthed to the lyrics as she slid her hand into my pants, "Gimmie gimmie your hands; gimmie gimmie your minds…"

Cher pulled out her hand and lifted her shirt over her head, exposing her defined stomach and perfect breasts under a black bra. Then she seductively slid off her miniskirt, revealing lace garters framing her exquisite hips and straps holding up fishnets. Her body was perfect. I lay in disbelief, thinking I was the luckiest man on earth as the music raged on. She was more beautiful than Mikultra Skalla. Why couldn't anyone see this?

Cher climbed onto the bed, pulling my shirt off and unbuckling my black Bockscar dress-code slacks. She sat up, smiled at me then went down, pulling me into ecstasy. After a few minutes, she climbed on top, still wearing the garters and stockings, and started to grind. Watching her ride, I knew I would never have it better. She was the best a human could do, a true mortal devi of flesh. The feminine ideal, capturing my soul with her motion.

After we finished, we lay there, holding each other. I was happier than I had ever been. I would never be the same.

"This was my first time," I told her, laying on my back as she propped herself up with her arms.

"Really? I don't believe you."

The side of the record ended, and the turntable arm automatically returned to its rest, leaving her house quiet.

"It's true," I said.

I'd barely uttered the words when we heard a cabinet slam in the kitchen. Cher leapt up, completely alert. "Shit, it's my dad! You've got to get out of here."

Terror shot through me. Cher slid open her window, motioning me to go. I grabbed my clothes and stood on the bed to climb out. Landing in the back yard, I could hear him calling her name. I ran across the lawn, threw my clothes over the fence, and pulled myself up.

With one leg over, the wood ripped my naked flesh and genitals. I looked back to the house to see a man in a police uniform step out the sliding glass door. "Hey!" he shouted, running towards the fence, pulling out his gun.

My alarm increased as I saw the intensity in his face. I lost my balance and fell, my skin ripping as I landed in a pile of tumbleweeds, crying out in pain.

"Get back here!" he yelled.

I jumped out of the tumbleweeds and collected my clothes. I could hear Cher and her father screaming at each other inside the house. I distinctly heard him hit her and shout, "Whore!"

Needing a place to hide, I ran down the street naked, clutching my bundle of clothes. There were some tall bushes ahead, so I crouched behind them to get dressed. I went to put on my shoes when I realized I had left them back in Cher's room.

"Dammit!" How was I going to go to work tomorrow without those black shoes? Sharon would write me up and send me home.

I cowered in the bushes for about twenty minutes and emerged into the blazing Eastern Washington sun, my feet burning on the concrete. It was so hot you could cook an egg on the sidewalk. There was no way I'd make it home, and I didn't have enough cash to take the bus.

Down the street was a 7-11 where I could make a call. I plugged the payphone with a quarter and dialed. "Bone? It's me, Deacon."

"Hey man, how's the job?" he said, mumbling over a cigarette.

"Listen, my scene is shot. I was fucking Cher Hanson, and her father came home."

"Cher Hanson, eh? That gal is hot."

"Bone, listen to me. You've got to come and get me. I've got no shoes and the street is burning my feet. I'm at the Sev on Jadwin."

"Sure man, be right there."

I sat down on the curb in front of the crushed ice freezer to wait. It'd been about five minutes when a police cruiser pulled up. Out stepped Cher's father, holding my shoes. I could've died. He stood above me, hate filling his eyes, his ripped muscles pushing out from under his bulletproof vest. "Forget something?" He dropped the shoes on my bare feet. It stung, but I didn't dare move.

Just then, Bone pulled into the parking lot next to the cruiser. He looked at Cher's dad, got out and headed into the 7-11, pretending not to know me.

"Lucky for you, my daughter is over the age of consent in this state," he said, breathing heavily, "so I can't bust you for statutory rape. She invited you in so I can't bust you for trespassing." He looked around to see if anyone was watching. "But I will bust you for something. Now stand up!" He pulled me up by the shirt and shoved me onto the hood of the cruiser, pushing my face into the hot metal hard enough to bruise. He patted me down. "Any weapons—a little weed?"

"No, sir," I said, frightened.

He knelt to whisper in my ear. "You touch my daughter again, I'll shoot you and claim I thought you had a weapon. Understand?"

It was hard to nod with my cheek on the car's hot hood.

"In the meantime, watch your back when you walk at night. I'm liable to pick you up and drive you out beyond jurisdiction where your body will have decayed by the time they find you. Maybe I'll dismember you and bury the pieces all over the desert. You follow me?"

"Yes," I said, my heart pounding.

"Now get out of here and quit loitering in front of the 7-11," he said, loud enough for people pumping gas to hear. He got in his car. I didn't bother putting on my shoes and ran down the block, feet blistering on the pavement. My shirt was soaked, and I was having trouble breathing.

The Duster pulled up beside me with Bone holding a Slurpee. "Hurry up and get in."

I threw my shoes through the passenger window and opened the door.

"What the hell was that about?" Bone took a sip of Slurpee and winced from the brain freeze as I sat down.

"That was Cher's father."

"Man," said Bone, shaking his head. "That's fucked up. I thought he was going to cuff you."

"He threatened to kill me."

"You better quit fucking her."

"I think I'm in love with her."

He shook his head. "That's fucked up. You better rethink that one."

I rested my head on the glass, watching all the government letter houses pass by, wondering if I'd ever see her again.

CHAPTER 19

THE COLLABORATOR

I t was the next day at my RADD job that the inconceivable came to pass.

Adonai and I started work at 4:45 in the morning. I couldn't concentrate on the job, all I could think about was Cher, how it ended with my face pushed against her father's police cruiser. I was scared shitless; her dad had threatened my life. I wasn't sure how moving forward with her was going to work, or if I'd ever see her again. These thoughts made it hard to get through the day.

Crispin showed up around eight to help us with the morning rush. We were desperate for breaks. At ten, Sharon walked in, greeting us, beaming with positive affirmation. "Good morning, Collaborators. Ready to make a positive impact on our community?"

"Yes," I said, immersed in despair.

"Don't sound so gloomy Deacon," said Sharon. "We are the most important part of our customer's day. They depend on us to set the tone."

I didn't doubt her sentiments. It seemed the types that frequented the Bockscar were addicted to caffeine and vamp like branding.

Instead of sending us on our much-needed breaks, Sharon announced, "I'm going to have a feedback conversation with Adonai in the back room, then we're going to have a Collaborator's meeting."

"Fuck off," I mumbled under my breath as she walked to the back.

Crispin frowned at me, arms crossed. "You don't have passion for what you do," he said. "You're not interested in sharing in our success."

"I show up and work for my pay. Isn't that enough?" I went to the espresso machine, trying to remember what Adonai had shown me. "We closed last night at ten and opened this morning. We've been working for five hours without breaks. It's bullshit."

"Sometimes we have to go above and beyond," said Crispin, "We're the most important part of our customer's day."

"Oh, come on," I said; "we are not. This is just a low wage job where we serve overpriced coffee."

He seemed insulted. "It's more than a job; it's a lifestyle."

"You sound like you've bought into a cult."

"A cult? You and Adonai are just jealous because Sharon's going to promote me to shift manager, and I'll be your boss, even though the two of you are older. That's what happens when you don't have a future."

He was about to continue when Sharon walked out with a moody Adonai. "Collaborators, I have an announcement. We have a new addition to our team. He's reporting for training in about five minutes, and I expect a warm, legendary Bockscar welcome."

"Yeah, real legendary."

"Adonai, what did I say? We were just talking about this in the back-room."

"Respect, Dignity, and Diversity: RADD. Look, I get it. Okay?" Adonai huffed.

Sharon continued, "As I said, I have an announcement to make. Your shift manager, Deloris, is getting promoted to assistant manager."

"Deloris is going to be our Ass Man?" said Adonai, eyes bulging.

Crispin began to bob up and down in excitement. "Does this mean I'll take her position as shift manager?"

"I'm sorry, Crispin. You're not ready in your development. If you want, we could fill out a Collaborator Development Form when you finish your shift and are off the clock."

"But?"

"I've had to hire externally for that position. The new Collaborator will start today in a few minutes."

Crispin was distraught. "So this person has management experience?"

"No; this will be his first job."

"But you promised me that position."

Adonai and I looked at each other, relishing his pain. I smiled, and he winked.

"Crispin, we have to do what's best for the company. Sometimes we must step aside to acquire talent. But don't worry, we'll keep developing and fast-tracking you. Oh, wait, here's our new shift manager now."

We looked up in horror as Steve Hannity emerged in full dress code. He walked behind the counter with the confidence that comes with ownership. It was the first time I'd ever seen Adonai at a loss for words. Gone was his usual self-assurance. He seemed more like Crispin, polarized by shock.

"Everyone," said Sharon, beaming as if he were her discovery, "this is our new shift manager, Steve."

Crispin's mouth was gaping, waiting for a fly to enter.

"Steve, let me introduce you to Crispin. And this is Adonai, our bar star," said Sharon, "and this is..."

"I know these guys," said Steve in a tone that spelled out his contempt for us to everyone but Sharon.

"Steve is new. This is his first job, so I expect every one of you to contribute towards his success. Adonai will train you on the bar, and Crispin will coach you in customer service and POS. And when you've mastered that, I'll train you in your managerial duties."

Sharon went to the back, and Adonai whispered in my ear. "We're going to train him to be our boss. Get real."

Steve turned to face Adonai. "You got somethin' to say, faggot? Say it. Otherwise, quit whispering in the loser's ear. You write-offs want to keep your jobs? You better show some respect and fly right. Remember, I'm wise to you." He walked up to me. "And we'll see how you fare. I'm sure stealing kegs, punching cops, smoking weed, spitting on school mascots, and carrying guns violates this business' moral code of ethics."

"You did all that?" said Crispin, looking at me as though I were a monster.

"Yeah," I said with contempt, "so no one better fuck with me, or they'll go down like that cop."

Steve gave me the stare-down.

"May I ask you something?" said Crispin to Steve. "How did you come to be hired into a managerial position without any prior experience? I'm sure you're making more per hour, too."

You see, Crispin went to the other school, and wasn't aware of Steve's power, or the unspoken understanding that one didn't ask him such questions. One merely tried to stay out of his way.

"I approach life as a competitor," Steve answered. "Understand?"

Crispin shook his head.

"During the job interview, I told Sharon that if she wanted me to work here, she would have to give me the shift supervisor position. Simple as that."

I listened to this talk. And for the first time I understood the main difference between myself and Steve. It wasn't that Steve was a better reader or mathematician. It wasn't that he excelled in sports. It was self-confidence.

How would I acquire this thing I lacked?

I watched carefully as Steve walked over to Adonai. "Alright, you heard the lady, time to show me the ropes. Let's start with a latté."

Adonai pinched his features. "Okay, you begin by pouring milk into the pitcher."

Steve put up his hand. "Don't talk. Just show."

The chains of uncertainty that shackled the rest of us weren't apparent in Steve. We would've worried about screwing things up. Steve just went for it, his brazen attitude softening his mistakes.

Within an hour, Steve had mastered the art of the espresso bar to the level of an old-world artesian. He poured his cappuccinos with silky foam into the espresso's crema. No one had seen anything like it. I could barely pour a latté, and here he was, a master. He was that gifted—witty with customers and quick to deliver. Crispin and the rest of us didn't stand a chance.

After an hour of watching Adonai train Steve, we started rotating lunch breaks. Adonai and I had been working for six hours.

When it was Steve's turn to go on break, Adonai motioned for Crispin and me to gather around. "Look, we've got to do something. My work-life already sucks. We have to stop this Neanderthal. He has no place in café society."

"What are you suggesting?" I said, hands in my pockets, watching Steve sitting in the café, enjoying his mocha.

Adonai lowered his voice to a whisper. "I suggest that we organize and revolt. The café can't run without us."

"You mean go on strike?" asked Crispin wide-eyed.

"Yes. Collective bargaining is the only way the proletariat has any power."

"Uh, I don't think so." Crispin snarled and shook his head. "You losers do what you want, but I'm up for promotion."

"Our manager gave your promotion to that lug-head," said Adonai. "You worked hard, and he steps up and takes it, with no prior experience. It's his first job for chrissakes."

Crispin crossed his hands over his chest and stood defiant. "Sharon will come through for me. She always does."

Adonai exposed his teeth in a hiss. "When has Sharon ever come through for you? It's all promises. Behave, and good things will come down the pipe. She'll keep stringing you along because you've let her. You've shown her that you're willing to give more for less. The only way an employer comes through for the worker is when collective bargaining forces them."

"You're not pulling me in with your subversive attitude," said Crispin. "I happen to value this job. Besides, going on strike is un-American. Any more of your socialist talk, and I'm going to report you to Steve."

"Suck up," said Adonai. "Come on Deacon, Crispin is cut off."

The rest of the day was dismal. Adonai was furious; he didn't talk until we got home.

"Thanks for the tips on the espresso bar," I said, getting out of the car.

"You're welcome," he said, slamming the door, "but remember, when I'm on the clock, I work bar. When you're working with Crispin, do what you want."

"Thanks for the ride."

"Maybe now that you've got a job," he said, marching up the steps, "you can start saving for a car."

I stuck my key in the door when I heard someone say, "Deacon?" It startled me. I jumped around. It was coming from the bushes next to the front door.

"Deacon, it's me, Cher."

CHAPTER 20

BEYOND NEPTUNE

Cher had a black eye, and there was a handprint bruise on her right forearm. She had no makeup on, and her white tank top was dirty. It was the first time I'd seen her without the thick black eyeliner. A duffle bag was slung over her shoulder.

"Cher, my God, what's happened?"

She began to cry and rushed to hug me. I held her tight.

"I'm so sorry," was all she could say through her sobs. She was crying into my shoulder. I could feel her precious tears through my shirt.

"Did your father do this?"

She continued to sob.

"Come inside." I opened the door. "My parents won't be home for hours."

I led Cher up to my room, my arm around her with her face on my chest. I sat her on my bed and knelt at her feet, taking her hands into mine. She sniffled and became distracted by a cheap print of Jesus that my mother had hung.

"I can't stay," she said. "I only came to say goodbye."

A cold, intense feeling came over me, like a fox hearing dogs in the distance. "You're leaving?"

"Yes. I need to get away from him. It's only gotten worse since he caught us."

"I have a job," I said, kneeling further down to look her in the eye. "I could rent an apartment and take care of you. I want you to be my girlfriend."

"You don't understand," she said, "I can't see you anymore. It was stupid of me to think I could. You and I shared something, so I felt it best that I come here and offer both of us some closure."

"Cher, don't do this. I'll move to Seattle, and we can be together."

She braced against what seemed to be a mountain of yearning, and bit her lower lip, as if trying not to say something mean. "I can't be anyone's girlfriend," she whispered, her voice quivering. "I'm too dirty." She let her head drop, trying not to cry.

I pulled her to me and held her tight. "I want you to be my girl."

"Why would you want me?" she said.

"I believe you're the one. I just wish I were good enough for you."

"Don't say that," she said. "You're too good for me. It's hard for me to believe someone like you would ever want me?"

"Why not?" I said, desperate.

"Because of who I've been with." She turned her body to look away in shame.

"You think I care about how many guys you've been with?"

"It's not that," she said, getting angry.

"How many guys have you been with?" I insensitively asked.

"That's none of your business," she said. "And besides, that doesn't matter. It's who my first was that matters. He's the one I've fucked more than anyone, and because of him, I'm foul."

"Who? Danny Lau?"

The room became still. Whoever this guy was had damaged her. The words barely escaped my mouth. "Who?" I asked, frightened of the answer.

She paused, straightening her back, and sucked in her tears with a quick stuttered breath. "The man I'm referring to is my father."

146

My bedroom seemed to transport into dead space, somewhere beyond Neptune, cold and orbiting the sun once a millennium. My skin bristled. I had no idea, but it all made sense, the secrecy, the running away, her father's intense reaction as if he were a jealous lover, her rebellious nature, her allure.

What does one say to this sort of revelation? If I had to do it all over again, if I could go back to that single moment, there were about a thousand things I could have said—anything—something. But I would not have stayed silent for as long as I did because everything after that silence was met with suspicion.

"You see," she said after she could no longer take me sitting there, mute, "you see why I can't be with you?"

"No, Cher. I think I love you."

"Think?" She tensed and turned to stone, refusing to face me. "I'm leaving town. This time, I won't be back."

"Cher, please don't go. There must be something we can do?"

"Deacon, I told you from the start that I was going to leave Richland. Well, now is the time."

"Then let me go with you."

She shook her head. "Deacon, I need to be alone, and I also told you that I wasn't going to be your girlfriend."

"Cher, don't leave me." My lower lip was quivering, despair boiling in my chest.

"Deacon, we never had a commitment. You need to accept that."

"Cher, just spend the night with me; think it over. My parents won't be back until late. I'll leave a note saying I'm sleeping. They know I've been working crazy hours and will leave me alone. I go to work before they get up and could sneak you out."

She seemed unsure.

"I'd like you to stay."

"Alright. I'll stay. But after that, I'm gone."

I pulled her towards me and put my arm around her, laying her head on my shoulder. "I really like you Cher," I said.

"Don't talk about that. After today, you won't ever see me again."

I started to speak, and she pulled my head down with her hand on the back of my neck. "Shh... Just kiss me."

Her heat burned through me, yet it was like holding the wind; I would spill her any moment. I instinctively knew that her leaving was for the best. Even if she agreed to let me see her, it wouldn't matter. I could marry her, tattoo her name on my neck, or lock her in a cupboard, but she would never truly be mine. It was breaking my heart.

"Cher, I'm sorry I made you uncomfortable."

"I'm sorry I can't be what you want," she said. "If I were capable of love, it would be with you."

I lowered to kiss her again. I wasn't sure she'd want intimacy, but our tongues went deep, and we began pulling off each other's clothes. This time was better than the first, and the first time was beyond measure.

We lay silent for many minutes, holding each other until I said, with enough sincerity that her defenses didn't push me away, "If I make it to Seattle, can I see you?"

She smiled but seemed sad. "No. I opened up to you, and that was a mistake. It's made leaving harder."

"Then I'll go with you."

"That fact you said, *If* I make to Seattle, means you're not ready. You want to sing in a band, but if you were serious about it, you would have done something to make it happen. There are plenty of bands right here. You haven't even tried. You know you're not ready. You have your own things to straighten out, and I have mine."

My heart went solemn. Cher put her hand on my cheek.

"Deacon, I want you to understand that even though I said you aren't ready, this isn't about you; I need to be alone right now."

She was full of trauma and defenses. There would be no getting through. I knew then, despite my young age, that if I were to love her, I'd have to accept her and let her go.

"I understand," I said. "You won't forget me?"

"Never," she said. "I've never been loved by anyone. How could I forget?"

We held each other until we fell asleep.

I dreamt that Cher and I were naked in bed. In the dream, she came to me and whispered in my ear as we made love, "Together we have yearned for death—you and I. As we wander through the trough, pigs will eat our flesh."

When I woke up, she was gone. There, sitting on the pillow was a 45rpm record with an envelope. It was the *We Got The Neutron Bomb* single by the Weirdoes.

I opened the envelope.

Dear Deacon,

You are the only person I have willingly shared my true self with and the only one who has ever wanted me for me. It breaks my heart to have to leave you. I cannot love; therefore, I should not be loved. Anyone who loves me will only get hurt. I am unworthy, and the path I'm on must be taken alone. Please don't look for me, and if you see me, walk the other way.

So there are no hard feelings, I left you the Weirdos record. I know it means something to you. I hope it makes you happy because I cannot.

Cher

Ps. Darby Crash couldn't sing, but he believed in himself.

I put the record and letter under my pillow and spent the rest of the night tossing and sweating, my thoughts seeking out darkness, my light lost in despair.

CHAPTER 21

THE PASSION OF DEACON JONES

I dreamt my bed was in a desert field, and thirty feet away was a small graveyard surrounded by a chain-link fence. Tumbleweeds collected around it.

Cher was standing over me as I lay in bed. I felt a mouth on my penis, but this time, it did not feel good. I looked down to see my dick in a large snake's mouth. The fangs were injecting me with venom, paralyzing me.

My mother walked into my room and grabbed Cher by the arm. "You can't have Deacon."

Cher looked at me, repulsed. "I don't want him, he's married."

My mom let go of her arm, and Cher walked off.

"No," I cried, "I love her."

"Do you?" said my mom.

I tried to answer, but my voice had no sound. Feeling ashamed, I turned my head away and saw the graveyard. In the distance was a dormant nuclear reactor, looking more like a black shadow than a building.

"Don't look over there," said my mother. "That's the BC Crib, where we buried your father."

I closed my eyes and a pure tone resonated out of my head. The snake recoiled in pain and my mother's skin boiled like water, turning her to steam. Lights of the dormant reactor burst open, and vapors started rising from the chimney. I could stand up and move, but I was not free.

The snake sat coiled, ready to strike. I started to run, and it chased me. I tried to flee to the east, but there was the river. The south was blocked by the snake, north were cliffs. The only direction I could run was towards the reactor. I didn't want to go. Oh God, anywhere but that reactor. If I made it to the reactor, would I lose myself? Would I become something hideous, be thrown into molten plasma?

The snake was catching up, so I kept running towards the reactor.

I woke in a feverish state, my sheets wet. Desperate to cool myself, I tore off the pajamas that my mother insisted I wear to be modest before the Lord. I looked up and saw my reflection in the mirror, crouching like a gnome in my tighty-whities. Disgusting and void, flesh with zero prospects, someone who lost the affections of Cher Hanson, the only victory this loser had ever achieved.

The Ritalin kid kept staring at me, so I lunged at the mirror, smashing the glass. I held up my bloody hand, enjoying the pain, and understood why Adonai relished his broken fingers.

I looked back at the mirror, which was nothing but a few shards.

The Ritalin kid was dead.

My parents burst into the room.

"What's going on?" my father shouted.

"Oh my God." My mother rushed to me. "You're bleeding. What on earth happened?"

I calmly looked up from my bloody hand. "I must've been having a nightmare."

"What were you dreaming?" said my mother.

I smiled. "I dreamt that I had to murder the wicked part of myself."

CHAPTER 22

REACTOR MAN

It was going to be a busy day at Bockscar. Thousands of people were descending into our town to witness the grand festival called the Water Follies. The climax of this celebration was the Columbia Cup, an Unlimited Hydroplane race. This event was held in high anticipation by locals and tourists alike, drawing huge crowds to watch a handful of noisy boats chase each other around the Columbia River. Each of the Tri-Cities—Richland, Pasco, and Kennewick—participated in hosting the event.

People would flock to our town from all over the Pacific Northwest to participate in drunken mayhem. Nights would be spent high, cruising, and hanging out in parked cars at the carwash on Court Street in the town of Pasco.

This whole weekend of good times started with the Atomic Frontier Days Parade. Each year, Bone and Fenix would attend the parade then trawl along the riverside, ignoring hydroplanes while checking out bikinis. I, of course, was never allowed to go.

When I got to work, it was utterly insane. There was already a line out the door. Things were moving too fast; I didn't have time to decipher the tickets, and I kept making mistakes.

I was pouring ingredients into cups for Adonai. "This is some kind of hell!" He slammed the milk pitcher down in frustration.

"How long did you say it's taking you to save up to get out of here?"

"Too long," he sputtered. "Years."

I knew then that this job wasn't cutting it. With this wage, it'd take forever. Three years could go by, and I'd still be there, being humiliated by Steve and rude customers. Maybe I was better off mopping radioactive floors for my father. Six months at Hanford and I could leave Richland in style.

"What's a matter with you," Steve shouted in front of the customers, "can't you read?"

I ignored him and continued pouring coffee while Adonai worked espresso.

"Go switch with Crispin," Steve said, "You're better on cash, anyway."

His comment floored me. The color coding had worked. I had overcome my disability to master something. Maybe I could work at Hanford and succeed, get the fuck away from this hell.

I began ringing in customers, fast and accurate, taking pride in what I was doing. It was the first time I'd felt self-esteem since I was a kid. I looked down at my bandaged hand and knew I had changed. Dyslexia would no longer hold me back, I just needed to come at things from a different angle that worked for my brain.

Thanks to Adonai, I had overcome a major hurdle.

As the morning progressed, it got busier and busier. The Bockscar was packed and we could barely keep up. Just when I thought it couldn't get any worse, I saw Bone and Fenix towards the back of the line. The embarrassment of their seeing me working under Steve was mortifying. My newfound self-esteem started to diminish.

"Oh, sweet Jesus," said Bone when he got up to the counter. "You never told me you work with Steve Hannity."

"Not for long," I said. "This job is losing its appeal by the minute."

"Are you going to be able to sneak out tonight?"

"Yes," I said, "but I want to go to Carson's party."

"What?" He was shocked.

I pulled a copy of the flier out of my back pocket and handed it to him. He picked it up, staring at it. "Is this you?"

"Yep."

Bone chuckled. "You didn't tell me."

"I did, but you were stoned."

He smiled. "You know I don't mix with them."

"Come on, they put me on the flier. Carson asked me to invite you."

Bone seemed uneasy. "Yeah, sure. I'll go. But I want you to come with us to Court Street first. If we don't do a little cruising, Sparrow will kill me. It's our last date before I go."

"Go where?" I asked.

"I'm due at MEPS in Spokane Monday morning. I'm driving there after the boat races."

"What are you talking about?" I said.

"MEPS, Military Entrance Processing Center."

I was dumbfounded. "I don't understand."

"I'm shipping out. By this time Monday, I'll be a jarhead."

I didn't know what to say. I just stood there silent, trying to digest the situation. I'd been so wrapped up in my own scene that I forgot Bone and his father had been to the recruiter.

Come Monday, Bone would be gone, his head shaved, marching in the sun, and doing push-ups till every bit of who he used to be was gone. He would come back a different person who followed orders and violently furthered his government's interests.

This news broke what was left of me into a thousand pieces.

Steve came up from behind, yanking me out of despair. "Hey Deacon, quit talking to your friends. You're backing up the line."

I waved Bone and Fenix away, giving them their drinks for free.

How could this be? Cher—and now Bone?

I began to quiver and looked down at the cash-register which was a total blur. I mindlessly took the next order, trying not to collapse. My vision began to spin, and I gripped the counter.

When my world stopped swirling, I opened my eyes and saw Carson's flier on the counter. There I was, running from the cops. Run, Deacon, run!

At that moment, I was done.

Steve walked over and pushed a ticket towards my face. "You've let our customer down. They ordered a mocha, and you had Adonai make a latte."

I stopped ringing in orders and turned to face him, defiant.

"What are you doing? You're just standing there."

"Listening to your expert feedback," I said. "Anytime you want to settle this, I'll be there."

He backed down, and I continued taking orders. I was so upset; I wanted to give every person a drink on the house—the whole fucking world. "Yes, ma'am, your drink is complimentary!"

"Really?"

"Yes, it's free, to help you celebrate the Water Follies. It's how I can better serve you. Enjoy the parade, courtesy of the Bockscar Café! Next?"

I felt like that goon at the 7-11. I could've buried the entire business, stole every dime. One way or another, I'd get my due, reaching into the till, stuffing a few twenties into my pocket. It was the only way to numb the pain.

Steve came up from behind. "Hey, you screwed up another order." He pushed the ticket towards my face.

I swatted his hand out of the way. "You really want a problem with me?"

"Do you want to keep this job?" he said, inflating his body and moving close.

"No. Do you?" I took off my apron and pushed it into his chest. "Go ahead, punch me. Let's see you do it."

He backed up.

"What's a matter, don't want to get fired for fighting on the job, or are you scared?"

Steve didn't say anything.

"Hey," yelled a man, "I've been waiting in line for five minutes. Are you going to take my order?"

"Fuck off," I said. I walked away from the counter, headed towards the door. I felt a tap on my shoulder. Thinking it was Steve, I turned to punch.

It was Adonai. "What are you doing?"

"Quitting," I said.

He was shocked. "You can't leave me here."

"Watch me."

I pushed open the door and Adonai bared my way with his arm. He looked at me in a motherly sort of way. "It's Steve, isn't it?"

"That and other things. I just can't do this; I deserve better." I patted him lovingly on the back. "And so do you. I'll see you around. I'm going to watch the floats."

"Fine then," he said, fanning me off, "go enjoy your peasant parade."

I walked outside. The crowds were so thick I could barely move. I pushed my way up to where the action was. There were Jaycees on horseback, Shriners in go-carts, and a float that had a throne for Miss Tri-Cities. I'd never seen a parade before.

My vision started to blur, and I became dizzy. Then I heard it, the beating of tribal rhythms, tri-toms, and bass drums. It progressed on the horizon like an impending invasion. It was the sound of last night's nightmare, the spectacle everyone waited for each year, Reactor Man.

Marching in time to the beat, a team of troopers in white Hazmat suits flanked his float like pallbearers in a Louisiana wake. On the float's deck, men in white coats with clipboards paced before cardboard control panels, and above it all was Reactor Man, perched upon his nuclear core.

Reactor Man looked like a robot from a low-budget black-and-white sci-fi serial from the fifties. His suit was blown large with argon atmosphere, and a particle-mask shielded his face. He danced awkwardly to the driving rhythms of John Phillip Sousa, played by the Richland Bomber Marching Band, with added menace from the bass drums.

Everyone cheered as plumes of radioactive steam rose above the reactors upriver. I watched the float creep by like a hearse and gazed up at Reactor Man, boogieing in his puffy argon inert clothes. He had left my dream world and was haunting me.

Each jerky movement drove the crowd wild. I stood like an alien in the multitudes, viewing him as a Hollywood monster, the first person you see when you enter a doomed career at Hanford.

What did I do? I quit my job to work for my father so I could become a janitor that wears a Hazmat suit like Reactor Man? *Hey Deacon, when you're done mopping that atomic waste, we got another spill.*

Working out there was my worst fear. Was I the only person in town who had these nightmares? Everyone I knew thought it was all pretty neat.

Aside from the obvious worry of contamination, I had a deeper fear. Every time my folks would suggest I work out there, I was afraid I wouldn't be good enough and would bring even more shame to our family.

I turned around, ready to tell Steve I was sorry. I walked back to the café and stood looking at him barking orders at Crispin and

Adonai. It was a study in low wage humiliation. Being a janitor couldn't be worse than this. At least janitors don't have to read.

When I got home, I stood at the door, preparing myself to face my fears and dominate the shit scene with my parents. It was early. My folks were finishing their breakfast before they went to church. I walked into the kitchen to forage for food. They studied me like a suspect.

My father stopped eating. "Aren't you supposed to be at work?"

"I quit."

My dad put down his fork.

I turned from the cupboards with a physically menacing posture to remind him that I could kick his ass. He was afraid to cross me, and my punching the mirror had only deepened his insecurity. In an act of submission, he picked up his fork and resumed eating.

Determined to control the conversation, I poured some Fruit Loops into a bowl and sat, staring at them. I said a quick prayer to keep them off my case and maintain my advantage. We chewed our food in silence as if I were not welcome. It was five minutes before they broached the subject.

"Why did you quit?" asked my mother.

My father made a fist, ready for anything, uncertain of his role as household king in this new normal where he could no longer beat his son.

"It's not a Christian environment," I said.

They started to chew their food in silence, each contemplating what to do with this information, afraid it would blow up into a physical altercation that they couldn't contain.

"Is that job still available with your company?" I said, nonchalantly.

My parents looked at each other, speaking in the unspoken covert tongue mastered from years of marriage.

"This is quite the change in attitude," my father said, cutting his sausage after my mother signaled that he would broker the subject.

"You were right; it doesn't take long to figure out that minimum wage jobs don't cut it," I said, casually, as if the tension didn't exist. "Besides, Collin Fenix is finishing his training for the Hanford Patrol, and I thought I might give working out there a try, too."

"I also told you that all you'll get is janitorial work," my father said. "Even the most basic entry-level job requires a high school diploma. I'll convince them to make an exception since you're my son."

"Better than working in that café."

"Mark, maybe Deacon could take classes at the community college while he works as a janitor?" said my mother, trying to stay positive about my future. "He could study for the GED."

They just didn't get it; school wasn't my thing. I'd never succeed no matter how hard I tried or how much people helped. I needed to find my own way.

I gripped my fork, about to explode, then I came to my senses. I calmed myself, knowing I'd made the first steps towards my end goal, a life of self-respect and dignity, free of abuse. If I did things right, I could play my parents to my advantage and get the fuck out.

"Well," said my father, "I'll make a few calls and see what I can do."

CHAPTER 23

A STREET

After a long nap, I lay in bed, trying to recognize images in the popcorn ceiling, waiting to hear my father snore so I could leave for Carson's party. Despite personal setbacks, a wonderful feeling that I'd never had before filled my chest and spread through my body: I was in control for the first time.

Why? Carson's Boat Race Mosh was the hottest event of the year, and I would be attending as guest of honor. If I did it right, this would be the official start of a brand-new life.

A strange optimism spread through me. I felt that tonight would be the axis upon which all humanity shifted toward a new dawn. It may have been 1986, but for me, the Eighties were over. I lay in my bed, resolved to be something new, a force to get the message out. I truly believed that I was capable of something fantastic. It was the old crumbling away, and I was determined to stand at the epicenter.

Carson was a shepherd, and by using my image on his flier, he had knighted me. Up until then, I'd been this Ritalin kid loser. Now, I was the guy on the flier, the guy who punched cops.

There was also something interesting about the timing of my two closest relationships leaving. It was as if they had to get out of the way so I could emerge a chrysalis from my Ritalin past. Bone had to go his way, and I mine. As for Cher, was I really in love? I

160

found her inspirational and beautiful, but no, I was in love with the validation I felt from her touch.

I'd make new friends, meet new loves. Bone was right; all we had was now. It would never be better than now.

I held up the record Cher gave me and made a vow. As of this day, I was going to live full tilt. I would no longer be Deacon Jones; I would be the guy on that flier. And if Cher's dad crossed my path, he would be another cop for me to beat down.

When the time was right, I climbed out of the window, making my way through the dark greenbelt. The 7-11 glowed like a nighttime oasis. I walked in, headed straight to the Slurpee fountain, and topped it off with pop. The zombie behind the counter watched my every move without blinking. I reached for some round tortilla chips and slathered them with chili & cheese from the self-serve machine. I made sure I topped them with as many black olives and onions that the pile would take without spilling.

The clerk and I made eye contact as I slowly walked out the door without paying. He was too numb to do anything but watch me leave.

When I got outside, Bone was there.

Fenix met me by the Duster drinking a can of Bud. "Night before the boat races," he said, taking a gulp. "Biggest party of the year, right here in Tri-Cities. You ready?"

"Yeah, sure," I said, grabbing the can out of his hand and taking a swig.

Bone reached into the Duster through the open window. A girl handed him a joint. It was his recent part-time girlfriend, Sparrow. He tilted his head back in ecstasy, blowing out smoke, the lights from the 7-11 reflecting off his shades.

Sparrow had a healthy appearance. She was Bone's type, trim on the flesh and smooth on the eyes. She also turned a blind eye to his fooling around with other women. These attributes elevated her above all others in his eyes.

She'd been spending so much time at the Reinhold house; you'd assume that she lived there. Since graduation, he'd been getting bolder, sneaking her into the basement to drink, play video games, and fuck while his parents watched television upstairs. Either he considered his position invincible, or he knew he was doomed anyway.

Sitting next to Sparrow in the back seat was a mystery girl. I leaned over to see who it was. Mikultra Skala!

She waved at me and smiled. She was beautiful, but trouble. I felt her allure like an illicit drug that you regret taking, a sticky trap that ensnares you in cotton candy.

Bone slowly moved his head down, and our eyes met. He grinned, reveling in his decadence. A bag of dope and surrounded by the most beautiful girls in town. He was in his element. How could he say that this was his last party, or that this was the end? No one I knew had it better. Four years in the Marines, and he'd be free. He'd get through it. He always did. It was how he did things.

"I'm so glad you made it," he said, hugging me. "You're the best friend I ever had." He patted me on the back.

"I call shotgun," Fenix said, aggressively.

Knowing he was an idiot, I shrugged my shoulders and sat in the back between the girls.

Mikultra and Sparrow were each wearing matching spandex miniskirts that gripped their perfect bodies, showing off smooth legs. Their hair was teased to the extreme, held stiff by Aqua Net.

"Hey bro," said Fenix, turning to the back seat. "What's up?"

"Not much," I said, grabbing his beer and taking a swig. "I quit my job."

"All right," said Fenix, reaching over the seat to punch me in the arm and take back his beer. "The future's so bright, you should be wearing shades."

"Your dad is gonna freak," said Bone.

"Actually, he's helping me get a job with his company out at the Site."

"Don't do it, Deacon. You know what happened to my grandpa."

"Easy for you to say," said Sparrow in an annoyed tone. "Maybe you should apply out there instead of leaving me for the military."

Bone ignored her.

"My best friend Kendra says I'll marry a guy who works out at Hanford," said Mikultra. "She read it in my cards. She does tarot."

"Could be anybody," I mumbled, wondering why this church girl was messing with tarot cards. "It's not hard to predict; over half the men in town work out there."

"Our grandpa says he can get me on after I finish my security training," said Fenix. "Says he's already got a spot reserved for me. Least they can do since they zapped his shit. It's all who you know out there."

"That's so exciting," said Sparrow. "These two getting on at Hanford."

Sparrow was beaming at Fenix. He blushed and turned back to face the front. Bone looked in the rearview mirror, annoyed. His ecstatic state out in front of the 7-11 was waning. He drove in agitated silence while the rest of us talked like he was our chauffeur.

Mikultra leaned up against me. "You must be thrilled to get a job out there."

I reached up and took the joint from Sparrow. "Yeah, thrilled."

"Do you have any hobbies?"

"I like to sing." I passed the joint to the front seat.

"Horses are my thing," she said. "Do you like horses?"

I began to imagine how she'd look naked, mounted on the back of a horse. "Yeah sure; they're cool." What was I saying? I shouldn't be getting involved with her. She would make it harder to leave.

"Fenix, give me back that joint," I said, mad at myself for thinking about it.

After a hit, I passed Mikultra the spliff. She looked into my eyes, pouring on the sensuality.

"What other hobbies do you have?" she asked. "Kendra's tarot cards say that… blah… blah… blah…" I began tuning her out, just like I'd done with my teachers back in the day.

Cher began to permeate my thoughts. Instead of Mikultra's face, I thought of Cher's almond eyes and precious mouth, and how her essence had washed through me as I held her. Cher wouldn't expect anything from me, except that I stay true to myself. She wouldn't demand the fancy or overpriced swell. We could sit on the steps at midnight and make out till three in the morning. Cher would give me poetry.

But Cher was gone, never coming back. She didn't want me. And Mikultra was there, more beautiful than ever, ready to ease my pain. There was absolutely no reason I shouldn't go for it. At least that's what I told myself at the time.

When we got across the river to Court Street, cars were already cruising. Girls were dancing on the beds of pickups to hair-metal butt-rock records while drinking beer. Guys in baseball caps and flannel shirts were hanging out of windows, screaming, "Let's party," as if it were the only sentence in the English language.

We approached the carwash where everyone parked and hung out.

"Pull over, there's Carmen Stiles," said Sparrow.

The girls ran to meet their friend, and Fenix went to admire a monster truck with duel diesel chimneys.

I watched Mikultra and Sparrow talking to Carmen. They smiled at me and giggled. Mikultra waived.

"She likes you," said Bone.

"Nah," I said, not wanting to think about it.

"No, really. I know women." He sighed and kicked the pavement, looking over at Sparrow. "Or at least I thought I did."

"I don't want to get involved with a Tri-Cities girl. Mikultra's not my type. I'm moving in a new direction."

"You used to be crazy about her," he said.

"Well, I've changed. I've decided to take the Hanford gig so I can move to Seattle. She'll hold me back, keep me here longer. Besides, I just got dumped by Cher. I'm a bit broke up over it."

He patted me on the back. "The best cure for a broken heart is another woman."

"Maybe you're right."

"If I were you, I'd ride that wave."

My eyes followed the curve of Mikultra's miniskirt. "I just might do that."

"No sense worrying about a lost girl," said Bone, eyes glued to Sparrow. He turned and gave me an insincere smile. "I'm pretty sure Sparrow's about to dump me. I need to be reminded that there is no yesterday and I don't care about tomorrow." He shook his head and took out a cigarette. "At least that's what I thought before I got into this mess. Maybe tomorrow I'll look upon today with envy."

I watched Bone carefully. He had seemed out of place ever since we stole that keg.

"Sparrow thinks I should use my grandfather's connections to get on with the Hanford thing," he said.

"Maybe you should."

Bone smirked contemptuously and shook his head. "Nah. And nor should you. There's some spooky shit out there."

"It's a temporary measure. I want to get out of here, and I don't want to sleep on the street to do it."

"Hey," shouted Fenix, pointing towards a monster truck. "Check it out."

Sitting on the hood was a redneck drinking from a pitcher like it was a beer stein. He was gulping so fast that he was spilling it on his chest.

"Come on. They got a keg in the back," cried Fenix. "Eric's taking us out for a cruise. It'll be the biggest truck on the strip."

Mikultra and Sparrow were already climbing in.

"I'll pass," said Bone.

"Deacon?" Fenix said as if judging me according to my participation.

"I'll stay with Bone. There's a party on A-Street. You can meet us there." I handed him one of Carson's fliers.

We watched as the colossal pickup drove away, belching black spent diesel out of dual chimneys with everyone in the back, redneck still on the hood drinking from his pitcher.

"Let's ditch this scene and go to Carson's party," I said.

"Might as well." He sounded depressed. "I suppose my girl will eventually be there." He grimaced at his cigarette and threw it down, barely smoked. "Yeah, let's go. This is the last party before I ship off; let's make it mean something."

Carson's Boat Race Mosh was in a dilapidated house on A-Street, surrounded by a moat of dead grass.

The A-Street house was rented by a hoser who made money by charging admission to his keggers. I doubt anyone lived there.

There were so many people cramming into the little house that we had to park a few blocks away. Excitement churned in my stomach as we walked down the street. Loud music echoed throughout the neighborhood, muffled and murky in the distance.

It was typical Eastern Washington rock played at parties in those days, a unique amalgamation of Hardcore Punk and Thrash Metal. Isolated from the rest of the country, these Washington bands were left to their own devices, combining everything that came before them into something new and organic.

The music filled me with an inspired feeling. Considering my learning disabilities, the language of this sound was the only thing I could truly read. I knew its beat, the reason it cried, how it punched a gut, the intuitive quality of its rage. Though I was incapable of creating it, it was like I owned it.

Bone stopped for a second and looked around, frowning. "When I hear music like this, I don't look forward to the future," he said, sounding defeated. "We were born the year the Beatles released Sgt. Pepper. You'd think our generation could do better."

"Our generation hasn't come up to bat yet. I think we can do something great. One of us just has to step up to create something that defines us," I said.

"We'll see. I'm not sure our generation stands for anything."

I knew he was right; this would be the last time we partied together. It was more than him shipping off to the Marines; we were growing apart. I was changing with the times, and he was refusing to move forward, clinging to the past. We couldn't go on without some form of resentment popping up in the future. He couldn't understand where I was headed.

We started to walk towards the party, passing a guy feeling up a girl, pressed against the side of a pickup. He was sucking on her neck, giving her a hickey. She observed us as we passed, looking me in the eye and mouthing, "Hi."

"Listen to this guy who's singing," Bone said as we neared the party house. "He's just screaming. No talent. Either of us could sound like that if we were pissed off enough. This isn't Punk Rock; this is bullshit."

"It's Diddley Squat," I said.

"Exactly."

"No. That's the name of the band. They're local."

"Of course they're local," said Bone, pulling a hip flask out of his pocket and taking a shot. "Nothing but shit ever came out of Richland."

I listened to the singer. He did sound pissed, and it touched a chord in my soul. I wanted to lash out at anything or anyone—lash out at my lack of opportunity and options; lash out because we were the first generation in a century to have less opportunity than our parents; lash out because Bone and Cher had abandoned me.

The sounds coming out of that party made me feel exhilarated, confirming my resolve to live in a space where music like this pumped out of valve amplifiers every night of the week.

People were loitering in the yard smoking, and a couple of girls were sitting on a planter filled with dead plants, drinking beer. They smiled at me as we walked past them. "That's Deacon Jones," one of them said.

The band was guitar, bass, and drums, with a singer who wore a paper McDonald's employee hat, like the Garrison caps that soda jerks wore in the 1950s. He screamed into the mic, moving around with exaggerated ape-like movements.

In front of the band was a mosh pit, bodies thrashing in all directions, smashing into each other with violent abandon, occasionally denting the drywall. The group was so loud it was punishing. It hit me right in the chest, and the intensity of the music spoke to me on a primal level.

The sound pelted my skin, causing it to prickle, as the bass player jumped, maneuvering around the fretboard with rapid notes. The drummer was thrashing his kit with accelerated precision. The guitar raged with semi-automatic fire. The singer lurched then thrust upward in a scream that sounded like it came from a traumatic existence.

Bone watched the wild scene with disgust, but I wanted to jump into the maelstrom of male angst. In my Ritalin life, I would have been afraid to get hurt. But now, I yearned for physical pain. Like Cher's cutting, I wanted to feel something. I had lived my whole life in fear, but it was time to stop. I would submit to the tornado.

I shouted into the din as I entered the mosh pit.

The pit pushed me into a hundred directions within a second. Fists in my face and bruised flesh, my adrenaline exploding, releasing everything that had been pent up within my Ritalin fog. All my anger, compacted into a white dwarf star, was ready to explode. It all came out. Round and round.

The song finished, and the pit came to a halt. I knelt, putting my hands to my knees, trying to catch my breath while laughing. It was the most fun I'd ever had.

Bone looked at me with concern and repugnance with the scene, knowing that there was no place for him in this new world.

I took a deep breath, my blood dripping down from my nose onto the beer-stained carpet, reminding me that I was very much alive.

CHAPTER 24

MIKULTRA

I remained there, breathing heavy, hands on my knees, allowing the blood to form a small puddle between my feet, occasionally glancing at Bone who stood at a distance with a disturbed look on his face.

Carson came and put his hand on my shoulder. "Alright! You came. That was some sweet action in the pit."

I smiled at him, completely exhilarated, trying to catch my breath, blood dripping down my face. If I could relive the feeling over and over, I would. Standing among these thrashers, I felt comfortable socially for the first time in my life.

Chaos would be my new mantra. Anger, my principle. Freedom, my offensive. Anarchy, my gospel.

Carson stepped up and took the mic from the singer. "Hey mother fuckers, we got Deacon Jones in the house!" The crowd cheered. I couldn't believe it; this was the best day of my life.

The singer grabbed back the mic. "This one's for Deacon Jones, someone who knows how to handle a cop. It's a cover by the Vandals. It's called, the Legend of Pat Brown. Deacon and Carson are gonna help us sing."

Carson grabbed my arm and we gathered around the mic as a crunchy riff came out of the shitty amp. The band hit full gear, starting the rumble. Joy burst out of me as the three of us shouted, "Pat Brown... ran the cops down."

The mosh-pit went nuts and I pushed forth the voice of hell, singing the lyrics. This is what I wanted to do with my life, it felt so good.

When the lyrics were over, and the music started to drive, I leapt into the pit. The kids held me up, passing me from hand to hand as I lay on my back, looking up at the moldy ceiling as though it were heaven.

I was finally pushed off and joined the maelstrom, slamming in a spiral, like gravity to a black star. The mosh-pit began to churn with sacred geometry, swirling into perfection, drawing me into its ferocity. I could exist in this storm that was better than a carnival ride, more focused than Ritalin. Round and round, this music was my Kaaba, my Mecca. I was so in the moment, thrashing in the most primal of tribal dances.

The band suddenly stopped, but I kept going with the human tornado for a couple of rotations. Then a deep older male voice came over the microphone. "Alright, break it up. Time to go home."

It was a cop, shitting on our scene.

Carson shrugged his shoulders as the pigs pushed their way through the kids. My disappointment that the music had stopped far outweighed my fear of being arrested.

While Carson negotiated with the police, I faded into the crowd that was milling out the door. I found Bone on the other side of the street, tucked away from the action. He had a talent for avoiding heat.

I could see it in his eyes: this change in our culture, the death of the 80s, the end of the Cold War, the end of our childhood. It was the end for him and the beginning for me. Maybe we didn't know it consciously, but subconsciously it was there. The era of the loser was upon us.

We stood looking at each other, communicating without speaking, when up walked Sparrow and Mikultra, arms crossed and looking impatient.

"Good, there you are," said Sparrow. "This party sucks. The police are here. We want to go, and Fenix wants to stay with Eric."

Bone looked visibly upset. "What does Fenix have to do with it? I'm the one who brought you. I'm the one driving."

The girls saw the blood on my face and rushed over to me.

"Oh My God," said Sparrow. "What happened?"

"Mosh pit," said Bone, annoyed.

"A bunch of savages," said Mikultra. She pulled a pocket-pack of Kleenex out of her purse and lovingly started to wipe the blood from my face.

"I'm alright," I said, pushing her hand away.

She stopped and looked into my eyes. "You're cute. I never noticed that until recently."

"Yeah," I said, "what's so different?"

Determined to get around my cagey responses, she reached up and stroked my cheek, sending black magic energy through me, turning my distrust into desire.

"You're a naughty boy," she said. "And the way you hit Dick Jameson with your skateboard," she stood on her tiptoes and whispered in my ear, "it kind of turned me on."

I chuckled.

"I bet you thought I was a nice church girl," she said.

"You got that right."

"Well, I thought the same about you... boring! Oh, but how I was wrong." She slithered her arm into mine. "All the boys at church are dull, but not you."

"Then why date guys from church?"

"If I date a Christian, my parents don't ask questions."

I hadn't thought of this. Dating her could buy me some freedom till I was ready to leave town. I reached my arm around her waist. It felt like perfection, my hand fitting perfectly on her hip. She didn't seem to mind, so I held her tight.

We became distracted by Bone and Sparrow fighting. "All you had to do was go inside and find me," he shouted. "You know I'm always happy to take you home."

"We didn't want to go in there," she said, angry. "It's loud and violent. Look what happened to Deacon."

"You're the one who wanted to ride in that stupid truck." Bone turned to Mikultra and I. "You guys want a ride home? I'm leaving."

We followed the angry couple up the street at a distance to give them space to fight. Mikultra moved her body close to mine; her presence put me into another world. Bone's drama did not exist in our little sphere. I wanted to grab her and make her mine. With each step, her body brushed up against me, pulling me in with desire.

She stopped walking and spread her fingers though my hair. We kissed passionately. "My parents are away at Lake Chelan," she whispered. "They won't be back till tomorrow night."

I looked down at her miniskirt and started to melt like a western witch under Dorothy's water pail. If I got validation from Cher, Mikultra would make me a man.

Fuck it, let her cure my broken heart.

"Douglas, you need to get a job," we heard Sparrow shout as they got to the car ahead of us.

"I've got a job," he said, sounding desperate, "I'm a Marine." Bone slammed his hand on the roof of the Duster.

Mikultra pulled away from our kiss and looked over her shoulder at Bone and Sparrow. "Can you believe the way he treats her?" she said, looking up at me as we started to walk towards the car, arm in arm. "I bet you know how to treat a girl."

"You'd do far better getting a job out at Hanford like Fenix and Deacon," Sparrow shouted.

I didn't like her using my name in their argument.

"Fenix and Deacon don't work at Hanford," he said. "They haven't even applied. Get in!"

Sparrow slumped into the passenger seat and slammed the door. "You don't care about me," she screamed at him as he walked around the car.

Bone opened the driver door for us. Mikultra and I got in the back, and I put my hand on her bare thigh. She moved it further up her skirt and put her leg over mine. We started to kiss, and she moved her hand to my crotch as Bone and Sparrow sat in strained silence.

When we got to Mikultra's, Bone let us out. "I'll see you later, buddy." He sounded completely dejected. "At least one of us will be having a good time tonight."

"Sorry man," I said.

"It's not your problem." He gave me a hug and a sad smile. "This was going to be my last night of good times as a free man. I was looking forward to this."

"Maybe you placed too many expectations on it," I said.

"Nah, it's just an omen that my time is done."

"Will I ever see you again?" I said, filled with sorrow.

He laughed. "Of course. You'll see me after boot camp."

I knew that on the surface, it all seemed so simple. Bone could go, cut his hair, and get a job through his grandfather's connections, pleasing his woman and family. He'd be set. But sometimes you have to do what feels right—no compromise. I know that working out at Hanford didn't feel right for me, but with my hands on Mikultra, I convinced myself that I was making wise choices and Bone was being obstinate. I didn't even watch Bone and Sparrow drive off; like a fool, I just madly kissed Mikultra.

She led me up their designer driveway that curved through a professionally manicured lawn. I marveled at the immensity of Mikultra's house. I could see a pool with a slide poking out from around the back yard. The house had a red clay tile roof and stucco walls. The foyer was massive. Mikultra pulled my gaze away from the art on the walls to make out.

"I want you to sleep with me in my parent's bed," she said after we parted lips for air.

"What does your father do for a living?" I asked, amazed, glancing at the opulence of the house.

"Doctor Dimitri Skala," she said with a smile that I wasn't sure if it was laced with respect or contempt. "He's a prize-winning nuclear physicist." She took my hand to lead me upstairs. We entered the master bedroom, and she motioned to a California King waterbed with a silk comforter and large pillows inside frilly cases.

Mikultra pulled back the sheets. "Sit."

She proceeded to undo my pants as I bobbed up and down on the water mattress so she could slide them off. She knelt, holding my hard member in her hand, smiled, and put it into her mouth while maintaining eye contact.

A rush of euphoria shot through my entire frame, causing my inner spirit to hover in bliss, making me momentarily immortal.

How did I arrive at this moment? And why did I feel like such a sellout, despite this glorious feeling, this trial in beatific ecstasy? We had nothing in common, but did it matter? Could I possibly be happier? Yes, if she were Cher.

But forget that. I was in the moment, and this was one of the happiest nights of my life—a glimpse into my future.

Mikultra got up and guided me to lie back on the pillows. She lifted her miniskirt to reveal a perfect set of legs coming out of hips that commanded my innermost instincts to make her my property. It was the animal in me.

To my surprise, she was not wearing panties. She was religious, a real church girl. I'd never imagined she would put out. I was like those jerks down at the Delta keg; I'd put money on her being a virgin.

She climbed on top of me and put my cock in her hand, lingering there, waiting to put it in. "Before we go any further, I need to know if you have a personal relationship with Jesus."

"What?!" I found this a very odd thing to say at a time like this. I knew where this line of talk went. My desire to fuck her overcame my disgust and contempt for my parent's god. "Of course," I said, willing to say anything just to get inside her.

If I weren't so young and horny, I'm sure the thought of Jesus watching us would've been real boner death. "We go to the same church. Why would you ask?"

"I just need to make sure we're forgiven, and that you are serious about being in a God-centered relationship because what we do offends Christ." She lowered herself and started to thrust in concentric motion as she peeled off her dress, revealing firm buds.

She began fucking me with confidence and skill, licking her lips, half laughing in a purr as she grinded. She reached over, took a cigarette out of a pack, and proceeded to light it without skipping a thrust. "Also, if you get me pregnant, I need to be sure you won't pressure me to get an abortion."

"Of course not," I said, gripping her hips.

She must've seen the look on my face. "Don't worry, I'm on the pill."

Mikultra tilted her head back and released the smoke in an erotic haze. Then she took the cigarette and put it to my lips. "Suck it," she said.

I breathed in the resin tainted fumes and coughed, causing me to thrust deeper. I enjoyed the taste.

She took back the cigarette, sucked in, and started to fuck rapidly. "Together, we will bring out the fruit of the spirit." She blew out her smoke, letting the cloud fall upon me.

That night, asleep in her parent's bed, I had a dream. I was driving Bone's Plymouth Duster down a long straight highway that passed through a massive stretch of seeding wheat. Adonai Garcia sat next to me in the passenger seat. The skies were blue with occasional clouds, and the sun was shining. We were driving towards a range of jagged mountains.

There was a flatbed trailer without railing, just a black frame holding together wood planks. The trailer was hitched to the front, with the Duster pushing it down the highway. Placed meticulously in the center of the trailer was a black oil drum.

Bone was standing on the trailer bed, fretting about the wheat we passed at speeds exceeding fifty miles per hour. He kept walking around the oil drum, completely stressed, trying to grab some of the grain, only to have the stalks brush against his palm as he tried to grasp in vain. He would rush around the oil drum to the other side of the trailer to make an attempt at grabbing a bunch of wheat. Each time, they alluded his grip, over and over.

He would curse and declare that he'd lost the stem of one grain while a million others passed him.

"What's he doing?" said Adonai, calm as Buddha.

"Fretting about what's behind him," I said.

Then I woke up.

CHAPTER 25

THE HANFORD MAN

I woke around 3 a.m. to Mikultra snoring. Despite spending the past twelve years as a bullied dork, I had just fucked one of the most popular girls in school. I lay there, determined that from now on, everything I touched would be a win.

Mikultra must've sensed me stirring and rolled over, putting her hand lovingly on my chest, reminding me that this ecstasy wasn't imagined.

"Hi," she said in a sleepy voice. "Last night was fantastic."

"Yeah," I said, wanting to get the hell out of bed and race home. My parents would be up soon and discover I was gone.

"Are you going to be my beau?"

I was halfway out of bed and looked back, baffled by what she was asking. "Beau? Like a boyfriend? Yeah, sure." It felt wrong saying it, a bit like selling out.

She pushed herself up, revealing her perfectly tanned torso. "Do you want to fuck me again?"

I looked at her breasts and followed them down to her stomach and hips. Part of me wanted to run, but I just couldn't stop myself. I reached over her hip and cupped her naked ass, pulling her close, caught in a barb.

My parents and everything could go to hell, I was into now.

After sex, she rolled onto her side and looked me in the eyes. "Are you going to the boat races?"

"No," I said. "I've got to be home before my parents get up, or I'll be in a similar situation to Bone."

"I think I'll skip church and go. You'll call me?"

I knelt and kissed her. "Of course."

Walking home from her house, I felt terrific, doomed, and strange. I gazed upriver to the Energy Northwest Cooling Towers in the distance, steam rising like a pumping plume, raping the virgin sky.

When I got home, my parents were still asleep. All was as it should be. I jumped in the shower to wash the blood and sex off and get ready for church. If this bullshit was going to make my life easier, I should go all in. Besides, going to that fucking church just got me laid.

I came downstairs and took my place at the table.

"You look nice," my mother said, admiring the cheap suit I usually wore on Sunday mornings. "Up early, too."

"I'm just excited to go to church, that's all." Since I was going to spew bullshit, I might as well go all the way, use their stupid religion to gain more freedoms.

My father squinted, not buying it. "What's brought about your change in attitude?"

"To be honest, I met a girl at church."

My mother perked up. "And is this young lady anyone we might know?"

"Her name is Mikultra."

"That's Dimitri's daughter," said my mother, exaggerating her face so my father could see that she was impressed.

"Pretty girl," said my dad, focused on his food.

"To be honest, this is one of the reasons I want a better job. I was thinking," I continued selling out, "I know I'm not supposed to date and receive calls, but now that I'm eighteen, maybe we could relax that restriction. After all, Mikultra is a good Christian and believes in Christ-centered dating."

They looked at each other. My father smiled at my mother and held her hand. "Deacon, it was a beautiful woman who brought me to Jesus. Before I met your mother, I was a lot like you."

My mom blushed, and I about barfed.

"May I be excused?" I said, standing up. "I need to finish getting ready for church."

After service, I left my parents to their Bible study and walked home. The streets were empty. Everyone was down at the river for the boat races. I could hear them in the distance, a good mile away, screaming pistons blaring.

When I got home, I was surprised to see Bone parked out front. "Thought I'd stop by and say so long."

"Shouldn't you be at the boat races?" I said.

"I decided not to go. The last thing I want to see is a bunch of people having fun. Besides, I needed to finish packing." He took a hit off a joint and forced a smile. "Get in. There's something I want you to see."

"Where are we going?"

"To see my grandpa," he said, joint hanging off his lip.

"I thought he was quarantined out in the Eleven-Hundred Area?" The thought of his radioactive grandfather scared me.

"He was. A few years ago, they moved him to a secret trailer by the hospital to make his treatments more convenient," he said. "Now they got him in a trailer park on Photon Avenue."

Years later, after Grunge and Alternative Radio helped make skateboarding acceptable, the city built a skate park on the spot where Harlan Fenix's personal contamination had seeped into the ground.

"Are you sure," I said, "I thought no one was allowed to see him?"

"It'll be okay. His contamination is coming down."

"Isn't he dangerous?"

"No, not for short periods. I see him all the time. Don't worry; they chelated his blood. Now he's only dangerous to his pets. He's on his tenth cat." He handed me a few joints. "Take 'em, I bought a whole bag. Got twenty dollars from pawning Travis' Mexican Stratocaster. There's no way I can smoke it all before I leave."

"You pawned your brother's guitar?"

"He's a jarhead now," said Bone, slurring his words. "He doesn't deserve the same guitar Hendrix played. He can take his GI money and buy an Ibanez, if he ever gets back." He took a hit and laughed. "He'll probably be shipped off somewhere and get shot. Maybe I'll get shot. That's what happens to jarheads."

We drove to the north side of town where the streets had names like Neutron, Argon, Cosmic, and Nuclear.

Bone's grandfather lived in a doublewide mobile home with an American flag hanging off the stoop. The lawn had gone to seed, and Bone looked embarrassed.

"He doesn't mow the lawn because he can only go outside at night. The accident made him sensitive to light." He knocked on the door and poked his head inside. "Grandpa, it's me, Douglas."

Reynolds Aluminum foil was taped to the windows, allowing faint streams of light into the room. After my eyes adjusted to the dark, I made out a man, smoking in an armchair with a throw over his legs. Each puff illuminated his face. He squinted behind thick-rimmed Penguin glasses. If he'd had hair, you could almost visualize him greasing it back, combed fine with a black unbreakable comb. But all he had up top was a bumpy ulcerated scalp that looked like it would never heal. I swore I could see silver pieces of americium lodged in the right side of his skull. Light glistened off them when he'd turn his head.

He coughed, spraying cigarette smoke everywhere.

"Grandpa, this is Deacon."

"Pleased to meet you," said Harlan Fenix, nodding at me, pushing his cigarette into the ashtray. "You'll have to forgive me, but I'm not allowed to shake hands."

I stood, silent from fear. This could happen to me, or my father. I thought about the BC Crib and the spill.

A toothless cat with a bald-patch coat hissed and jumped off his lap. "What can I do for you, Doug?" he croaked.

"I've come to say goodbye. I'm shipping out."

"I heard. Can't believe you're going through with this nonsense," said the old man.

"What can I do?" said Bone. "They were going to throw me in jail."

He shook his head, making it sparkle. "What on earth were you thinking, stealing beer? Stupidest thing I ever heard. I ought to tan your hide."

Bone shrugged.

"What are you, an alcoholic?" coughed the old man. He calmed himself and shook his head. "Doug, it's not too late. You need to reason with your father. His anger is a culmination of frustration from years of irresponsible behavior on your part. Show him you're willing to put your life on track. Tell him you'll enroll in college."

"He's made it clear for years; if I want to go to college, I'll do it on the G.I. Bill. Besides, I've signed a contract."

"Should've never let a soldier marry my daughter," Harlan mumbled. He poured a finger of Bushmills into a dirty glass. "You could get a student loan."

"What would be my major? And where would I live while I studied? My old man has made it clear, and I've made my decision. Besides, it's part of my parole. I've come to say goodbye."

Harlan sighed and took a sip of Bushmills. "Doug, you don't have to do this. The Marines is not for you."

Bone stiffened a little, his posture becoming tense.

"Your father is serious, but he's reasonable. When you get home, present him with a plan, like school. You'd be able to afford to live the way you want on a Hanford paycheck. Your cousin Collin has almost finished his security training, fresh out of high school." He fiddled with the butt in the ashtray. "Tell him you'll apply for the Nuclear Waste Apprenticeship Program. Your father and parole officer will go for that. You're too smart for the military Doug."

"Come on grandpa, can you see me handling nuclear waste?" said Bone.

"More than I can see you crawling through the jungle with a rifle in your hand." The old man's rant sent him into a painful fit of coughing.

"Doug," Harlan continued, "please, I don't want any grandson of mine in the military. There are far better ways of serving one's country then manning a weapon. War should be obsolete. We live in a nuclear age, where you can resolve conflicts with diplomacy, backed by a nuclear arsenal. I'm urging you to go to school and help design the future; don't give in to some antiquated idea of military strength."

I stood there listening to the old man, his health and skin destroyed by the progress he was pushing on his grandson. He sounded like he had razors embedded in his throat, a victim of his pristine nuclear age. I wanted to bolt, get as far away from this horror as possible.

"And if school isn't your thing," he continued, "then find a trade. You fixed up that motorcycle; there's skill in that. I'm sure your father will accept any form of effort, just as long as you're working."

Bone stood stoic, letting him speak, his eyes damp in the faint light of the mobile home. "Well, grandpa, you know we'd like to stay and talk, but I'm due at MEPS." He grabbed my arm, ushering me outside, slamming the door behind us. "Now you see why I chose the Marines over working out there?"

I didn't know what to say. I thought about what Adonai said, that there are always options. As horrible as it all seemed, I wasn't sure either of us had a choice.

We sat in the car before he turned the ignition. "I endured that humiliation because I wanted you to see him before you took that job at your father's company."

"Thanks," I said. "But it's sort of like you and the Marines; at this point, I can't see that we have many options."

CHAPTER 26

THE LOLLYPOP GUILD

When we got to Bone's, he motioned for me to have a seat on the worn-out couch. He took a Corona out of his bar-fridge and handed it to me. "Deacon, by the time we finish these beers, things will never be the same. Before I get behind the wheel of that car, I'm fallin' down the hatch." He clinked my bottle with his. "Better to die drunk on the road then sober on a battlefield."

I was blown away by what he said. I'd never seen him so negative.

He walked towards a bookshelf filled with videotapes. "There's one last thing I want to do before I'm a full-fledged Marine. I want to watch the Wizard of Oz."

"That a kid's show." I was sure he'd lost it.

"It's not a kid's show," he said, annoyed at my lack of stoner sophistication. "It's one of the most perfect works of art, totally in alignment with the universe, or what your parents might call God. If you watch it while listening to Pink Floyd's The Dark Side of the Moon, you will see what I mean. It'll give you spiritual alignment."

I was convinced his years of partying had finally driven him insane.

"You're in for a trip." He took a Betamax cassette off the shelf. "It's an even better experience when you burn a little dope." He reached over to a series of milk crates that housed his collection of vinyl records, erected as a shrine to better days.

"The Floyd designed this whole album to go with the first forty-three minutes of the Wizard of Oz. If you start the record by the lion's third roar, it syncs up beautifully. It's a real fuckin' trip," he said, pulling the vinyl out of its sleeve.

He opened the album jacket and placed it on his coffee table, put a pinch of bud into the fold, and proceeded to roll a joint. "If you live your life in alignment with the Wizard of Oz, you'll be at one with the universe, and you'll be amazed at what you can accomplish. I used to do this once a month for three years. That's how I restored the motorcycle. It's all about alignment. When I finished the bike, I stopped the Oz ritual. Now my whole world has gone to shit. Today, I will attempt to get it back."

"What do you mean?"

"If you are in alignment with the universe, magic happens. You'll lead a charmed life where everything comes to you. Right now, I am completely off with the universe; been that way since graduation because ending school is a shift. I always followed these vibes, now my path has taken a turn. I've lost my way. I'm hoping this will help me realign."

"I don't know. Sounds stupid to me."

"No, it's real." He took a lighter from the watch pocket of his tuxedo vest, put the joint into his mouth and bent into the flame, then held the joint towards me. "Get high and see."

I took a deep hit and passed it back. He set the record on the turntable, looking me in the eye. "Line up the Betamax Deacon. We got to synchronize it just right."

I turned on the television and took the joint as I loaded the cassette. I put the spliff to my mouth and breathed in the resin-tainted air. It burned my lungs, and I seemed to be hovering over myself like a bystander. The weed high pulled me back in time to a memory of the pharmacist handing my mother a bag with the bottle of Ritalin and explaining the dosage.

The first time I took Ritalin, the high was the most potent— the initial hit, like MDMA, meets cocaine. With each dose, I became further reduced, inching my way to becoming a minimum wage dropout. Visions of them taping electrodes to my head and observing me through a glass window appeared before me in a haunting hallucination. I didn't remember much other than feeling like a freak and tuning them out, just like I did with everyone at school.

"What is 2 + 2?" the EEG nurse had asked.

"Huh?"

"What is 2 + 2?"

"Mm… dunno."

I picked up the cassette box and stood there looking at Dorothy and her friends on the yellow brick road. Maybe everyone thought she had learning disabilities. Perhaps when she told people about her trip to Oz, they attached EEG diodes to her head?

"What am I doing here?" I'd asked the EEG nurse.

"You have a learning disability," she'd said, writing on her clipboard.

My mind returned to the present. I started to hover over myself and imagined my body in a giant cocoon, like the core in a mini nuclear reactor where I was cooking, baking into a bomb, ready to explode. I passed the joint back to Bone. I looked at him and could see the uncertainty that had been growing inside of him since the arrest. It was like his power had transferred to me, and I finally found out what it was like to be him.

He stopped laughing, and the room went silent within the moment as the astral procession of the stars seemed to stop.

"Douglas," I said in a trance. "Be true to yourself, lest your spirit dies before its time."

Bone laughed nervously. "I should've never given you pot. Now you think you're a fucking philosopher."

We heard the start of the movie. Bone came to life, holding the needle over the grooves of the record like a vein, letting it drop on the MGM Lion's third roar. I killed the volume on the TV, the heartbeat coming out of the stereo speakers paralleling my own.

I took the joint from Bone to *Breathe* in the air, watching the film's credits as the weed-filled my lungs with its lore. "For long you live and high you fly… run rabbit, run…" I watched the hounds of society nip Dorothy in the heels. And then, the cyclone of God tore up her town, destroying her enemies and family farm, killing the inadequate person she was.

And yet, she joined the fury, submitting to the inevitable, becoming one with the fractal of universal perfection.

Dorothy's home was in the cyclone, the *Great Gig in the Sky*. Then she dropped it on the wicked witch that resides in the East. I watched how chromium reality turned to Technicolor Nirvana during the clink of the song, *Money*. Dorothy walked out amongst the Munchkins, her mantra ringing out in the West to the chimes of the Lollypop Guild.

The cyclone seemed like chaos to everyone but the witch of the North. To her, the fury represented peace. To the governing evil, it was destruction.

Bone was right; everything in that movie synced up beautifully. I gazed at the synchronicity, knowing that life is perfect. And to share in its perfection, one merely had to accept and go with it.

I pulled another hit, soaking in the sublime integrity of what I was witnessing, chasing it with Corona.

"Do you think the Floyd really planned the whole album around The Wizard of Oz?" I asked, watching with stoned eyes. "It's crazy; the music lines up to the events of the movie perfectly."

"I don't think so," said Bone. "But this I know for certain, there is a sequence to everything. Every person has the potential to be an underdog or a winner. It all depends on if they can align with the river of flux. Hard work and intelligence have little to do with it. Whether it's a good film or an album with each song paced right, when you submit to the universal vibration, everything lines up. God's muse angel sings it, standing on high, repeating the same message throughout time, waiting for us to listen. Pink Floyd just played along."

Sitting on Bone's couch, with the weed moving through me, I could see my path. It was music, but it seemed so remote. I had no talent or ability. Did it matter? I had vision. Maybe I could influence people who had talent and skill, get them to combine Bone's music with Carson's, creating a whole new genre from the tastes of the two people I admired. Maybe I could start an independent record label? Why not? Adonai had his perfume. I would sign bands and put out records.

Then the pot high faded, stealing the vision. I sat there depressed until Bone stood up. "Deacon, it's time."

Feeling heartbroken, I followed him out to his grandfather's car, somehow completing the tragic cycle that had befallen his family, putting his free-spirited life in danger to advance the ambitions of others. We didn't speak, and he wouldn't look at me, just got in the car with the remaining Coronas and drove off into his personal oblivion.

I stood in the road until the Duster rounded the corner.

CHAPTER 27

TEN-THOUSAND THINGS

Watching Bone leave was depressing. I felt defeated. I didn't want to go home, so I stopped by the drug store to grab a Snickers and got caught up looking at magazines. There was Creem with Prince on the cover; Hit Parader with K.K. Downing of Judas Priest; shit with articles about the Cure, Keel, Jesus & the Mary Chain, Madonna. I wanted my music, not this crap.

Disgusted, I put the Hit Parader back and perused the film counter. A box on the shelf caught my attention. It was a Sony Walkman cassette deck, complete with headphones.

I was struck with an electronic epiphany. This portable tape deck could fit into my pocket, be hidden from my parents. They would never find it, and I certainly could afford it.

The Walkman called to me. I bought it with a blank cassette and ran home, searching my dresser for any leftover Ritalin. There were three pills that had fallen behind the dresser. I changed clothes and took the Weirdoes 45, skating to Carson's. His hot mom let me in.

Carson was in the Basement, drinking beer with some punks while listening to records. A crazy guitar riff tore through his stereo, spy rock meets punk and metal. The lyrics and the song's vibe reminded me of my life on Ritalin and the hopelessness I now felt:

Ten-thousand things
chasing me
I could've screamed
I could've died
but nothing
was happening right.

The song's intensity was like an apocalyptic omen. This music was the future, my future.

Carson looked up from his pontificating. "Deacon Jones! Outta sight." He grabbed my hand and pulled me into a hug. "Dude, it's good to see you."

"You too. What are you listening to?"

"Deep Six, man," he said, reaching over to the stereo and handing me the album cover.

It was a compilation of six bands: Green River; Malfunkshun; the Melvins; Skin Yard; Soundgarden; and the U-men. The cover looked like a crack in a blue-black wall where you could see inside to a world of hard-hitting music—a Xeroxed collage of bands, mosh-pits, guitars, and cheap amps. I wanted to leap through the crack and enter that world.

"This is where it's at," said Carson. "Fresh from Seattle. Wanna hear the future of music? It's not Punk Rock; it's this shit."

Carson was a prophet. I handed him back his album jacket as the next song played. It had heavy guitars, with a singer whose voice tattered the speakers. He couldn't sing, not in the conventional sense, but it was the voice of my people.

"So, what brings you to the Basement?" Carson motioned for me to sit in the exalted position directly across from his spot on the couch. "Got any more Ritalin to sell?"

I reached into my pocket, pushing the skaters out of my seat, and handed him the pills. "It's not much—three tabs. It's all I have left."

"How much?"

I handed him the blank cassette. "I just bought a Walkman, and I've got nothing to listen to. Tape that record you're spinning and this 45, throw in your latest issue of Milk-Bone, and the Ritalin is yours."

His eyes glowed as he inspected the Weirdoes record. "This is a fantastic song. Where did you get it?"

"Cher gave it to me."

He stuck out his chin and nodded. "She must like you if she'd part with a sweet side like this. Cher's a cool girl, a bit fucked up, but aren't we all." He reached over to a shelf and pulled the latest Milk-Bone off the stack, tossing it to me. "We got a deal. I'll tape it for you right now."

I handed him the cassette, and he lined up the turntable. "Because you can dig this futuristic shit, I'll throw in a bonus. It's a demo tape I bought off a band I saw at Gorilla Gardens. They're called Polychrome. You'll like these guys. They're another band to watch. They'll go huge if they can ever get their shit together." Carson made a motion of shooting up heroin while rolling his eyes. "The singer's got a bit of a drug problem. Only made it through half the set when I saw them. The key is to make it big before you OD."

As the music recorded, Carson sat down and popped a pill. He tilted his head back in ecstasy as if the drug's effects had already kicked in. "God, I love this shit." He pointed to me. "Deacon Jones has got it. This dude knows where music is headed. You saw the way he tripped to Green River's 'Ten-thousand Things.' The world will answer to his musical taste someday."

"I don't know," said a skater, lurched over the coffee table, rolling a joint, "seems like shitty butt rock to me."

"No, it's true," said a guy, brooding in the corner. "Carson is right."

He was puffing on a clove in an effeminate manner like he was Oscar Wilde. He wasn't like the others. He had curly hair hanging over one eye, sort of a cross between Prince and the singer of Ratt, but he dressed like Peter Murphy, black stretch-jeans and a paisley shirt that hung past his waist like a dress. His legs were crossed at the knees, making one of his sharp toed John Fluevog boots point right at me. They used to call these types Goths, but idiots in Richland called them Bat-Cavers.

"This record is the future," said the Goth, puffing his cigarette. "I know it's hard to imagine, but it's true. I should know."

"Deacon," said Carson, motioning me towards the Goth, "this is Rex."

Rex smirked and reached out to shake my hand, palm down, sizing me up sexually. "So I finally get to meet this anarchist who pushes cops." He feigned a slight swoon. "You're all I've heard about since I got back."

"Rex ran away from home," said Carson, looking up from grinding one of my pills. "Made it all the way to Seattle. He's been gone for a month. You can read about it in that issue of Milk-Bone."

"Yeah," said Rex, as if his deviance was a source of pride, "I was living on the streets and partying at the Monastery."

"But now Rex has returned," said Carson. "You can always get the fuck out of Richland, but Richland has a mysterious way of pulling you back. Ain't that right, Rex? No place like home."

The Goth laughed, coughing up smoke, pushing his cigarette into an ashtray. "That's for sure."

The thought of leaving Richland, then being lured back by some satanic magnet, terrified me. Never. Not on Thanksgiving, not on Christmas, never. I didn't want to think about it, so I sat and focused on the voice of the future coming out of Carson's stereo.

When I left, I could see the billow of steam rising above the nuclear reactors in the distance. Hanford, genesis of the atomic weapon, most polluted and evil place on earth. I would be filling out an application for my father's company tomorrow. I had to do it, I had to get out.

Soundgarden started to blare on my new headphones, cutting through my anxiety.

CHAPTER 28

FOOT, PAW, AND MOTHER'S LOVE

After a background check, my father's connections came through. It was only a matter of days after I had applied that I found myself sitting in front of the recruiter of Pearson House. She was a roundish lady, stuck in the early 70s with mousy, shoulder-length hair—Jan Brady in middle-age.

The offices were inside a trailer home—defying all things permanent, as if they needed the option of moving their operation if things got too contaminated.

I was so scared; I could barely talk.

"You'll have to fill these out," she said, handing me a clipboard.

I took the forms over to a desk. The place was sterile, white walls and short knobby carpet, the kind you see in a hospital waiting room. I imagined I'd come there to die.

The forms sat before me. I stared at them as if I had to decipher the dark angelic script in the heavenly chapter of doom. My heart raced, on the verge of seizure, arrested by the ominous prospect of Hanford employment.

I looked at the papers with distrust, my inner instinct telling me to get the fuck out. It was some sort of release. The page was a sea of print that I was too anxious to decipher. I closed my eyes and told myself that I could read well enough to get the gist of these forms if I took it slow.

I carefully looked at the beginning and end of each jumbled word, trying to sound them out: Uondarshend the daggers of izoning radioteeon… I languished over the sentence, reciting the gibberish in my mind, over and over, trying to match a word to the sound. I was eventually able to decipher *I, Deacon Jones, understand the dangers of ionizing radiation.*

"Dangers?" I looked up from the release. "Where will I be working? I thought I was going to be a janitor?"

"You'll be stationed in an area that has a high level of contamination," she said, dryly, not bothering to look up from her writing. "It's out at the B-Reactor."

"I thought the B-Reactor was decommissioned?" I said, unable to imagine why they'd need a janitor.

"It is, but contaminated areas need to be dust and rodent-free," she said, over her typewriter. "Dust and vermin can spread contamination."

"Is it safe out there?" The words barely came out of my throat.

"Why, dear, it's as safe as a mother's love."

"Oh my God, what have I done?" I said in a whisper.

I sat back and calmed my breath. "Okay, I've got to do this. I've got nowhere else to go."

The first line of the second page required me to fill out my name: Deacon Jones—easy enough—but then came a section that I read easily, employment. My heart sank. I don't know why this question was so hard. I'd only ever had one job.

My head started to swim. On autopilot, I laboriously spelled out, *Bakscer Cafae*, carefully forming each letter. I glanced over my shoulder at the woman, knowing I was taking too long.

I started to imagine that I was smart, handsome, with a chiseled chest and ripping abs. I had a beautiful tall gal by my side and was in a famous band. Then my vision began to dissolve into memories from ten years ago—the EEG test.

I'd been in a white room, strapped into a padded chair, much like those they have at a dentist. I remember two women in white coats, lacking emotion. They took diodes attached to long wires and taped them to spots on my head.

"What are all these wires?"

"Don't worry about those," one of the women said. "They will tell us things about you."

Each wire had a different color: red, blue, and green.

Another woman came out in a white jacket, cradling a clipboard in her arm. "I will be asking you a series of questions. Please answer as simply as possible."

"Okay," I said.

"If a man crosses the road with his dog, how many feet are striking the pavement?"

"Two," I said, "Men have feet, dogs have paws."

She raised her eyebrows and looked at a nearby screen that faced away from me. "Do you exist?"

I was about to answer the question when I emerged from my flashback and found myself faced with the task of writing my education on the next line of the questionnaire.

Richlind Hi Skool.

Did you graduate? *No.*

The form was humiliating. It took me an hour to answer a few embarrassing questions. After I finished filling it out, I nervously handed the recruiter the stack of papers, worried I had misspelled everything.

"Took you a while to complete these," said the woman, probably wondering what was wrong with me. "You'll need a physical. Then you'll have to go for OSHA training to prepare you for emergency response to hazardous substances."

"Alright," I said. "When do I start?"

This reactor was a death house, home to Lucifer, Angel of Light—temple of torture, a womb for the thing that could destroy us all. Here, men played God with a radiating core that glowed like a star, molten and plasmatic.

CHAPTER 29

SHIVA THE DESTROYER

My shift started at 10 pm. My father drove me on the first day. After that, I would ride a shuttle bus to the farthest reach of the Hanford Site. It would take over an hour. My dad didn't have to work in the morning so he thought it would be a nice gesture, nurturing me in my new role as a provider.

"What am I going to be doing out here?" I asked. The uncertainty was killing me. Nobody seemed to be able to tell me anything.

"You'll be the janitor in a decommissioned nuclear reactor," he said, the dashboard illuminating his face. "How hard can it be? There won't be much to clean up. It's just you, a couple of security guards, a nurse, a radiation tech, and the plant manager, Jamesy."

If it was decommissioned in 1968, why did they need a nurse? Why did they need to guard it? And most importantly, if the dust in these contaminated areas is toxic, what would protect me from what I'd be sweeping?

We finally got to a gate where a paramilitary guard checked our ID badges. We drove further down a lonely gravel road with pockets of ancient, eroded asphalt. The headlights illuminated the darkness twenty feet in front of us, along with the occasional tumbleweed.

My father parked next to a moonlit silhouette of an immense concrete structure. It looked like a cubist sculpture of unimaginative design—or a crude ancient Mesopotamian temple built with Legos.

A lofty chimney, over twice the building's height, loomed behind it, flipping off the moon. I looked around; there was nothing but sagebrush, dirt, rock, and this heinous cyclopean structure—not even a proper paved road. The asphalt had disintegrated back in the 70s.

The land was beautiful, strange, a desolation that chilled your heart. It had an eerie vibe to it as if the ghosts of Japanese dead lurched among the barren landscape—miles of brown grassland with odd mounds and outcrops of jagged basalt.

I thought of the model down at the Science Center with its greenery and trees. None of that. This reactor was a death house, home to Lucifer, Angel of Light—temple of torture, a womb for the thing that could destroy us all. Here, men played God with a radiating core that glowed like a star, molten and plasmatic.

This structure, made from millions of CMU blocks, sealed in spots where the masonry had broken, entombed the genesis of the Atomic Age. It was right in this building that they had made the plutonium for the first atom bomb detonated at the Trinity Test. Standing before this massive construction, I could hear the ghosts of eighty-thousand cries.

I didn't want to go inside.

My father and I stood looking at the B-Reactor in silence. In the front of the building was a large dark green metal door that slid open on a rail. Within the large bay door was a small regular door, illuminated by a single light bulb. Its only security was a substandard deadbolt. Above it was a yellow sign with a purple trefoil that read: "CAUTION: Internally contaminated systems within."

"Safe as mother's love," I grumbled under my breath.

My father casually opened the door as if he'd been there a thousand times. The hall was lit with punishing fluorescent lights. The walls were painted two-tone: emerald-green and white. The place had the distinct smell of old electronics and particles.

"Anybody home?" my dad yelled.

"Jones, is that you?" came a voice from the approaching room. "I'm in the Front Face."

We walked down the hall into a room about the size of a gymnasium. The two-tone green/white wall motif continued, but the top white portion kept rising about three stories. Ladders within tubular safety cages were mounted to the walls next to an American flag, leading up to scaffolding.

I turned to my left, instantly floored with awe.

There was it, the core.

Lights illuminated the face of a bronze box that had two-thousand tubes for uranium rods fucking their graphite holes— their sex encased in a biological shield. Each pipe was capped and tagged, reflecting the light with a warming sepia.

It was the most remarkable thing I'd ever seen, an electric deity from an evil alternate universe. The opposite of the Big Bang—the heavenly deconstruction, a human-made Molech. A monolithic cube, once liquid, now cast and tempered to be a real-life Shiva the Destroyer, lying dormant to be woken by some human imp.

This is where it all began, right here before me, the birth of our potential atomic winter and extinction. It was so breathtaking I almost fell to my knees in worship.

"What's the matter," came a voice from above, "never been in a nuclear reactor?"

I looked up at the scaffolding. I couldn't see who was talking, blinded by the fluorescent lights attached to the underside. Hydraulics started to lower the scaffolding.

The voice came from a fat ginger-headed guy who wore thick coveralls, rubber shoes and a cap, sort of like a line cook. When the scaffolding got to the floor, he hopped off.

"Jamesy," said my dad, shaking his hand and hugging him. "This is my boy Deacon."

The fat man's whole demeanor changed, and he put his hands on his hips, looking me up and down, frowning. "Ah, the rookie. You may be a Jones, but there'll be no special treatment on my watch."

He led us down the hall. "Here's the locker room. Yours is number thirteen. You won't need a lock. You're workin' in one of the most secure places on earth. Inside you'll find coveralls and boots. You get hot suits and masks in the cubbies. Here's some barrier cream for your gloves." He tossed me an apothecary tube. "Get suited up in your coveralls. When you're done, I'll be in the break room with your father. Then I'll show you how to put on a hot suit and use the Mask Testing Station."

What did he mean by mask and hot suit? I was the janitor, not a radiation worker. What the fuck was I going to be doing at this job?

I began to get anxious as I approached the dark military green lockers with pleated vents, the kind they had at Richland High. Next to these were a wall of cubbies with face masks staring at me, filling me with terror.

My father and Jamesy were sitting around a table. A box of doughnuts sat between them.

They looked up from their conversation and coffee. "Hey rookie," said Jamesy, "sit down and grab a doughnut. They're from the Spudnut Shop in the Uptown."

"Sure," I said, grabbing a classic. Maybe this job wasn't so bad?

"That's it. Sit down and relax. There's not a lot for a janitor to do around here, but they do earn their money." He and my father stated to laugh.

202

Jamesy turned to face me and became deathly serious. "As I said, there's very little for a janitor to do. Mostly check rat traps, but we don't want you touching them. That's contamination's job. You just report to me if you see or catch anything. Each night you'll go out with a Geiger counter and make sure there's no rabbit shit by our cars, mop the halls, then do a patrol of the traps, occasionally clean up a human mess. That'll be the daily routine. Easy peasy. Get your work done early and you can lounge till morning."

"I best be off," said my dad, standing up. "Be good Deacon. I'll pick you up in eight hours. After today, you can ride the bus."

"Mark, come by anytime." Jamesy shook his hand. "I'm about to take your son out to the yard for crap patrol. Show him the ropes; see how he does."

Jamesy proceeded to give me a tour. "Here's the latrine." He pointed to a restroom with three stalls and a urinal. The sinks had their knobs removed from the spigots. "Don't worry; you won't be cleaning here. You gotta take a dump, we got a 'Honey Bucket' out back. You don't want to shit in these toilets."

"Why not?"

"Why you think? Everything's contaminated out here. We got a raw water sink by the front door if you need to wash. You need coffee, make it with water from the Arrowhead cooler. Ok, no more fucking around; time to get to work."

He led me back to the locker room. I was given a white suit with a trefoil symbol on the back and a pair of special rubber boots. With my HAZMAT particle mask and puffy suit, I looked just like Reactor Man.

"Don't forget to tape the seams," Jamesy said, pointing to my wrists.

He gave me this thermal box with a strap, just like my mom used to do when handing me my lunch pail on my way to school. I slung it over my shoulder, and he led me out to the gravel yard.

"Here's where we send the new guys," he said with a laugh. "Kid, you're gonna love this job. I used to do it myself back in the drinking days. I want you to pick up rabbit shit in the yard within the chain-link fence. I'm not sure why they endured the expense of erecting a fence. No one in their right mind would trespass out here. Pay close attention to where we park. I don't want to be stepping on any hot turds when I get off work. Capiche? You got the Geiger counter, just try and be thorough."

I could see bright lights illuminating a compound to the east. "What's that building in the distance with the plume rising above it?"

"It's a reactor—PUREX," said Jamesy.

"Sounds like a detergent."

"Plutonium Uranium Extraction. We use it to pull all the good stuff out of the sludge before we send it down the pipe. Did seven million gallons just yesterday."

"And what do they do with the good stuff?"

Jamesy chuckled and tilted his head back. "They're fueling warheads, baby. We're celebrating a major milestone tomorrow morning after work. We just passed the 70,000 mark in warhead production. Too bad you're not twenty-one, you could go to the 9 a.m. toast down at the Ol' Stalag. Maybe you can get your old man to buy you some beer. It helps you to pee out the rads."

"I think he's a little too Christian for that," I mumbled. "Is that plume radioactive?" I pointed to the cloud rising out of a tower.

"Nah, just steam. When the Columbia gets too hot, the chief phones upriver to the Grand Coolie and has them open the dam to cool it off. Heaven forbid killing a few salmon. Now back to business." He pointed to my thermal pail. "Inside that, you'll find a poop scoop. Like I said, all you gotta do is pick up scat."

"What's scat?"

"You know, rabbit shit. Rabbits love radioactive sludge, especially Strontium. They crave the salt in the waste, so they burrow down to get at it. They've even been known to breach the thin walls of the antique tanks. Then they go and crap all over, leaving radioactive shit."

"You've got to be kidding?"

"No. The vermin even make it into town. It's a real problem. That's when our job gets interesting. When these hot rabbits wander into Richland, crapping in school playgrounds and such, we're the ones who have to pick it up. We call this a 'Priority.' When this happens, we drop everything and go. Since we're an unknown operation way out here, we're the ones who get the hush-hush jobs. Understand?" He smiled and patted me on the shoulder. "The boys in Special Ops call us the crap crew."

"You're kidding, right?" I started to laugh at him, causing his already red face to turn redder.

"Look, the only reason you got this job, is because your dad is a good ol' boy. Get serious. These rabbits are a big problem."

"Sorry, I never heard of such a thing," I said.

"You don't hear about it 'cause the Plumbers keep it out of the paper," he said. "One time we cornered a radioactive mouse down at the Richland Food Bank. They managed to keep it out of the Herald, but the Seattle Times got hold of it. One of those black suits lost his gig over that one."

"How did they know it was radioactive—by looking at it?"

Jamesy laughed. "Talk to me tomorrow, and you tell me. Look, all you have to do is wander around the yard over by our cars. If you see rabbit pellets and that counter starts to squeal, scoop them up and put them in the thermal pail. At the end of your shift, take it to Dean down in decontamination. Make sure you put the poop scoop in the bucket before you zip it up. Oh, and watch where you step, cause this is a contaminated area."

"What do I do if there's contamination?"

"Stop breathing," he said, walking off, laughing.

CHAPTER 30

POTASSIUM IODIDE

I stood watching Jamesy leave, feeling abandoned. I coughed, fogging up the glass on my face shield, breathing damp air. A series of bright halogens burst open, spraying white light all over the yard, veiling the darkened sky in vivid contrast. Taking my new job seriously, I began to walk the yard, patrolling like a security officer on his beat.

It was a half-hour before the Geiger counter squealed. There were some droppings next to the driver's door of a Dodge pickup.

"For fuck's sake," I said. "How many people step in rabbit shit out here? What if my dad brought some home on his shoe?"

I scooped the contaminated feces out of the gravel, depositing it in my thermal lunch pail.

The wind was blowing fierce off the Columbia, but I couldn't feel it underneath the radiation shield covering my face. I watched it uproot a tumbleweed, blowing the radioactive bush off into town to end up in some poor sap's backyard.

Bored, I started to sing. A deep, resonant tone filled the mask, fogging up the eye ports and amplifying my voice's subtleties. It was raspy and seemed to paint pictures with emotion. I surprised myself with how it sounded and how good it felt to unleash my feelings with the human voice.

I began to picture a mosh-pit before me and a powerful band at my back. We were a swirling force at one with our audience. I started to scream, "We got the neutron bomb... We got the neutron... Gonna drop it all over the place... Gonna drop it on your face!"

Then I heard the front door open. Startled and embarrassed, I saw a lone man in a security uniform emerge from the B-Reactor. He neared and waved. "I've come to fetch you. Jamesy spilled some coffee and needs you to come in and mop the floor. Find any scat?"

"Yep, I've got a pail full of hot poop."

We walked into the B-Reactor, and the paramilitary guard started to move a Geiger counter wand around my body as I held up my hands. It felt like I was being arrested. When he got down towards my boots, the thing squealed as if someone had pinched it. A couple of the guards started to panic, running in all directions away from me.

"What? What?" I cried, arms out pleadingly as I turned around in circles.

"Just stay put Jones," said a voice over an old tin horn speaker. It was Jamesy. He and some other guy came out in hot suits. "Take it, easy kid. We're radiation techs, versed in NRC approved procedures."

"Sir; looks like he's stepped in coyote feces," said the tech.

"Didn't I tell you to watch your step out there?" said Jamesy. "Frickin' newbie steps in coyote shit on his first day. All right people, nobody panic; get him to the mop basin and clean up his boot."

They had me stick my boot into a large, low mounted porcelain basin, plumbed with raw river water. Jamesy pointed to a yellow clothes hamper with a trefoil symbol. "Your outers are no longer good. Put them in this lead acrylic hamper for disposal, then go see the nurse in room twenty-six. Tell her to hurry up. I need a floor mopped. Oh, and while you're at it, mop everywhere you stepped when you came in. Maybe next time, you won't track coyote shit into my reactor."

Like most doors in the B-reactor, Room 26 had a window, but this one was reinforced with a diamond grid of wires so it wouldn't break if someone hit it. Why you would need such a thing in an infirmary made me nervous. Stepping inside, I felt pangs in my chest. The room was narrow with blinding fluorescent lights. Against the wall was a wooden exam table upholstered with leather; they still used expensive and beautiful materials for such things back in the 40s.

Seated at the desk was an old lady who wore a nurse's hat that sat atop a mound of hair styled like Lucille Ball's. She silently pointed to the exam table and had me sit. She started passing the time by telling me about the days of the Manhattan Project as she moved a Geiger counter over my body. "I was just a girl back then, giving out Potassium Iodide pills, thinking they were vitamins," she told me through cracked lips, accentuated by red lipstick. "We didn't even know why we were out here. My husband, Dan, God rest his soul, worked out on the crew that housed the core."

The Geiger counter started to hum at a low, unobtrusive level around my clenched fists that sent me into a state of terror. She seemed unconcerned. "Did you forget to wash your hands after you dumped your suit?"

"Yes," I said, voice quivering in panic. "Am I hot?"

"You'll be fine," she said indirectly. "You'll have to have a shot. Just take a shower when you get home." She took out a syringe of something and got ready to stick my arm, continuing her horror story. "They had no idea what they were building out here, just given a piece of blueprint and told to make it so. They built this reactor that way, and it only took 'em eleven months. Can you imagine the day after Nagasaki, when they announced that it was the bomb we'd been working on, and all the lives we'd saved through our efforts. It was our community that ended the war."

"Yeah," I said, "but those bombs killed over 200,000 people."

She turned wide-eyed at my comment and jabbed the needle into my arm with disdain.

"Ouch!"

"Maybe you'd better watch where you step next time, rookie."

I was mopping up Jamesy's office when my father burst in. "Boy, you still hot?"

"They say I need to shower when I get home," I said, shaken.

"You'll be fine." He patted me on the arm. "It happens. Now you're officially one of us."

We walked out to his car, and he smiled at me as he unlocked the door. "Now that you've got clearance, I figure we can take a detour through the 200 Area, and I can show you where I work."

We drove by his building as he spoke about what he did at Hanford. Around it was a parking lot with rows of Japanese autos. I saw a chain-link fence in the distance, surrounding a basin of gravel with sagebrush and Russian thistle collecting around its base. "Is that the BC Crib?"

"Yes," he said. "Those pinko environmentalists got congress focused on the river for the next eight years. Sure wish they'd move some of the cleanup efforts out here where we park our cars."

We left the gate and started the long commute home. "I'm sure sorry that you got a low-level contamination Deacon. Thank Jesus you weren't hurt. Wouldn't want my boy to end up like Harlan Fenix."

I slumped in my seat, listening to him.

"When I got the call about you, my heart stopped. I called your mother, and we prayed over the phone. I keep considering the modern way of doing things, and how we've been conducting our lives as a society, putting our careers before health and family.

Did you know the average pension payout here at Hanford is two weeks?"

"No, I did not."

"They're working us to death."

"Then why do you do it?"

"For you and your mother."

I wasn't sure how to respond and looked out the window, not accepting his answer. Maybe if he genuinely cared, he'd be a nicer father.

He began talking about how runaway consumerism was causing people to withdraw from Jesus. My mind began to wander, silently reciting lyrics to "We Got The Neutron Bomb."

CHAPTER 31

THE CRAP CRÜE

Janitor work at the B-Reactor was simple. If you based it on the skills required, the amount I made was ludicrous. A ten-year-old kid could've done it and in half the allotted time.

Why was I making thirteen dollars an hour? Because I had to stay up all night and expose myself to radiation in a concrete box.

Whether I was working my ass off for nothing, or risking my health for something, a lack of education can only lead to one thing—exploitation.

My day started with scooping rabbit poop around the cars; this would take me an hour because I fucked around. Then I would spend the rest of my shift pushing a mop while checking traps.

The form I used was natural for me. It was a map of the reactor with three boxes: clean, scat, or vermin. I initially struggled with the words on the form, but after I had deciphered what they said, it was easy. I used the same form every day, so no one ever suspected that I was a challenged reader.

If there was a rodent in a trap—usually one per shift—I went to the nearest terminal and called it in over the PA system. The radiation technician would come and handle it. I never once had to touch a trap. The only hot material I ever had to deal with was rabbit shit in the parking lot.

The B-Reactor's intercom system was comprised of strategically placed terminals, each with a telephone receiver that looked like it came off a World War Two battlefield radio. It had an aviation switch that selected the control room or the PA. On the side was a little crank that you could turn to generate a signal. This was the only primitive technology in the place.

On the other end, what they had accomplished was marvelous, dwarfing the achievements of today. They had taken progress to the human limit, assembling a core of such sophistication that it could produce a weapon capable of destroying humanity.

They kept on fueling warheads in this building right on through the Summer of Love until January 1968, before I could walk.

During my shift, I was left alone. I spent most of the time practicing singing. Each day I got better. On the bus ride home, I wrote lyrics. As time went on, my confidence grew.

On the weekends, I would see Mikultra.

I cruised like this for about a month before the inevitable came to pass; we were given a "Priority." It happened at about 1:30 in the morning while I was in the Valve Pit, checking traps.

The Valve Pit was the room where water from the Columbia River would enter to cool the reactor. It was a collection of large metal pipes, covered by aluminum grate flooring. Poking up from each tube was a valve the size of a steering wheel on a semi-truck. It looked like it would take all your strength to turn off the water.

I was checking traps beneath the pipes, singing along to the Polychrome demo that Carson taped for me:

"Gonna come, a come, a come to you
depression hits
all, all the whole way through-hoo."
Jamesy appeared on the grate above. "Jones?"
"Down here," I shouted back, taking off my headphones.

"Hey, rookie," he said, his voice echoing through the pit, "quit your singing; the whole reactor can hear that crap. Besides, it's time to earn your pay. Finish up your patrol and meet me in the Control Room. We got a Priority."

I climbed out of the pit and went to check traps by the Intake Fans, then made my way to the other side of the reactor.

The Control Room was solid electronics, diodes, displays, and every type of control known to humans back in 1942. There was an entire wall of NASA-green panels with thousands of knobs from the floor to the ceiling, each with a rotating numeric display.

To the left was a wall of displays that looked like clocks, some designed to record information onto paper charts like lie detectors. There were also brass lever switches, each with a keyhole in the center so only qualified nuclear physicists could use them to control the fission. Like much of the equipment in the B-Reactor, the gadgets looked brand new despite being forty years old.

The main instruments were in the center of the Control Room on the far wall, laid out in a trapezoidal recess, resembling an old mixer board in a recording studio from the nineteen-fifties. I imagined Elvis Presley singing "Burnin' Love," gyrating out in front of the core while being mixed and equalized in here.

Jamesy sat with his back to the controls, reading the June edition of Hustler Magazine. The cover had a tan blonde in a black ballerina tutu pulled up around her waist, crouching down and sticking out her ass.

"Interesting article." He looked up at me and let the swivel chair fall forward. "Who's Killing The Star Wars Scientists? This is crazy shit." He set the nudie mag down on the nuclear reactor's control panel. "Did you know over twenty scientists who worked on Reagan's Star Wars Defense System were mysteriously killed?"

"No," I said with a blank stare.

"Strange stuff. It's too bad ol' Dutch can't get Star Wars going. The world would be a much safer place."

"Maybe the world would be a safer place without nuclear weapons?" I said.

"Aaaah!" He slapped my stomach. "You young pricks think you know everything. Listen, Dean's out sick so you're coming with me. We don't normally utilize non-certified personnel, but I'm desperate. Besides, these are hush hush operations so no one will hear about it anyway. There's no union rep out here." He laughed. "Just do as you're told, and things will go smoothly."

He walked into his office, unlocked the cabinet, and took out a set of keys. "I need you to go to the Storage Basin and load the van. It seems a contaminated rabbit took a shit in the playground out at Lewis & Clark Elementary. Chaps my ass. My cousin's kid goes to that school. Thank God it's summer break."

"That's down the street from my house," I said, mortified.

Jamesy fanned me off as I followed him down the hall. "Ahh, you'll be alright. You get more exposure from your microwave oven."

"Did you tell your cousin?"

"Are you kidding? This situation is classified on a need to know basis. And you better remember, loose lips sink ships. Talk about this, and the Plumbers will be visiting you in your dreams."

"Who are the Plumbers?" I asked.

"You don't want to know," he said, holding the door open for me. "Just keep your mouth shut, and you'll never have to meet one."

He pointed to a van parked inside the bay where a bunch of flight cases sat in front of a large open door. "Load the gear, and when you're done, come and get me. I'll be in my office."

The side of the van had "ATZ Landscaping" silkscreened onto a magnetic strip. Inside was a console with video screens and various gauges that I assumed measured radioactivity. I loaded all the gear and went to Jamesy's office.

Jamesy was in a radiation suit, resting his fat arm on a bookcase. He was chatting jovially with two men in black suits. Both wore sunglasses as if they wanted to hide their identity. One was leaning back in Jamesy's chair, away from the desk. The other was slumped on the edge of a drafting table.

"So I told the drunken bitch," said Jamesy, "come over here, and sit on pappy's lap."

They all broke into laughter.

When they saw me, the laughter came to an abrupt halt, and the two mysterious men stared at me from under their sunglasses. I slowly walked into the room. The one leaning on the draft table reached over to a black safe that looked like it was designed to withstand a nuclear meltdown and shut the door.

"Finished?" said Jamesy.

"Yes,"

"Go get suited up and meet me at the van."

They watched me leave.

I had seen these men before. They were the two men in black suits at the Federal Building, the night of Reese's crank. I worried they would recognize me.

When I got back to the van, Jamesy was in the driver's seat, and the mysterious men were nowhere in sight. "Close the bay door behind us when I pull out."

After we were on the road, I asked who the men were in his office.

"Those are the Plumbers," he said, tilting his head back towards the rear of the van in a couple of quick jerks as if to make sure we were alone. "They're here to make certain we do this pickup with the utmost discretion. Capiche? No talking about this to the girls. If the paper gets wind of it, those two will have our ass."

"You can count on me," I said.

"I know I can; you're a Jones. This is why we're handling it and not the Contamination Department out in East 200. Those pricks talk too much."

On the way into town, Jamesy spoke about sports and how he felt Ronald Reagan should be able to serve as many terms as elections allowed. "Reagan's the best president this country's ever had. The Great Communicator," he said. "Lincoln and Washington pale in comparison. It's a shame this will be his last term."

"I thought FDR was the best president," I said, feeling warm in my suit. "Didn't he end the Depression and get us through World War Two?"

"Where'd you learn that liberal crap, school? FDR was a communist and loose on morals," said Jamesy, annoyed. "I'm telling you; Dutch is the best we've had—the Gipper."

It was strange rolling through town in our Hazmat suits behind tinted windows in a landscaping van. At every light, the people next to us just stared straight ahead. They couldn't see through the dark tint if they bothered, but not one person looked our way.

When we got to the school, there was a group of skaters hanging out around the swing-set, smoking weed. You could hear them talking and laughing.

"Goddam punks," said Jamesy, turning off the engine. "It's three in the morning. They should be home in bed." He opened a box of Spudnuts and took out a maple bar, lifting his particle shield to stuff it in his face. "Let's give it a minute."

"How long are we going to wait here?" I asked.

"You're on the clock," he said, with his mouth full. "What are you complaining about? Grab a Spuddy and shut up." Then a big smile spread across his face. "Hey, watch this."

Out of the shadows emerged two cops, surrounding the skaters. They grabbed the kids by their shirts and threw them in the sand, kicking them and smacking them with their batons. Jamesy watched with delight. "Oh-ho yeah!"

I witnessed the scene with disgust. How many times had I prayed during church that I could smoke weed with friends at 3 am, sitting on my board, soaking in the night? Now I sat next to this fat fuck, listening to him talk about the fucking Dutch. I was a sellout. I felt shame. What would Jello Biafra say?

The cops dragged the skaters to two police cars that were hiding in the darkness next to our van. One of them punched a skater in the gut.

"The Plumbers," said Jamesy, chuckling to himself, digging in the box for another doughnut.

"They're not real police?" I said, chewing on a chocolate Spuddy.

"Nope, government-backed disguises. They'll rough 'em up and drop them home with a warning. One of the cars will come back and make sure no one comes upon us while we work."

One of the cops pushed a skater by the top of his head into the back of the cruiser. It was Carson!

Total despair. What was I doing? I had become poser shit. Even though he couldn't see me, how could I ever face him again?

After the cops left, we stepped out of the vehicle and Jamesy pulled a Geiger Counter out of one of the flight cases. "I'm going to locate the contamination. You bring that empty case and a shovel. We gotta take any sand that gives a reading."

I followed him out to the playground, dragging the large case behind me with one hand, shovel in the other. I was worried that Carson had been contaminated and was going to get cancer.

"We've been waiting for the site to clear since noon," he said, watching me drag the case. "It burns me up to think of all the kids who were playing here today, not knowing they were exposed. The Plumbers waited until sundown, then a couple of teenagers came here to make out on the jungle gym. At least they were high up instead of in the sand."

I thought about where I sat with Cher down on the river. I wondered if radioactive rabbits had pooped out there. I pictured Jamesy and some young sellout, waiting in the shadows for us to leave.

"After the teenage lovers," continued Jamesy, "those punks showed up smoking dope. Maybe a shot of radiocaesium will burn some sense into their brains." He laughed.

"Will they be okay?" I said.

"Oh sure. They only got a mild dose. Should be out of their systems in a couple of months."

I looked up while Jamesy moved about the playground with the Geiger Counter. The stars littered the sky, illuminating our Hazmat suits. I stood wondering if there was life up there. And if there was, could they see us, and did they think we were fools?

What sort of madness had we conjured upon ourselves? Insanity... and then the sound of the Geiger counter screaming at us, shouting, "You idiots! God gave you fire, and you forsake it for the cauldron of hell? Now rabbits will shit on you, and Mother Nature will seek her revenge."

"Over here, kid," said Jamesy, pointing with the Geiger wand to some scattered pellets. "Start digging."

I pulled the lead-lined flight case through the sand, close to the scat.

"Pick that up," said Jamesy, disgusted. "Quit dragging it and get some life about you."

I lifted the flight case and dropped it next to the pellets. I opened it and started shoveling shit and sand while Jamesy supervised. "Deeper, at least ten inches."

When I got done, he shut the lid and checked the area with the Geiger counter. "Shave off another few inches of sand," he said over the counter's slight whine.

I opened the lid and shoveled more. When the counter was silent, we carried the case, each of us holding the handles, satisfied that we'd done our part in protecting our community.

As we loaded the flight case into the van, I heard the rooster crow. I felt low; I had betrayed everything I believed in.

By the time we got back and delivered the van to Contamination, I had just enough time to catch the shuttle bus into town.

CHAPTER 32

RAT SHIT

Despite stealing kegs, underage drinking, and general contempt for the law, Colin Fenix had the odd ambition of becoming a cop. Unlike Bone's side of the family, who felt that you should serve your country through armed conflict, Fenix felt it his patriotic duty to serve as a police officer. Fortunately for punks, skaters, rockers, and ethnic minorities, the police deemed Fenix unfit to serve.

"When I become a cop," Fenix used to say, "the first thing I'm gonna do is bust Bone."

This lust for domination over his fellow humans didn't end with his failure to get into the Police Academy. After they put Fenix on the five-year plan, he would spend his mornings training for the Hanford Patrol, then commute to school, where he'd finish out his day.

I'd been working at my father's company for three months by the time Fenix had finished training and was hired. Like my family, Fenix's people had worked at the Site since the Manhattan Project and were Hanford royalty. Even still, lawyers had to get the keg debacle removed from his record before they would hire him.

Unfortunately, they stationed him at the B-Reactor.

I was checking traps under the North Intake fans when Fenix approached me for the first time at work. I'd been avoiding him all night on purpose. I was writing illegibly on my clipboard when he came up from behind and whispered, "So, have they given you the pills yet?"

I had my headphones on and pretended I couldn't hear him. I started singing along to Green River.

He tapped me on the shoulder. "Hey, have they given you the pills yet?"

"What are you talking about?" I said, taking off my headphones.

"I was told they give you pills to keep you awake."

"Who told you that?"

"The dudes I trained with."

"Well, they told you wrong." I didn't want to talk about this. Now that I had a job, I was beginning to consider him reckless. "The only pills you'll be getting are Neumune tablets."

He stood, looking dumb.

"Look," I said, "this job may be a cakewalk, but you have to be careful. Just watch where you step."

With his head shaved, army fatigues, and black bulletproof vest, he looked half cop, half soldier. The Hanford Patrol was a private army, employed by my father's company and run by a retired general. It was a tight outfit, and they didn't fuck around. Despite his family's connections, how they managed to take on Fenix is beyond me. I guess the Fenix name was gold out there among the sagebrush and basalt.

With his holstered gun and handcuffs, you could tell he was drunk on power. Who would he arrest out in this loathsome desert? Who would he beat with his baton? I felt I no longer had anything in common with him, and seeing him like this only cemented this feeling. I was sorry he got the job.

I ignored him, bending down to check a trap. Empty. I glanced to my right and noticed a scattering of rat shit on the concrete floor next to Fenix's boot. "Dammit!" I said, noting it on my triplicate contamination report.

"What?!" said Fenix, worried. "What's wrong?"

"Hot turds," I said in a calm voice.

"What does that mean?"

"What it means, is that little scattering of debris that you almost stepped in is radioactive and dangerous. I told you to be careful."

"Oh shit!" He jumped back like a fool. "What are you gonna do?"

"Report it to Contamination."

He followed me down a hall to a 1940s telephone booth made of dark wood, its thick walls lined with acoustic pressboard. It had to be soundproof because back when the reactor was pumping "hot feed," it was too loud to hear anything with all the fans and water rushing through the cooling pipes.

I selected Jamesy's office with the aviation key and turned the crank. "Hey Chief, I finished my patrol, and there's hot turd under the North Intake."

"I already got Contamination coming in from the 200 Area to try and catch that lizard you saw yesterday," he said. "Dean took the day off. Fucking slacker. If it weren't for the goddam union, I'd can his ass."

"The scatt caught me by surprise. I was in proximity."

"I'll be right there with a thyroid blocker. Meet me in the break room."

"You better bring some for the new guy," I said, "he was in proximity, too."

I stepped out of the phone booth, and Fenix resumed his bullshit as he followed me around the corner to the break room. A box of Spudnuts was sitting on the communal table.

"This is a sweet gig we've got here," he said, grabbing a doughnut. "I can't believe you're makin' thirteen bucks an hour to log traps and scoop rabbit shit. Free Spudnuts too."

"You want to scoop radioactive crap for thirteen dollars, go right ahead."

"I saw Mikultra Skala the other day," he said, oblivious to the fact he was annoying the hell out of me. "She was talking about you with Sparrow. I don't know what you did, but she sure is into you."

I rolled my eyes, pretending to read the safety bulletin. I couldn't read it, but I could tell by the pictures I should be wearing rubber gloves and cup-type goggles when I mop the Front and Rear Face floors.

"I don't know about Mikultra," I said, feeling dirty. "I'm not sure it's going anywhere. I'm tired of listening to her talk about Jesus."

"What? You don't like her? Out of all the guys in school, you're the one who scores her as a girlfriend. She's pretty fine." He took a deep breath and hesitated. "Sparrow seems impressed too. I think I've got a chance with her."

"What are you talking about?" I said, shocked.

"They've broken up," he said.

I had a horrible feeling. It's not that Bone was ever in love with one woman. Though Sparrow was his favorite, there were others. It was because Bone had been slipping. His rate of decline before he shipped off was shocking. He had lacked his usual confidence and wasn't fitting in at social functions. He had gone from being the coolest guy in school to some guy who has problems, just like the rest of us.

"Yep," Fenix said, pushing out his chest, making it look grotesque in the bulletproof vest, "Sparrow is in the market for a new boyfriend."

"She's your cousin's girl," I said, disgusted.

"Not anymore." He chuckled to himself, sitting down and manspreading in one of the swivel chairs. "He's coming back from boot camp today, and she's refusing to see him."

"He's coming back? Fenix, you should've called and told me."

"I thought I'd tell you when I saw you here." He stuffed a doughnut into his face.

"Keep eating those and you'll be as fat as Jamesy," I said.

Fenix had been on the job for only an hour, and I was already sick of him. He was killing my serenity. How was I going to practice singing with him following me around?

He'd never annoyed me to this degree before. I used to think he was cool when we were kids. In high school I started to dislike him. Had he changed? No, I was the one who had changed.

Fenix was gazing at the doughnuts. "I owe grandpa big time. Won't be sponging money off him now that I've got this job." He was going for a maple bar when Jamesy rounded the corner, looking red against the green and white walls.

"Jones, here, take this." He handed me a pill. He tossed one to Fenix. "Make sure you two hand in your dosimeters before you check out and take a shower when you get home."

Exposure didn't seem to bother Fenix. It worried me every day.

I held up my pill in front of Fenix's face. "This is for our thyroid, not our hi-roid."

"So, you two are friends?" Jamesy said, walking up to the table and grabbing a Spudnut. He'd been eating a lot of them, and I could swear he'd grown even fatter. "I'll tell you right now, I've got no patience for slacking," he said with a mouth full of Chocolate Spuddy. "Jones, I want to see those shit buckets nice and full. And Fenix, just 'cause there ain't shit for you to do doesn't mean you shouldn't be patrolling." He pointed his doughnut at Fenix. "The only reason you got this job is that the DOE owes your grandfather for what happened to him. Capiche?"

CHAPTER 33

THE LEATHER

I went to see Bone the minute I woke up. A heavy curtain covered his open window, blocking the light.

"Come in," he said in a soft voice after I knocked on the sill.

I climbed through the basement window. The room smelled of booze.

After my eyes adjusted to the dark, I could see he had on his blacklight, making his velvet Elvis poster glow in the dark. It had Elvis surrounded by marijuana leaves, fat, stoned, and sweating, but still spewing passion—a full-on Romanic Scientist. He wore a superhero suit that made him look like Marlon Brando when he starred as Jor-El in *Superman*.

Bone lay on the couch with a near-empty bottle of Jameson in his hand. The black light reflected off his mirrored shades. He was wearing a skintight Marines t-shirt, military fatigues, and had a shaved head. Even in the dim light, I could tell he'd grown buff from all the push-ups. His lean rocker look was all bulky.

"Hey man," he said, taking a shot off the bottle.

"Douglas, what is this?"

"They're sending me to the Middle East." He laughed and took another swig. "I'm going to spend the next two years guarding the U.S. Embassy in Riyadh. You can't even buy alcohol there or have sex. This is so fucked up."

I didn't know what to say. I just stood there, my heart sinking. He was my hero.

"I can't even get laid before I go," he said, head bobbing to the right and left. "Sparrow's left me for Fenix."

"That fucker."

"He's a skunk." Bone took another shot.

"What does she see in him?" I said, standing over him in the dark.

"He's a fucking dick," said Bone, forcing himself to sit up.

There was a bong next to a half-eaten Plutonium Burger that was being devoured by ants. He held a disposable lighter over the bowl and sucked hard until the water gurgled like a tummy.

"She says she loves him," he coughed.

This was blowing my mind. How could a worthless dime-a-dozen Richland jerk like Fenix steal a girl from Douglas "Bone" Reinhold? If Fenix could take Sparrow from Bone, what hope was there for me? Self-doubt began to creep back in.

I watched him, drunk on the couch, all his former mystique seeping into the cushions.

"Come on," I said, "I've got a couple of hours till I catch the shuttle. Let's get some coffee in you."

"I can drive," he said, standing up and knocking over the bong. Rancid water flowed off the coffee table onto the carpet.

"How about we walk," I said, pushing him through the window. I climbed out to find him lying on the lawn.

"What's become of me?" he said as I helped him up. "I'm done."

"You are not. You've got your whole life ahead of you."

"Do you see me out in the desert, holding a gun and shooting people?"

"No."

"They've tried to change me, make me into something I'm not." He sounded desperate.

"You're still you."

"Nah." He stumbled and started to ramble. "I'm fucking Peter Pan! Remember that!"

"What are you talking about?"

"Forever young, man," he said, looking straight ahead with rigid and determined body motions as we neared the cafe. He stopped, blocking the entrance. "I'm not getting drunk over Sparrow. I mean it, Fenix can have her. I'm drunk because I'm only here for two days. I'm shipping out the day after tomorrow."

His words drained all vitality from my blood.

"It's awful Deacon," he said, barely able to stand. "They broke me. I can't do four years of this shit."

I looked at him as he swayed in the doorway to the cafe. We stayed like this until a woman came to the door. I pushed Bone out of the way. She gave us a dirty look.

"When I ship off," said Bone, swaying. "I want you to have my leather jacket."

"You'll need it when you get back."

"Nah, I'll buy a new one. Take it. I'll bring it over to you tonight. You can sneak it past your parents."

I ignored what he was saying, knowing it was drunk talk.

"Fenix has my girl," he mumbled, "and you can have my leather, then all will be as it should. She's better off with him anyway. I shouldn't be so selfish."

We approached the counter, and Crispin was there to greet us. "Hello, it's a great day at Bockscar. How may I better ser… Oh, it's you, the quitter."

"Are you going to take my order?" I said, throwing down five dollars.

"That's right, you've been promoted to customer," he said in an effeminate voice. "How may I better serve you?"

"I'll take a large vanilla mocha and a latte."

"Bunch of fucking princesses here," said Bone under his breath.

Adonai had his eyes on Bone, upset by his decline. "Here's your drink, sir," he said, handing Bone his latte.

I walked up to the drink handoff. "How's it going'?"

He dropped his usual customer service pout. "Your friend is a wreck. He's only finished boot camp, and it's like he's a Vietnam veteran."

"I don't know what to do," I said. "He's got four years ahead of him."

Adonai shook his head with concern. "Call me if you need me."

"Thanks."

I found Bone by the door with an unlit cigarette in his mouth. We sat outside under an umbrella. He lit up, coughing, looking small in his chair. He stared into the ashtray, the sun burning his shaved scalp. Then the corners of his mouth turned downward, matching the slump of his body. He began laughing at the ashtray with an air of menace that gave me a sick, uneasy feeling.

He put down the cigarette and pulled a joint out of his wallet, placing it in his mouth. "Maybe I could go to jail?" He laughed. "Better to die in prison than the Middle East."

"Douglas, put that away!"

He giggled, then got sad again, and slid the joint back into his wallet. Then he put out the cigarette and unraveled it, playing with the tobacco. "I'm going to quit smoking," he said.

I couldn't take it anymore. Bone's decline was too hurtful; it was hard to see. He had deviated too far from his proper path.

Then it dawned on me—so had I. I closed my eyes to visions of Mikultra's body and my handsome paycheck, and how I'd been avoiding Carson and the punk scene after that night. I didn't want to face it.

"Look," I said, standing up. "I've got to catch the shuttle, and you need to sleep this off. Let me walk you home. I'm off tomorrow.

I have to attend a picnic at my boss' house around two. I'll make an appearance then come over and spend the rest of the day with you."

"You're a good friend Deacon," he said, looking up from his empty cup. "The best friend I've ever had."

CHAPTER 34

THE FLESH OF PIGS

I had worked at the B-Reactor long enough to get invited to one of Jamesy's famous pig roasts. It would be the last outdoor soirée before fall. I didn't want to attend, but everyone told me that social functions were a part of the job.

If I had to go to lame parties on my days off, maybe I should get paid to attend.

Jamesy owned a modest one-bedroom house in a neighborhood called the Richland Y. It got this name because the freeway exit created a Y in the road. This was the first time people had seen an off-ramp in this part of the world, so the name stuck.

The Y was Richland's white trash ghetto, surrounded by swamp and river delta.

Jamesy's house was a paradox. It was so cramped that you knocked your knee on the wall when you got up in the middle of the night to go pee. There was no room for hospitality—but the yard was a different matter. The house was a tiny cube among a sea of crabgrass, with enough space for all Jamesy's friends to park their pickups on the lawn. He had set up a movie screen with a projector outside to broadcast the Seahawks game. All this, and there'd still be room enough to dig a pit to roast a pig and four picnic tables.

It was perfect for a confirmed meat-eating bachelor like Jamesy. Less space meant less house cleaning. More yard meant more party—nothing that couldn't be conquered by a riding lawnmower.

Even though there would be drinking, my parents let me go because it was a "work function." They were still controlling me with their Christian bullshit as if I were a child.

Mikultra picked me up in her father's BMW, and we drove through the back streets to get to Jamesy's. "If you only want to stay for an hour, we should've met for coffee," she said.

"I told you, I'm going to spend the evening with Bone."

"This is your career. Social functions are a big part of success. I had to find out about this picnic from Sparrow."

"That's because I wasn't planning on going."

"Deacon, you need to grow up," she said.

We walked through the rows of parked trucks on the grass to get to where people crowded around the pig. All heads turned as I approached with Mikultra, holding hands.

"Hey, rookie!" Jamesy said, walking through the crowd to meet us. "Who's the little lady?"

"Jamesy, this is Mikultra."

"You can call me MK," she said, flirting and shaking his hand.

"Y'all come over here and pinch a little pig," he said, his light skin red from the sun. "Your buddy Fenix is over there." Jamesy pointed to the other side of the pit.

There they were, Sparrow and Fenix, devoid of guilt. I felt as if I were betraying Bone just by being at the same party.

"Try and have a good time," she said. "I'm going to say hi to Sparrow. When I get back, maybe I can get a smile."

I stood about, nursing a can of soda, watching her talk to Sparrow and Fenix while everyone put away the warm beer like it was the elixir of life. I watched the three of them laugh and talk, disgusted as if they'd shat on a sacred vow.

Fenix led the girls to the pit and piled their styrofoam plates with meat. Mikultra sat with the others, dishing with all the girlfriends about celebrity gossip and television. "That daughter on Roseanne is such trash. A little makeup—hello?"

"I know, and the way she dresses? Baggy pants and flannel shirts," said Sparrow, talking like she was in the movie *Valley Girl.* "It's gross."

"Totally agree," said Fenix, stuffing his mouth with pig flesh. "Bitch looks like a skank."

"I often wonder what the world is coming to," said Mikultra, picking up the roasted corn cob with her fingernails and taking a dainty bite. "The sixties never should've happened. If those Communists hadn't protested the war, we'd've won Vietnam."

"Obviously," said Sparrow. "Don't tell that to my ex. All he thinks about is sixties music."

"Eck...." Mikultra almost spat out her meat. "You are so better off without him."

Jamesy came over and sat next to them, enthralled by the girls.

"Your house is so cute," said Mikultra.

"Thanks," said Jamesy, blushing under his sunburn. He got up and walked over to me, beer in one hand, his gut hanging over his belt. "Hey, rookie. Guess I can't call you that anymore; you've been mopping the reactor for a while."

"Yep, I'm a true member of the crap crew," I said with a faked smile.

"Man, your gal is hot," he said, eyeing Mikultra. "Guess pussy comes easy with the Hanford buck. Even a fat slob like me can score." He slapped me on the back, spilling my pop. "Come on," he said, "let's go and pinch some of that pig. Sure you don't want a beer?"

"I'm good."

"I won't tell your old man. Come on." He pulled my arm, guiding me over to the pit of coals. He was so fat, he waddled across the lawn.

The carcass lay there, searing in the sun, apple in its mouth. It looked at peace like it was born for this, feeding the insatiable need of Fenix, Jamesy, and the others. Mikultra was delicately holding the meat, stuffing the fatty flesh into her beautiful mouth.

I felt a slap on my back and turned around. It was Fenix.

"Hey buddy," he said, spraying particles of spit in my face. "We're all frickin' drunk. You're the only one sober enough to drive. Would you go and get some ice, if you'd be so kind, so?" He handed me a twenty, swaying in his step. He forgot I didn't have a driver's license or a car.

"Sure," I said, willing to do anything to get away from the party. I'd even walk for a bag of ice.

I took the twenty, watching Mikultra trying to eat pig without getting grease on her face. I wondered if she would even see that I was gone. Would anyone notice?

Around the corner was a small bait and tackle shop with an ice cooler. Lottery stickers and prices for beer covered the windows. Frustrated, I opened the cooler door and grabbed a bag of ice. I saw a girl walking on the other side of the road by the river. She reminded me of Cher Hanson.

The thought of Cher made me disgusted with myself. I was a false person who had no personal truth or criteria. I'd been sleeping with a girl I couldn't stand because she was hot and being with her helped me imagine I was cool. I was the opposite. I was a sellout, a typical Richland asshole. I'd been working this job for months. I had enough money to leave but I kept telling myself, some day.

When I got back to Jamesy's, no one even realized I'd left. I stood there watching Mikultra talk to Dean from Contamination with the melting bag of ice in my hand. "He can have her," I said to myself. "I can't stand her."

I threw the bag of ice in the cooler and approached them, determined to leave.

Mikultra turned and smiled. "Hi," she pointed to the guy. "This is Dean."

"We work together," I said.

"Yes," said Dean, "I've contained Deacon's shit many times." He and Mikultra laughed.

"Oh come on, Deacon," she said, still laughing, "don't be a sourpuss."

"I think we should go," I said.

Mikultra's energy changed as she smiled at the Chemistry-Tech. "Dean, would you please excuse us."

"Yea, sure," he said. "I'll be around."

Mikultra pulled me by the arm to an isolated spot under a tree. The shade felt good, distracting me from her bitchy face. "Deacon, the game hasn't even started."

"We talked about this when you invited us to my work party," I said, getting angry. "We were going to make an appearance, then I was going to see Bone."

She calmed herself and began stroking my arm. "But I'm having a good time. I want to watch the Seahawks."

"Bone is leaving tomorrow for an overseas assignment. It could be years before he's back," I said. "I'd like to see him before he goes. I'm not making you leave. You can stay if you like."

She smiled and put her hand on my hip, pouring on the sex. "Are you a little jealous I was talking with Dean?"

"No," I said without emotion.

"Is it because he has a university diploma?"

I looked the other way, not wanting to scream. "Look, I'd just like to go and see my friend before he leaves. I'm worried I'll never see him again."

She realized I was becoming immune to her allure and tried another tactic. "I know he's your friend, but after the way he treated

Sparrow, I think the Marine Corps is the best place for him. It'll improve his character."

"He didn't make her any promises."

"What about your job?" she said. "This is a work function. You can't leave before the game. It would be bad for you politically."

"Look, Bone is my best friend. Besides, they're all drunk. No one will notice if I leave. Come or stay; I don't care."

I didn't wait for her reply, just turned and walked away.

At the bait and tackle shop, I called a cab. In twenty minutes, I was at Bone's. The breeze was blowing the curtain into the room, and I could see that Bone had his light on, making his basement walls look like the color of butter. I knocked on the sill and knelt, waiting for a response with my arms crossed.

"Hey, Bone... Bone!"

Thinking he was passed out, I pulled back the curtain and peeked in.

There was Bone, hanging from the basement rafters, his face swollen while the hemp rope cut into his neck. Time didn't move him. He was frozen.

I was still, lifeless as stone, yet I can recall my palm sweating as I held back the curtain.

My thoughts ceased because nothing made sense. I couldn't function; no impulse or cognition; just a blank node.

It looked like he'd been hanging since the night before. His tongue was huge, the color of a plum—purple, black, and maroon, all at the same time. Miniature blood vessels had burst on his skin and eyes as if he'd stuck his face onto a bed of needles.

The realization of what I was seeing hit me. My entire being burned and shivered, causing my arms to shake. "Oh God," I whimpered, turning away, letting go of the curtain.

I stayed there on my knees, crying, digging my fingers into the lawn until I got control of myself. Realizing I should do something, I decided I would enter the house. I started to climb through the window, but my nerves got the best of me, and my quivering arms gave out. I fell to the floor, knocking over beer bottles.

I stood up and saw a vinyl record spinning on the runout groove, the turntable arm being hit back to spin out again. It was the Doors' first album.

I looked at the ground beneath him. Under the overturned chair were five vinyl LPs laid out in a hexagon on the floor: Love's "Forever Changes," The Beatles' "Revolver," "Dark Side of the Moon," "Sabotage" by Black Sabbath, and "Zeppelin IV." They were his favorite albums. In the center of the records was the gun that Bone's father had given him and a note that said:

> *"I have lived during the best time in history; now, I am dead. I would have shot myself, but my coming-of-age present lacked bullets. Without me, you will all know winter. Travis can have the family's honor; Fenix can have my girl; and to Deacon Jones, I bequeath my leather."*

I set the overturned chair upright, sat down, looked up to my dear, dear friend, and cried.

CHAPTER 35

LOSER

Birds were chirping outside my window. I woke up to the leather jacket draped across my dresser. It looked like a shrine to the musical era that Bone worshiped, where anything was possible, world peace was an inevitability, and every human was created equal. It was a past whose future expectations never happened.

This leather shrine also reminded me that Bone was gone forever. How could I succeed when someone like him had failed?

Depressed, with a headache from crying, I got up and put on a flannel shirt. I took out some white paint leftover from my days of making model rockets. I wanted to paint something on the back, something that spoke about my era of white, suburban, newly minted adults. I wanted to make that jacket mine and honor Bone by carrying on his legacy.

I took the jacket outside and sat on the curb, staring at nothing, imagining the universe held within the nooks and crannies of the asphalt. I couldn't figure it out. What drives a person to end their life? Was he that desperate? Were there no other options but death or serving in the Marines? And would serving for four years have been that bad? There had to be something more.

Adolescence had been a great time for Bone. He'd had more fun packed into five years than most had in a lifetime. He'd had sex with beautiful girls, never having to grovel or work, never having to answer to anybody. He'd had access to an existence that people only dreamt about, but he'd felt that the life he led wasn't sustainable.

Maybe he was Richland's answer to Peter Pan and wanted to immortalize his youth like his idol, Jim Morrison? We never got to see Jim with wrinkled skin and a saggy belly, struggling to hit the highest notes in "Riders on the Storm." Like Bone, his memory would be forever young.

I'd thought about suicide myself after quitting Ritalin. I overcame those urges, and my life had been more of a struggle compared to his. Couldn't he muster the strength to carry on?

Could I muster the strength?

My world is smaller without Bone. I knew things would never be the same. But then they never really are.

I still can't believe he's gone. I expect it to be an elaborate hoax designed to prolong his youth. I've never accepted that he's dead.

And what of his parents? Did they blame themselves? I remember my mom and dad talking about it.

"I can't imagine losing a child, especially in that manner," said my mother. "It's unthinkable. I worry about his soul. Suicide is an awful sin. Jesus—El-Shaddai, spare his spirit from the unholy flame and forgive his trespass on his hallowed temple."

I was so comatose that I didn't even freak out on her for saying such shit.

To honor Bone, I wanted to paint the words "Truth" on the back of the jacket. I spread it out and was ready to start when my hand froze. I didn't know how to spell, Truth. I threw down the brush and sat on the curb weeping for about half an hour.

A shadow fell across the jacket. I looked up half expecting it to be Bone, but it was Adonai. He sat next to me on the curb.

"Cool jacket," he said.

"It was Bone's." I wiped my tears and runny nose with the back of my hand.

"It's sexy," he said. "Bone did have a certain style. It was when he started to second guess himself, that's when he lost his mojo."

I looked at him. "You always condemned his fashion sense."

"Okay, I'm admitting it," he said in a huff. "I always thought Bone was sexy, if not a little unkempt." He looked up at the sky. "I feel so terrible about him. I feel so bad for you, his parents; it's just tragic." He turned to look at me, face contorted.

I wasn't sure how to respond. Stabbing pain was twisting through me, like burning oil in my veins. I was trying not to cry in front of him. "Nothing's ever going to be the same."

"Nor should it," he said, reaching over and giving me a hug.

"You're artistic. Can you help me?"

"Sure," he said.

"I want to paint the word "Truth" on the back in arched gothic calligraphy, like the Hell's Angels have on their jackets, but I'm afraid I'll fuck it up. Can you paint it for me?"

"Of course." Adonai took the brush.

"Wait," I said. "Write Loser instead, block letters, all caps."

Adonai gave me a confused look.

"If I'm a loser with learning disabilities who can't make it in a reading-based world," I said, "then I want to own it."

Adonai looked at the jacket, deep in contemplation. "Hmm, Loser. I like it—conjures disenfranchisement."

He painted LOSER in a straight line, as opposed to an arch. It was perfect.

Adonai sat back and gripped his chin, deep in thought. "Put it on."

I stood up, and he squinted at me from the sunlight, motioning for me to turn around like a fashion model.

"Remember when you accused me of wearing the clothes my momma bought me?" I said. "What you don't know is that she would measure my size and buy the clothes while I was at school.

I'm going to leave Richland, and when I go, I want there to be nothing left of Deacon Jones the Ritalin kid. You still want to be a fashion designer?"

He nodded.

"Good, because I need a new look."

"Then come with me." Adonai started walking towards his house.

"Where are we going?"

"You'll see." He opened the door to his shed and plugged in some electric shears that were sitting on a workbench used to groom his mother's Bichon Frise. He went for my hair. I jumped back. "Woah! What are you doing?"

"Look," he said, pointing the shears at me, "each of God's creatures is given a time where anything is possible. Most people let it pass and don't heed the signs. For you, it started the minute you stole that keg."

"What do you mean?" I said, skeptical.

"Think about it; why does that popular girl want to attach herself to you? She would have scoffed at the thought of even saying 'Hi' to you six months ago." He became earnest. "Look, at any one point in time, on any given day, somewhere there is a convergence. Be it in the stars, a convergence of solar energy or gravities, or just getting caught in the eddies of fate where the air sizzles with perfection. It comes to a person once in a lifetime, but they seldom see it. It is happening to you, right now, and I can feel it. Deacon, this is your time. If you can go with it, anything is possible."

He lowered the shears. "You know I grew up Catholic. In Ecclesiastes 3, it states, 'A season is set for everything' and 'God brings everything to pass, precisely at its time.' Ecclesiastes also says, 'The only worthwhile thing is for you to enjoy yourself and do what is good for you in this lifetime.' So be true to yourself and your path shall be revealed."

"That's all great," I said, "but what does that have to do with the razor?"

"If you are going to take advantage of this convergence, you need a haircut."

I started to laugh. "You think shaving my head is going to place me into some convergence?"

"No," he said, in a severe tone, "but it will help if I only shave the sides. This is your time; are you going for it?"

In my heart, I knew he was right. My alignment had changed. I could feel it.

I dropped to my knees, and he started to shave. My longish locks fell to the floor. When he shut off the razor, I stood up. He grabbed a pair of scissors and knelt, cutting my pants mid-shin.

"There," he said. "If you buy a pair of combat boots from Sgt. Bub's, you'll be ready to go out and preach the gospel of now."

I saw my reflection in the glass window of the garage's side door. I was unrecognizable. The Ritalin kid was gone. There, staring back at me was something rugged, an approach new and untested, yet spot-on. Adonai was right. This was my time.

How would I be martyred? What gospel would I preach? It would be one of rage, disenfranchisement, and dissatisfaction, a doctrine designed to disseminate everything that my upbringing held sacred.

While others wrote books, some played guitar; I would get the message of my generation out through anger.

I looked at Adonai. "I have to leave for Bone's funeral."

"When is it?" he asked.

"In an hour."

"If you're going to buy combat boots, I better give you a ride."

CHAPTER 36

PRISON BUS

Adonai and I stayed towards the back of the funeral. They were honoring Bone as a veteran, with a flag and everything. They should've displayed his urn with a Led Zeppelin album instead.

They were going to spread his ashes on the river. It would be like he was never here, erasing everything that he was, so they could remember him the way they wanted him to be.

People gathered around the boat dock where Bone's father was giving the eulogy. He wore a Navy dress uniform, standing stoic, as if at attention. He looked like he had aged twenty years. His skin had a waxen pallor.

Travis was back from the Marines for the funeral, letting his mother cry into his uniform. It was as if she had become a different person, completely unrecognizable from the woman I knew. Grief had changed her.

Sparrow had her head on Fenix's chest, filling me with charged anger. I wanted to go and punch him in the face. How could they come to Bone's funeral as a couple?

Mikultra was standing next to them. Why was she there? She always talked shit about Bone. She saw me standing next to Adonai and walked through the people to approach. She strutted up and took hold of my hand.

"Why haven't you called?" she whispered.

"Mikultra, this is not the time." I attempted to free my hand. She wouldn't let go, gripping it hard so I'd be forced to stand there and argue with her.

"What have you done to your hair?"

"Shh," I said.

"That's not going to go over well with your job." She shook her head while watching the family suffer, pretending to listen to Bone's father speak. "I can't believe you dressed like this for a funeral. It's embarrassing. Does this have to do with your singing fantasy?"

Revulsion for her seeped through me as I watched the whole scene in a fog. My only sensation was disgust with her clammy hand. I began to imagine her flesh as rotten meat. I kept pulling away, but she held tight.

"I hope Jesus forgives him," said Mikultra as Bone's father took the urn and started to scatter his ashes onto the water. "You know how the Lord feels about suicide." She sighed. "But then again, He can be merciful."

She glanced over and saw Adonai. "What's he doing here?" she whispered, letting go of my hand to light a cigarette. "Jesus, El-Shaddai, I hope a homosexual doesn't show up to my funeral."

"You know, I've had enough of your bullshit," I said, turning in anger. "Why don't you go and comfort Sparrow and leave me alone? You shouldn't be here anyway."

"You're right," she said, regaining her composure. "She loved that boy, though he didn't do right by her."

"He was my best friend," I said, clenching my fist, voice filled with hatred.

"I'm sorry, honey," she said, trying to save face, blowing out smoke. "It's just a shame the way things have turned out."

"I'm not your honey," I said, filled with spite. "Fuck off... and don't ever call me again."

"Fine," she said, shoving me back. "I wouldn't want to date someone who looks like a loser anyhow."

I ripped the cigarette out of her mouth and pressed the cherry to my wrist, burning a Germs circle into the flesh. I looked her in the eyes as the smell of burnt skin surrounded us. "Shouldn't smoke at a funeral."

Mikultra stepped back in disgust, twisted by an attempt to cry. "You're sick. I never want to see you again."

"Good," I said, relishing the pain shooting up through my arm.

People gasped and looked at us, upset that we'd have a domestic spat at a wake. But why not? This funeral was a real horror, a spectacle of crass showmanship. The whole affair was unbelievable.

I watched Mikultra walk towards Sparrow and Fenix. I despised her and hated myself for being with her in the first place, and for waiting until Bone's funeral to dump her.

How could this be happening? How could Bone be dead? I turned to Adonai. "Let's go before I get violent."

"You don't want to stay?" he said, shocked that I'd want to leave in the middle of my best friend's funeral.

"I'm disgusted by everyone here, except you," I said, huffing up the hill towards the car.

"That's because they're all trash," he said, unlocking the door.

I looked at my watch. "I have to catch the bus to work, anyway." Rage shot through me. "Ah, fuck it!" I took off my watch and threw it across the parking lot, determined to be free of it. "I'm going to quit my job tonight. I'm done. I'll see you around, I need to walk and cool off."

I left Adonai and went to the café. A new girl greeted me, "It's a great day at Bockscar. How may we better serve you?"

"I'll take one of those caramel things, and can I borrow a paper and pen?"

244

I spent the next two hours at the Bockscar, trying to compose a letter of resignation, smearing ink as I wrote with my left hand.

It was dark when the shuttle bus arrived, headlights cutting through the fog. It was like an otherworldly leviathan, mutated by radiation, with glowing eyes, pulling up like a hearse. It was painted white with black bumpers. The driver wore a fluorescent green reflective vest. The only thing that differentiated it from a prison transport was the illuminated sign that read "Hanford" like a marquee.

I stepped through the service door, depressed and angry. Most of the seats were full, reminding me of my last ride on the school bus when I had to sit next to Adonai. I located the first empty seat in the dark and sat down. I looked to my right and it was Fenix.

"How dare you show up to my cousin's funeral with a fag and pick a fight with your girlfriend," he said. "I oughta kick your ass for making such a scene."

"And you show up with his ex-girlfriend? Go ahead and try."

"Right when we get to work, buddy."

"She was your cousin's girl. How could you?"

"Look, she got tired of wasting her time. She was just a lay to him. Besides, we're serious," he said. "She wants to get married."

I gave him a dirty look in the dark. "Good Lord Fenix, have you no shame? They broke up the day he died. Do you even love her?"

"More than the others," he said, looking away from me to stare into the black.

I took a deep breath, thinking about what I'd say. "You don't get it, do you? Sparrow was Bone's girl. You just don't do that."

"What about you?" he said. "What's this bullshit with Mikultra? She's about as good as you'll ever get, and you show up with that faggot, causing a scene, dressed like a loser."

"Mikultra can go to hell. I'm in love with someone else."

"Don't tell me you're gay."

"No. I'm in love with Cher Hanson."

Fenix laughed. "That slut? You dump a fine-looking broad like Mikultra so you can tap that crazy skank?"

"Better than stealing my cousin's girl."

He grunted and turned back to the window, ignoring me. Then after a few minutes, he turned around. "What did you do to your hair?"

I ignored him.

He turned back to the window, resting his arms on the gym bag that sat on his lap. "Jamesy isn't going to like it. Besides, it looks stupid."

"I don't give a fuck. I'm quitting. When we get to work, I'm handing him my two weeks."

"You're an asshole. And what the fuck are you wearing? Only a scumbag dresses like that."

"Fuck you."

"Yeah, we'll see."

We spent the rest of the bus ride in silence.

After we got to work, I stood in the locker room, looking in the mirror at my new appearance. People in Richland didn't look like this. You couldn't get a job with unusual hair, and the cops would harass you.

What were my parents going to do when they saw it? There would be no turning back.

"You look like a faggot," said Fenix, walking by, already in his bulletproof vest. "And you're stupid. Only an idiot dumps a fine bitch like Mikultra for a complete skank like Cher."

"Cher's not a skank, and it's you and Sparrow's fault that Bone killed himself."

"How dare you?" Fenix lunged at me, fists flying. Pain shot into my jaw as he beat the shit out of me.

I took it, hit after hit.

Then a rush of anger I hadn't felt since my days before Ritalin rushed through me. I punched Fenix right in the face, knocking him back against the wall.

Out it came, years of pent-up anger, unleashed in a tsunami of hate. I started to pummel Fenix, beating him around the locker room as he stumbled and attempted to hit back. All my anger from years of abuse focused upon him. Blood was flying as I bashed the bones in his face.

He was the teachers who had no patience; the pastor; the EEG nurses; the pharmacist who bottled my Ritalin; my father and the cottonwood switch; my mother's stifling prayers; he was Steve Hannity and all the other bullies; and lastly, he was Bone for giving up. This is why I wanted to beat him till he was dead like his cousin.

"You killed Bone, mother fucker, son of a bitch!" I kept punching, unable to stop. "You fucking killed Bone!"

"Hey," cried Jamesy, running over, pulling me off him. "Save it for the parking lot at the Ol' Stalag. You want to go home without pay?" His hand gripped the leather jacket, and he pushed me back against the wall.

"He won't mind," said Fenix, readjusting his bulletproof vest, wiping the blood from his nose. "He's quitting."

"What?" Jamesy looked at me in anger.

"Yep," I said, resolute, pulling an envelope out of my pocket and handing it to him. "It's my two weeks."

Jamesy opened the envelope and grinned in a factitious manner. "You can't even spell, quit." Then he pointed the letter of resignation in my direction with a smug look and tapped my chest with its edge. "Quit starts with Q, not K." He laughed, amplified by anger. "Way to make your father proud."

"And he spelled, two, t-o-o," laughed Fenix, pointing at the letter.

Jamesy patted me on the shoulder. "You're too stupid to work here anyway. Two weeks accepted. Oh, and nice haircut, punk."

"Moron," said Fenix.

I opened my locker and stepped into my HAZMAT suit, the leather jacket, protecting my inner core from my reactor man shell.

CHAPTER 37

BLOOD MOON

It was a slow night for rabbits. I'd been searching the gravel parking lot for an hour, and only an inch in the pail. I was about to give up when I found a batch of pellets scattered in a loose circle, like spilled Trix cereal.

I held the Geiger counter over it, letting it squeal.

Tired of the job, I kicked the radioactive rabbit shit across the yard and sat on the edge of a valve lid, thinking about dumping my scat pail where Fenix might step in it.

I didn't want to go inside, so I just sat.

Fenix walked out of the main entrance and made his way towards me. He stood with his hands on his hips, trying to think of something witty to say, some sharp burn.

He gazed at the moonlit river. His facial expression changed. I followed his gaze to the moon. It had a strange reddish hue to it, reflecting off the Columbia like a grapefruit. I'd never seen a moon so red.

"You think you're gonna last two weeks without an ass beating?" he said.

Suddenly everything went quiet. I became alarmed by the abrupt silence and wanted him to shut up.

"Shhh," I said, looking around. "I don't hear any crickets."

"So?"

"It's too quiet," I said, unnerved by the lack of noise.

"You're a fuckin' idiot," he said. "Nothing but bullshit has come out of your mouth since you got on the bus. Cher Hanson? I dig you wanting to fuck her. Believe me; I'd like a piece of that myself. But please, don't get any romantic notions about her. She's a crazy fucking skank. Now you're telling me that it's too quiet? You're just trying to avoid an ass beating."

"Shut up, Fenix." I stood up, looking around.

Something wasn't right, and I was becoming concerned. There was always animal activity out at the B-Reactor, and the silence was unnerving.

"And what the hell is this stupid haircut you got going?" said Fenix, rambling on. "I oughta beat your ass for looking like a faggot."

"Fenix, shut the fuck up."

A herd of rabbits ran a few feet past us. Fenix didn't notice, just kept spewing. "I should shoot you right here and claim it was self-defense. You better rethink your life, or you'll end up like Bone."

Just then a group of deer shot past us along with a wild horse, all heading towards the river.

"Woah!" Fenix jumped back. "Did you see that? What the fuck?"

He looked past me with fear in his eyes. I turned around. Flames filled the distant horizon.

CHAPTER 38

THE MODERN BODHISATTVA

The wall of flame inched its way towards the dormant reactor. We stared at the fire like rabbits before speeding headlights. I don't know how long we were inert, but we didn't move until alarms sounded around the yard.

The sirens wailed in my ears. They were like the hum of the Universe—the sound of all sound—a great "hu," resonating within my subconscious. I closed my eyes and felt the vibration.

Like Dorothy Gale, I was going to be swept up in the chaos. I watched it in peace, not minding the catastrophe. To others, I may have seemed overwhelmed, but for the first time in my life, I was awake.

"Holy shit, what are we going to do?" Fenix whirled around, looking in all directions.

"There's nothing we can do," I said, sitting down on the valve lid, my ass covering a trefoil symbol, watching the flames surround us.

"What are you doing?" he cried, slapping me on the arm. "Get up!"

"I'm watching the fire," I said.

"Are you crazy? Do something!" Fenix seemed to be moving in various directions, mimicking the fractal nature of creation.

"You're the security officer," I said, "what would you have me do?"

"It's coming right at us."

The flame was advancing at an alarming rate, writhing like witches on Walpurgis.

"We can't fight this fire," I said, standing up. "We should leave."

"And go where?" screamed Fenix. "We're surrounded."

"Go inside," I said, calmly, "the reactor's made of concrete. It won't burn."

The front door burst open. Jamesy rushed out in a HAZMAT suit, gasping, running to and fro until he saw us.

"There you are," he shouted. "The road out is blocked. If that fire gets any closer, it's going to damage our cars. Come on. We've got hoses in the shop. Fenix, you need to go in and put on a hot suit. We're gonna fight this thing."

"Why do we have to fight it; where's the fire department?" I said.

"They're held up over by the N-Reactor. They've shut down everything to prevent a meltdown. It's up to us to fight it out here."

"What do you mean, meltdown?" said Fenix.

"Come on," cried Jamesy, "follow me."

We walked through the main door, and the Geiger counter alarm went off.

"Shit!" said Jamesy.

"What? What?" begged Fenix. "What does it mean?"

"Means we've been zapped. The burning tumbleweeds are spraying hot particles into the air."

"Zapped?" Fenix grabbed Jamesy by the arms of his HAZMAT suit.

"Radiated, you meathead. We're hot. Hurry up. We need to protect our cars. They're fucked if we don't fight that fire."

"Shouldn't we get scrubbed?" said Fenix.

"We'll be fine; it's like getting an x-ray. Go and suit up and you won't get radiated anymore." Jamesy grabbed three bottles of Neumune pills off the counter. "Stick these in your hip packs. After they come and help us out of this mess, make sure you dose yourselves, then go home and take a shower. You'll be all right once this thing is over."

Jamesy handed each of us a hose. We took them outside to attach to some river-water hydrants.

"Just let it burn," I said. "If we fight the fire, we'll get even more radiation exposure. The best thing to do is let the fire department handle it."

"Easy for you to say, you don't own a car," shouted Jamesy, screwing the hose into a fire hydrant. "We're going to fight this thing until they order us to evacuate."

"Evacuate?" said Fenix in despair.

"They announced on the radio that the President's called a national state of emergency. They're thinking of evacuating the Site."

"Then we should leave too," I said.

"Listen!" Jamesy turned to me, pointing his finger. "You may have two weeks, but this is your job, and we're going to fight this fire."

I aimed the nozzle towards the flame, waiting for Jamesy to open the valve and let the water fly. Fenix was still overwhelmed and lagging.

"Come on," screamed Jamesy, pulling on the hose. "We've got our backs to the reactor, and we're losing inches."

"I'm feeling pins & needles in my face," cried Fenix, spraying the fire with his hose, "and my mouth tastes like metal."

"Shit," said Jamesy, "radiation poisoning. Did you tape your seams?"

Flames reached around the entire nuclear reactor. It was too late; there was nothing we could do. We were spraying the blaze in vain. The fire was now six feet in front of us, cooking us in our suits. I stood on a cement lid, surrounded by an inferno. Why was I doing this, risking my life to honor a two-week notice, and protect someone else's property?

"I'm not radiating myself for your fucking truck," I said, dropping my hose. "I'm outta here."

Fenix gasped in horror as I inched my way along the reactor wall, unarmed against the fire that surrounded us.

"Where are you going?" pleaded Fenix.

"Inside," I said.

"Pick up that hose, or you're fired," cried Jamesy.

"Fuck you," I said, sweating from the blaze that was moving closer, "I'm getting out of here."

"Coward," shouted Jamesy.

Then the fire leaped forward and caught the sleeve of Fenix's HAZMAT suit. He began howling and swatting the flames.

I picked up the hose and turned to help Jamesy spray Fenix. Jamesy's backside caught fire. He dropped his hose. They both screamed in agony, flailing in all directions as their flesh cooked under their protective clothing.

"Deacon," screamed Fenix, "help me."

"I'm trying," I said, spraying them with the hose, watching them thrash their arms. It was ghastly; I felt helpless. Closing my eyes, I began to whimper. "Oh, God, please don't let this happen."

I stood with my back to a large metal pipe that ran through the yard and began focusing on anything but death and searing heat. I kept spraying until I extinguished the fire, and they stood there, blackened, and wet.

A wall of flame rose and separated me from the door. I could see Jamesy and Fenix retreat into the reactor. It surrounded me; I had no choice but to run through the inferno.

I took a deep breath, closed my eyes, and recited some apocalyptic scripture my father was fond of, "I saw an angel standing in the sun, and he cried with a loud voice," then I burst through the wall of flame.

My suit caught fire and began to melt, its mask filtering out the deadly smoke. I ran and opened my eyes to blinding orange light. I began to scream and ran faster, pushing through the flames until I made it to charred soil.

I threw myself onto the ground and rolled around in the hot ashes to douse my flaming suit, sending black soot into the air.

A helicopter flew overhead, spraying me with cold water. I lay there, my sweat mingling with my tears until my scalded skin itched, prompting me to stand up.

The fire was behind me, and I could see trucks and other vehicles in the distance.

Then an animal caught my attention. Perched upon a large piece of basalt, staring at me, was a rabbit. I looked into its yellow eyes. Its ears were round, like satellite dishes.

I took off my HAZMAT helmet and began peeling off my protective clothing. I was no longer Reactor Man.

The rabbit jumped off the rock, fleeing north to the river.

"Goodbye," I said. "Run rabbit, run."

In the distance was a fence that bordered the road like a salvation beacon. Firefighters were pulling hoses to spray the flames. Most of the fire trucks were converging down by the PUREX and other reactors. Helicopters sprayed water overhead, washing me clean and dowsing the remaining fire. Everything was out of control.

I left my cindered HAZMAT suit and hopped the fence to stand on the side of the road. Weak from radiation exposure, I could barely breathe; there was so much smoke, my lungs hurt.

A fireman ran towards me. "Are you okay?"

"I don't feel good."

"You've got smoke inhalation, probably radiation poisoning and heat exhaustion too. You'd better sit down."

He escorted me through a barrage of spray to the other side of the fire truck. Panic swelled within me. I felt an urge to escape the scene. Cars were slowing to look at the burning desert, so slow I could see the people inside staring at me like visions from a nightmare.

I began to freak out. The fireman forcefully grabbed my arm. "We're going to have to take you to the medic tent," he said.

"I'll be okay."

"Johnny," the fireman said to an EMT, "this one's delirious. Help me get him onto a stretcher."

I was in shock and too frail to resist. The paramedics laid me down to hoist me into the back of an ambulance. "But I don't want to go. Leave me alone."

"We need to help you," said the medic as the ambulance began to move. "Here's a pill to chelate your blood and make you better."

"What is it?"

"It will cure you of radiation sickness."

"I'm okay. I'm fine just the way I am," I said, taking the pill. "I'm not stupid. There's nothing wrong with me! I don't need Ritalin. I am not dumb!"

I quit shouting and started mumbling over and over into complete mental disarray, "I want to be left alone. Don't pray over me. Don't tutor me. I just want to be left alone."

No longer having the energy to fight, I fell asleep in the ambulance, dreaming of Cher Hanson. She was caressing my cheek, telling me that everything would be all right. We lived in a small cottage by the sea. She was pregnant, and I loved her more in that second than all the love I had given throughout my life. I watched her walk, large with child on the beach, the sun flirting with her hair. I would give anything for this not to be a dream.

I swore that if I survived, I'd find her and profess my love.

CHAPTER 39

THE EMERALD CITY

I woke up in what appeared to be a tent with a curtain around a cot. Bone's jacket lay across the metal frame at my feet, the white LOSER paint still fresh and bright. An overwhelming urge came over me to get up and leave. I put on the jacket and slipped out between the curtains.

Bodies filled the tent—a couple of burn victims and others suffering from atom sickness.

"They're evacuating the Site," said a nurse to her colleague, holding a tray of medication. She turned and noticed me standing there. "You need to lie back down."

"Where am I?" I said.

"You're in a medic tent at the Vernita Bridge rest stop. I need to get a reading off the dosimeter on your ID badge, see how much radiation you've been exposed to."

I ripped it from the lanyard and gave it to her. "You can have it," I said, anxious to leave the tent.

Cinders fell from the sky like rain as I burst out of the door, pushing aside the flaps. The floating coals burned my face and hands as I walked through the rest stop's parking lot toward the road.

A man with a bald head, defiant to the firestorm, stood holding up a bible next to an old pickup, shouting, "The end is near. Repent!

Repent before your coming Lord." He saw me and stepped forward to speak. "The Rapture is coming; have you been saved?"

"Saved from what?" I kept walking.

"If the flames reach those reactors, Jesus will return tonight."

"Fuck off."

In a daze, I stood on the gravel shoulder of the highway. A siren cried in the distance as a Black Hawk helicopter passed over my head. Its spotlight turned the ash into balls of light, like stars plunging to earth, radioactive fire and brimstone.

Despite the smoke clouding the visibility, I could see the giant plume of steam over the Columbia River rising from the cooling towers.

Cars slowed to look at the destruction that lined each side of the highway. The headlamps cut the darkness like a spotlight. The faces of the passengers were lifeless, like ghosts of manikins, unmovable from shock.

I faced the traffic going towards Richland and stuck out my thumb. Disoriented and frightened, I wanted to go home. Then I recalled going back to that alphabet house of hell and a life without Bone. I felt a pain on my wrist and remembered the Germs burn. I turned around and saw lights illuminating a sign, "Seattle, 165 miles."

Fuck it; this was it. Time to leave and not look back. There was nothing at home that I wanted. My Walkman was in the jacket pocket, and I had clothes on my back.

I ran across the street, waving my arms, blocking traffic going west. A station wagon stopped. The driver was an overweight man with a low forehead. "You alright?" he said, leaning over and rolling down the passenger window.

"No," I said, coughing, my chest hurting. "I need to get out of here. Can you give me a ride?"

"Um, I'm going to Seattle."

"Me too," I said, opening the door.

"I don't pick up hitchhikers." He put up his hand.

I forced my way into the station wagon. "Look, I need to get out of this place. The smoke's going to kill me."

"What on earth are you doing out here?" he said, driving over the bridge.

"I work at the B-Reactor."

"And you're going to Seattle?" He looked at the way I dressed and my haircut. I could tell he didn't believe me. "The B-Reactor is decommissioned. No one works out there."

"No," I said in a sleepy tone, resting my head against the window. "There are people out there."

"Where's your ID badge?"

I reached down for my lanyard, remembering I gave it to the nurse. He became uncomfortable and would've kicked me out, but I was nodding off. The radiation sickness and all the smoke I had inhaled made it hard to stay awake.

In my hypnogogic state, I kept thinking about Seattle... We were going to Seattle... Cher... Deja-Vu... She was going to work there... Stripper pole... Gorilla Gardens... Soundgarden... I could crash at the Monastery... I could see a band... Yellow lines on the road... Endless yellow lines on the road... yellow... road...

The last thing I remember was seeing the silhouette of imposing cliffs on each side of the Columbia River. We drove on, into the night, with Hanford burning behind us.

I dreamt I was the lead singer of Pink Floyd, and they had kicked me out of the band because I sang like a punk. I couldn't pay my bills, and the police were chasing me. I was so tired, I stopped running and fell into a field of poppies. My friends kept shaking my shoulders, trying to wake me, but I was too high from smoking the poppies.

"Get up!" he said. "We're here—the Emerald City—Seattle."

I opened my eyes. The guy who picked me up was standing over me, shaking my shoulder. "Look, you've got to get out. Here's thirty bucks."

In a haze, I took the cash, and he pulled me out of the car. I tripped on the sidewalk and fell to my knees, my hands still gripping the asshole's money. He hurried around to get into his car like he was frightened of me.

He sped onto a freeway on-ramp and disappeared into a sea of red taillights.

Confused, I took the time to check out my surroundings. I was leaning against the basement window of a brownstone, under a three-story wrought iron fire-escape. I'd never seen apartments like this except on television. Living in Richland was more like living on a military base. Most apartments there were newish bland structures.

It was misty, and the streetlamps pushed through the fog like alien beams from 1950s sci-fi saucers. The only people on the street were two drunk men who stopped to make out against a wall. I could see a streak of morning light. The sun would be up soon, and people would be going to work.

I stood up and shoved the cash into my pocket before someone jumped out of the shadows to mug me. I walked towards a well-lit street called Olive Way. The road cut an opening that gave view to the city skyline, the Space Needle glowing in the distance.

Here I was, Seattle! Was this the perfect ending to a bad dream? Was it real? Was I in heaven?

Still in a mental fog, I crossed a bridge over the interstate with no idea where I was going. I just moved like a bug towards the lights, in awe of all the skyscrapers.

An ocean of cars washed under the freeway.

I'd never been to a city before; my parents considered them sinful. It was frightening and mesmerizing at the same time. I continued for about a block when I came to an intersection.

Ignoring the red light, I looked both ways to dash through the traffic. Then I saw it, the dark silhouette of a church steeple a couple of blocks down. I had seen the picture in Carson's zine. It was unmistakable; this was it, the Monastery. If the legends were true, the kids would still be dancing, and after it died down, I could crash there.

As I approached, I began to feel nervous. The old church looked dark, the streets around it empty. Where was the muffled sound of pumping bass?

I ran up the steps to the front door under the belfry and found it chained. There was a paper notice glued to the door. I stood for five minutes, trying to read the first sentence, until a young metalhead walked by.

"Excuse me, can you please help me?"

"Yeah sure."

"I'm an illiterate person. Could you read this sign for me?"

He stepped up to the door. "It's a violation. '*City of Seattle; Notice of Closure for violation of City Teen Dance Ordinance, 112373. These premises are hereby closed until further notice.*'"

My heart sank into despair. I couldn't believe it. "What the fuck is a Teen Dance Ordinance?"

"Haven't you heard?" said the kid. "No live music or dancing in Seattle for people under twenty-one."

"Are you serious?" I reached up and felt the dark brown wood siding, letting my head fall onto the building in disappointment.

"Yeah, it's fucking stupid. We can get a lap dance on every corner but can't see a live band because it'll corrupt our minds. This town is nothin' but a strip show."

"Fuck everyone!" I screamed and kicked the door, spitting on the violation. The metal kid got nervous and split across the street.

I continued to walk towards the center of town, exhausted. The morning light was illuminating the city, causing the skyscrapers to glow in technicolor rays. I kept walking until I came to a large body of water where the city came to a halt. It was Puget Sound.

There was a park looking out to some islands. Mount Rainer was in the distance. Desperate from fatigue, I saw a lone tree surrounded by a fork in the road. Despite the grass being wet, I lay down and fell asleep.

CHAPTER 40

ARMY OF REVOLT

I dreamt I was alone in a classroom, and Fenix was the teacher. He was firm and bullish. He no longer had a shaved head, and he was back to his bread-loaf haircut. Despite wearing a pink Izod shirt, white pants, and cardigan sweater tied around his shoulders, Fenix still wore his dirty *Skoal* baseball cap.

It was as if he'd assumed the identity of our English teacher back in the tenth grade but was still Fenix.

Next to Fenix's desk was a pool table. He smacked the break shot into the stack, knocking the balls into random directions.

"That," he said, standing upright, "is just like fission in a nuclear bomb. The cue ball is the neutron that'll change yer life. Pow! Worse than a million cyclones."

Fenix pointed the pool-stick to a couple of equations on the blackboard.

$$^{238}_{92}U + ^{1}_{0}n \longrightarrow ^{239}_{92}U \xrightarrow[23.5 \text{ min}]{\beta^-} ^{239}_{93}Np \xrightarrow[2.356 \text{ d}]{\beta^-} ^{239}_{94}Pu$$

1/0 N + 239/94 Pu > [240/94 Pu]

"Understand?" said Fenix.

"No." My insides were churning with self-loathing. "I can't do math. I don't have that kind of talent."

263

The classroom door burst open. Bone strutted in, shades glowing with otherworldly fire. He was shirtless but wore an unbuttoned tuxedo vest.

"Bullshit, Deacon." He walked up to Fenix, grabbed the pool cue, and pushed him out of the way. He took a felt eraser and started cleaning the blackboard. "You don't need talent. You just have to be angry." Then he hit the table and began sinking balls like a shark, cigarette hanging from his mouth.

"I am angry!" I shouted at him. "Why did you have to die? You had a purpose. Me, I'm just a waste. I should've been the one who died."

"No," said Bone, looking up from aiming. He dropped the pool cue and held his hands up like Jesus. "You need to quit livin' against a wall. If you are going to be a flower, then you need to blossom. This is your time."

"Stop it!" I muttered, thrashing my head side to side.

"Shut up, Zeb," came a garbled voice. "You're waking up the kid."

I opened my eyes to the sun and immediately shut them.

"I am not. He's still asleep."

"Just try and be quiet. Okay? The kid needs his sleep."

"No, he needs to wake up," came a young voice. "If the cops see him sleeping like this, they'll harass all of us."

I opened my eyes and saw a shaggy man sitting under the tree with two street kids. One of the kids was chugging a tall-boy in a paper sack and threw it on the ground.

"Dammit, Zeb. Pick that up," said the shaggy man. "You know the cops are cool with us bein' here as long as we don't litter."

"Might as well litter," said the other kid. He wore a red flannel shirt and a Seattle Mariners hat. He looked about fourteen yet seemed to be on a different level of maturity. "If this guy doesn't get up, we'll all have to leave."

I stood, looking around, eyes adjusting to the light. Mount Rainier loomed in the distance and a ferry blew its horn as it docked below. Bums and street kids were hanging out. I crossed the street and a couple of boys in jean jackets with overgrown hair like Johnny Ramone blocked my path.

"Hey, got any change?" one asked.

I shook my head and moved on.

Just ahead were rows of merchant tables that lined the sidewalk, leading under an awning into an old-world market. It was open-aired but covered by an upper story, held up by ornate green pillars.

I mingled with the multitude that washed past stalls of every conceivable kind: fruit, meat, art, babies' clothing, and t-shirts with Native American designs. I'd never seen so many people. It was as if the entire population of Richland were crammed into a half-square mile.

At the end of the market were stacks of fish on ice. "One steelhead!" yelled a fishmonger. He threw the salmon over the display. It was caught by another, who wrapped it, then threw it back.

The market opened to a statue of a brass pig, the Emerald City's Marduk, its budding nipples spiritually nursing this city of heathens. The pig's brass hoof-prints were embedded into the sidewalk. They curved in a random fashion, as if the pig meandered stoned, craving slop.

The mouth of the market was a congested street. There were punks and street kids loitering, so I thought I'd linger and take it all in.

Two girls were leaning into an open car window. They saw me and started to fuss with their feathered hair. "Hey, you're cute. Want a date?"

I smiled. "I don't even know you."

They laughed.

I could see my reflection in the large shop windows. I was filthy, unprofessionally cut greasy hair, yet confident and imposing. I was Carson's future human, uneducated with nothing to lose, the glorious decline of Western hegemony—its final triumph, and most vile stance.

One of the girls got in the car, and the other stood posing on the corner.

No wonder my parents stayed away from Seattle. The town had emerged from the Gold Rush, and its origin in booze, gambling, and prostitution still hung in the air. Excitement was everywhere. It was even more glorious than I'd imagined.

I was about to walk up the street when I saw a glowing sign with a woman's legs in fishnets and heels. It had neon lettering towering above it. I didn't bother taking the time to read it. I knew what it was.

An icy feeling came over me. This was it. It's where Cher said she was going to get a job.

The old butter-colored building haunted me. Every inch of my being wanted to go into that den of sin and see her. But the memory of her letter stood like a wall. Cher had made it clear; she didn't want me.

For Cher, that letter served as closure. But not for me. I wanted to confront her, hundreds of miles from where we met, here on noble ground. The person she left back in Richland no longer existed. He was born a loser without a brain. I was free of that person. For me to have closure, she would have to leave the real me.

I ran across the street before the light turned green. Cars were coming at me, skidding and honking. I didn't care; I was chasing Cher down her path of destruction. I made it to the doors and mounted the crimson carpeted staircase. Thunderous bass moved through my chest with each step. I was frightened. What would I find? I wanted to run but couldn't.

My heart pulled me up the steps until I came to a man guarding the gate. He was stout, hair in a ponytail, and wore green-tinted glasses.

"Welcome." He smiled. "It's a five-dollar cover, twenty for lap-dances. Can I see your ID?"

"How old do you have to be?" I said, handing him my card.

"Old enough to vote." He opened the gate.

The place had a dank smell to it. They needed to change the carpets.

I looked, and behold, a whirlwind came around the brass pole. Lights, a great cloud of fire, infolding itself; a brightness the color of amber, as near-naked angels descended upon horny men.

And there they sat, facing the stage. Loneliness gave the room a heavy feeling of darkness.

Strippers approached, touching them, listening to their mundane conversation. These men consumed by the lust that coiled within, this serpent that climbs up a spine, commanding men to produce fruit and multiply. I watched as they debased themselves, paying for a woman's flesh and attention, allowing themselves to believe that the girls were enjoying their company. They were powerless.

The place was diseased.

I watched a young redhead leading an older man to an area partitioned off by a curtain.

Do not look behind the curtain, Deacon Jones! You will not like what you see. Ignore what lies behind that curtain.

I pulled it back to glance into the room. Rows of partitioned couches lined the wall, each with a girl grinding on some guy. My eyes went from couch to couch, looking, until they landed on her. Even with her back to me, I knew it was Cher. Though she was thinner, I would never mistake her. I'd replayed my hand caressing that back a thousand times.

She was on top of an unwashed man in his fifties who wore a sleeveless Seattle Sonics jersey, pushing her groin into his belly. He lay back in ecstasy as my entire life force drained from my ears to ankles. My heart fell to my stomach, spontaneously combusting as it encountered digestive juices.

I was hurt and enthralled at the same time. I couldn't move. I just stood and watched him grab Cher's breasts, breasts that I had cherished and yearned for. Her stomach was bare and pure, waiting for me to lay my head on and listen to her heart.

She kept swatting his hands away while grinding to Van Hallen's *Hot for Teacher*. This was Fenix's music, bringing me back to the inadequacies of my youth.

I was frozen until a young voice interrupted. "You shouldn't be back here unless you're with a girl."

"Huh?" I was startled and whirled around to see a cocktail waitress wearing a corset and fishnet stockings.

"This is the VIP Lounge. You can't be here without a girl. Find a table in the main room, and I'll bring you a drink. What'll you have?"

"I'm too young to drink."

She rolled her eyes. "We don't serve alcohol. State law. Soft drinks or juice."

"I'm not thirsty," I told her while watching Cher grind and rub.

"There's a one-drink minimum. House rules," she said.

"I'll take a Coke."

"That'll be five dollars."

"Five dollars?" I said, paying her, "Jesus."

"Thanks for the tip."

"Hey," I yelled after her. "Here." I handed her a couple of bucks. "Sorry, I'm new at this."

I went out and sat down in front of the brass pole, nursing my watered-down pop, listening to the loud music: "I wanna know what love is. I want you to show me..."

Song after song, Cher was grinding on that guy in the next room. I squeezed the plastic cup in agony, causing the pop to spill on my hand. Christ, would it ever end? What was I even doing here, anyway?

My torture was interrupted by a slender hand on my shoulder. I looked up. It was a stunning brunette with long hair in a fluorescent green bikini and red stilettos. "Want a dance?" she said, sliding her hand along my inner thigh.

"No, thanks," I said.

She stood up and walked off as I continued to watch for Cher.

After *You Shook Me All Night Long* by AC/DC, Cher emerged, stuffing a few twenties into her bra.

She walked from table to table, soliciting lap dances. She would stop, pretend to be interested in a guy, make small talk with him until he turned her down for a lap dance. One of the guys grabbed her arm, thumbed her cutting scars, and rudely turned her away with a motion of disgust. I wanted to kill him.

Cher made her way to my table and started stroking my chest from behind. I watched her hand slide down towards my crotch, nails painted blood red. I could see needle marks among her cutting scars.

She slithered around and sat, sliding her hands between my legs. "Hi, my name's Jinjur. Can I take you around the corner for a private dance?"

I'd never seen one before. I didn't have to; Cher was a junkie.

CHAPTER 41

GREEN RIVER

She looked as though she'd aged ten years. Her eyes were sunken. She was quite skinny and had lost her softness; her hard side had consumed her.

Despite the change, I would have known her anywhere, and yet she didn't recognize me. Had I meant so little to her?

"Cher, it's me, Deacon."

She looked at me, confused. I knew I'd lost her, but I just couldn't let go.

Then a momentary spark of light animated her face. "Deacon?" She said my name in a way that told me deep down in the isolated spot untouched by the wicked realities of this earth; I brought her some level of comfort. She pulled her hand from my body and sat in the chair across from me, stunned. She was silent for a moment. "What are you doing here?"

"I've left Richland." I put my hand on her arm.

She pulled away, then stopped. A strange spiteful look spread across her face. "Deacon, I don't want you here."

"I know you're working. Can I get your number and call you later?"

"No," she said, "I don't want to see you. I thought I made that clear when I left Richland."

"Can we talk?"

She shot out of her seat. I grabbed her arm, and she pulled away. A bouncer goon appeared from the shadows. "This guy bothering you, Jinjur?" He was muscular and veiny. He had combed his cruelly chopped bangs straight forward to hide his receding hairline.

Cher hesitated. "It's okay," she said to the bouncer. "Deacon, you'd better go."

The bouncer motioned me to the door. "Time to leave, pal."

"Cher, can I have your number?"

She bit her lower lip and shook her head. The guy grabbed me by the arm to escort me to the door. In a rage, I pulled free. "I'm leaving, okay."

Another bouncer came, and they lifted me, dragging me by the arms towards a back door.

"This is what happens to assholes," one of them said as they threw me down a concrete staircase. I refused to cry out in pain and just took it. One of them opened the door to the alley, while the other threw me out onto a pile of trash and cardboard. My head hit some pipes that led to an electrical box, mounted to the side of the building.

I writhed in agony, filling my nostrils with the smell of piss and rotten food. I just lay there, defeated.

My emotions were in control. I felt I should run, get the hell out of there, but my heartbreak was pushing me into obsession. My spirit hovered above my bruised body and said, "Run, Deacon; leave this poor broken daughter. You cannot fix her, and it would be wise for you to go. Close your heart and live on to love someone else." But this body, slow with math and unable to spell, stayed in that alley.

The door opened and out came a girl in tassels and a G-string, relishing the warm day. The bouncer that kicked me out followed, reaching over, lighting her cigarette. I could tell he liked her, but she was beyond him.

I hid behind some cardboard boxes and watched them, determined to stay there all day if necessary. I knew it wouldn't be long, and my instincts proved correct.

Out of the back door came a skinny guy with a greasy mullet, pockmarked cheeks, and a purple Polo shirt tucked into high waist jeans. He opened the door for Cher.

I sat forward, removing my back from the wall, but remained seated. They said "Hi" to the stripper and bouncer, then walked into the most private part of the alley where no one could see them but me.

Cher got onto her knees and unzipped his pants. I sat polarized, unable to move, my heart breaking, mortified and fascinated, all at the same time.

Embarrassment, fury, revulsion, disgust, and confusion about how this world could be so cruel spread through me like a fast-moving poison. I wanted to grab her and travel back to a time when the universal rule was love, but instead tortured myself by watching the woman I loved service this guy for junk.

My agony was short-lived. He zipped up his pants, reached into his pocket and pulled out a Ziplock bag of powder, throwing it onto the ground. Cher instantly lunged for the bag, and the guy put his tennis shoes onto her shoulder and kicked her back, causing her to fall on her ass.

"Junkie whore," he said, disappearing into the parking lot.

Cher quickly opened the bag and pinched a little snort to quell her burn, saving the rest for the needle. She sat there for a moment, savoring the rush, too absorbed to notice my presence.

"Hey, Jinjur," yelled the bouncer, "you know you're not supposed to give extras or snort junk in the alley."

"Fuck you," Cher said under her breath.

Nervous, I decided to make my presence known. "Cher," I whispered loud enough for her to hear.

She sat there bobbing back and forth, looking confused.

"Cher."

She slowly looked up, trying to adjust her eyes to the shadows.

"Deacon?"

I moved forward so she could see me.

Her features became distorted by an unstable rage, her skin bristling with an emotionally complex cocktail of shame turning to anger. "Fuck you," she said, with as much hatred a soul could conjure. She lunged and started hitting me. "You fucking son of a bitch! How dare you come here."

I backed away, trying to dodge her attack.

"Hank," she screamed.

The bouncer ran over to us, grabbing me by the hair and smashing his fist into my face, his rings breaking my skin. I could feel my brains jolt to the back of my skull with each hit. I fell to the ground, and he gave me a massive kick on the back of my thigh.

"I thought I told you to get lost."

Cher moved him out of the way and spat on me, pushing me back into the garbage with her sharp stiletto heel. "Get the fuck away from me, Deacon."

She went back into the club with the bouncer, wobbling along the uneven pavement in her heels, panties, and bra.

I lay in misery, my heart and body crushed, my face bleeding. My ribs hurt, and I struggled to get up.

Defeated, embarrassed and heartbroken, I left the alley. What was I doing? Where was I going to sleep? Seattle was turning out to be more difficult than I expected. The underage haven Carson had described in Milk-Bone no longer existed—if it ever did. I began to realize a life of freedom on the streets was just a fantasy. I was a fool.

Maybe I just needed to go home. I decided to call my parents. They probably thought I was dead. I kept walking until I came upon a payphone. I picked up the receiver and punched zero.

"Collect call... Deacon Jones... Hello? Mom?... Yeah, I'm fine... I know; sorry. I'm okay... I'm in Seattle."

"What are you doing there?" she said, almost hysterical.

"There was a fire."

"We know. We were so worried."

"It was horrible; I got scared and left. I had to get out of there. I was choking on the smoke. It was everywhere. I hitched a ride, and this is where I ended up."

"You need to go to a church right now," she said. "They can keep you safe until your father comes to get you."

Her words hit me like the bouncer's fist. What choice did I have? I had no job, no place to stay, yet the sound of her voice telling me what to do began to infuriate me.

"Deacon, hold on. We're getting you the church's address. There's one in an area called Ballard. The pastor is one of our friends."

This was it. I was like that Bat Caver Rex in Carson's basement, except I'd only made it a half day. That fucker made it a whole month.

I thought about Carson's words, the memory of them strong and piercing, "You can always get the fuck out of Richland, but Richland has a mysterious way of pulling you back."

There was nothing I could do; I let my mashed head hit the side of the phone booth, giving in.

As I stood there, waiting, I looked to my left and saw a lamp post covered in posters. One flyer stood out. It was a black and white Xerox of five scraggly guys in longish hair who looked like they never bathed. They weren't Butt Rockers, Metalheads, or Punks. They were something else, like me, born defeated.

They were part of the first generation in a century that wasn't going to do as well as their parents. There would be no union factory job waiting for the undereducated, no high-end tech job for the dropout. Looking into their Xeroxed eyes, I felt we occupied the same situation—brothers between universes.

The poster seemed to embrace the antithesis of everything my parents held sacred. They were unclean, not just in a hygienic way; they were sinful. Like Christians, their bodies were their temple, but this temple worshipped the erosion of all the morals put down by Ronald & Nancy. Gone were the values that stated you had to be clean-cut to get a job because there was no job worth being clean for, or that you had to study music to create it, or that your inner peace had to come through Jesus.

I took a long look at the poster, taking the time to read it, so I understood every word:

Gureen Riv… Liv… Voe… Polnome… Cat Butt…
Green River—Live at the Vogue, tonight!
With special guests,
Polychrome and Cat Butt

Green River and Polychrome! I had been listening to these bands on my Walkman for weeks. I knew their songs, and, like Carson, I knew they were the future. These bands were going to make it; a whole new sub-genre would come out of this moment in time. To be a part of something, to be there as it took off, to watch it from the very beginning—there must be some virtue in that?

Staring at that poster, I knew for sure I'd found my calling. I needed this experience. I had no musical talent, but I wanted to be a part of it, whatever it was. Just giving myself over to the music would be enough. I was beginning to see that destiny had pulled me to this very spot.

"Deacon, write down this address, and your father will come and get you." My mother's voice drew me back into the conversation. Then I thought about my parents' alphabet house in

Richland with Ronald Reagan smiling on the TV, speaking about his "Moral Majority," Jerry Falwell telling us how to live and what to believe, trudging out to work at Hanford, and getting married to Mikultra Skala.

No, I wasn't born to make bombs; I was born to be a bomb. I could live on the street, begging for change, avoiding the cops, never having to answer to one goddam person.

I turned from the poster and looked at the numbers on the phone and said, "Mom, I'm not going to the church. I'm going to stay here. From now on, Seattle is my home." I hung up before she could talk me out of it.

CHAPTER 42

POLYCHROME

The Vogue was down the street from the strip club. It was in a turn of the century brick building with wooden windows protruding from the upper stories. The ground level windows were blackened. People entered the club through a door off to the side that was used to access the apartments upstairs.

I loitered in line under the blue neon "Vogue" sign, looking at all the Xeroxed fliers that hung in the hall. There was so much music in this town. I never wanted to leave. I watched the bouncer at the back of the hall checking IDs. There was no way I was going to get in, so I went outside to see if I could somehow sneak in the back door.

The brick wall on the side of the building was illuminated by streetlamps. It was covered in graffiti, mostly band names: "The Accüsed," "Screaming Trees," "10 Minute Warning;" and strange, stylized writing that my dyslexic mind could not decipher.

I was standing there, worshiping the wall as if I'd arrived in Jerusalem, knowing I'd made the right choice. I had a few thousand dollars in the bank, enough to rent a room and survive for a few months until I found a job. In the meantime, I could sleep on the street. It didn't matter.

The sound of high heeled shoes clacking on the asphalt disrupted my thoughts. It was a stunning girl with a Vidal Sassoon bob. She wore black stretch jeans gripping perfect hips and a t-shirt with the arms cut off, leaving holes so large that I could see her bra. The writing on her shirt said 'J. Hadley Experience.' I recognized the logo. It was a clothing boutique Carson had mentioned in Milk-Bone.

She had round John Lennon type sunglasses and her fingernails were painted black. The only thing that wasn't black was her bright red lipstick.

The woman walked towards me like a wicked angel, looking me up and down. She took off her sunglasses, revealing an exquisite face filled with concern. "Are you alright?"

She was so beautiful that I forgot I had a cut-up face, stained by soot from the fire. "Yeah; why?"

"You're covered in blood. Who did this to you?"

"Some guy down the street," I said.

"Why don't you come inside and get cleaned up."

"I'm only eighteen," I said, embarrassed.

"Then you should go home. You're filthy and that cut could get infected."

I watched her leave then went around to the back alley where I saw a group of musicians hanging out in front of an open van parked under the fire escape. I sat down with my back against the graffitied bricks, listening to their conversation. They looked like they were straight out of the movie *Children of the Corn*, with long, unwashed hair.

"Fucking dick always disappears to get high when it's time to load gear," said one of them.

Two of them were struggling with a large speaker cabinet.

"I'll help you load up," I said.

They turned to look at me.

I stood up. "I'll be your roadie if you let me in."

They looked at each other. "Alright," said one with his hair in a side part, "but you help us before we go on and the load out too."

"Anything," I said.

"What's your name?"

"Deek Jones."

"I'm Oscar, and this is Tip and Sal."

"You guys Cat Butt?" I said, taking hold of one end of an Ampeg bass cabinet.

They laughed. "Fuck no. We're Polychrome."

"I know your music," I said.

Tip shot me a suspicious look.

"I got your demo off a guy named Carson."

"Don't know him."

When we finished putting all the equipment next to the stage, Oscar approached me. "After Cat Butt, meet us by the gear. You can help us move it onto the stage. We go on at eleven."

"See you then," I said.

The inside of the club was dark, and you could barely see the hundred-year-old bricks with random cement patches adding to the grungy nature of the place. Smoke collected up around the rafters. The ceiling was a series of thin cross beams covered by a wood slat floor, allowing the bands to blast the upstairs neighbors. The room was a long rectangle with the stage at the back and a bar off to the northern side.

I went to the bathroom to clean up, then went to explore the club. The girl with the Vidal bob was leaning against the bar. I stood next to her.

"I see you washed your face." She smiled. "And you somehow got in."

"Yeah, I'm Oscar's new roadie."

"Well I'm the Vogue's booking agent," she said. "I could have you thrown out."

I smiled at her. "I promise not to drink."

"You look like you need a drink." She flagged the bartender, a transgender girl with shoulder-length frizzy red hair, long earrings, and a tight leopard print shirt that hung above the navel.

"Two Jagers," she said.

I went to take out my wallet.

"I'm buying, you look like you're down on your luck. How old did you say you were?"

"Eighteen."

"Jesus," she said.

The bartender returned with our drinks.

"Well my little jailbait, here's to you." She handed me a long, slim shot glass. I took a sip; the sweet syrupy concoction of anise and citrus peel burned my throat on the way down.

"It's going to be a good show tonight," she said. "Green River has what it takes to put this town on the map." She downed her Jagermeister in one quick gulp. I followed her lead, trying not to cough it up. "You'll like Cat Butt." She motioned to the bartender for two more. "Polychrome's another band to watch, but you should know, as you're Oscar Diggs' guitar tech."

She handed me another shot. "So what's your name?"

"Deek."

"My name's Ann Soforth. Do you have a place to live?"

"No," I said, embarrassed. "I just got into town."

I was starting to feel the effects of the Jagermeister when a chunky guitar sounded out the call.

This was it; I was alive! We downed our drinks.

"Come on," I said, grabbing her hand.

"Oh no, I don't slam dance."

"Come on." I pulled Ann into the mosh-pit where we submitted to the maelstrom and entered the chaos.

When the song ended, Ann dropped into my arms, and my hands grabbed her sweaty bare midriff. She felt good and firm.

"Want to know something funny," she said. "I've never been in a mosh-pit until tonight." She reached up and pulled me by the back of the neck into a kiss of abandon. Then she pulled away, looking troubled. "I shouldn't have done that; you're only eighteen." She looked up at me, pleadingly.

"So?" I said, pulling her back towards me. "How old are you?"

"Twenty-three."

Something distracted me, so I let go of her and stood back for a moment, watching the crowd go nuts, swirling like a tornado. She looked at me, confused as if I felt twenty-three was too old, but I was distracted by the mosh-pit. There was a strange energy in the air; I could feel it.

I knew then that Adonai was right; at any one point in time, throughout our day, throughout history, somewhere, there is a convergence. Be it in the stars, a confluence of solar energy or gravities, or just getting caught in the eddies of fate where the air sizzles with perfection. This was one of those moments, and it was happening right there. Everything was in alignment.

Ann was about the most beautiful girl I'd ever seen. Instead of making me nervous, it felt natural. I was underage, in a bar, watching the birth of a movement. The mosh-pit started to swirl, and I could see beauty and order within the chaos. Though I couldn't understand math, I could harness the equation of this fractal.

Everyone is born with a season, a section of time where a person's potential matches the flow of what is happening, and anything is possible. Watching all those people swirl in that violent tornado, I knew this was my time. I was in control. I could be the shepherd that took this scene to the next level. My defects that society had invested money and effort into changing were now going to work to my benefit. I just knew it. My time had come, where everything I touched would be a win.

I failed school—but I wasn't going to be a failure. I was only capable of dead-end employment—but I would thrive as my own boss, and I would not be poor. I had made bad choices—jobs, girls, friends like Fenix—but now I had clarity. I was awake, and I was alive.

"Fuck it," I said, pulling Ann to me by her naked back just above her hip-hugging pants. She passionately kissed me, and we dragged ourselves into the darkest corner, giving over to the rush of the deafening din, making out until Cat Butt left the stage.

I stopped kissing Ann. "I have to go help Polychrome set up. I'll be back for their set."

The band wasn't by their equipment, so I stepped out back and saw them congregated by their open van.

"Get up motherfucker!" Tip was shaking a guy lying in the van's hull. He punched him in the arm.

The guy curled further into fetal position. "Leave me alone," he mumbled.

"Fuck you, Henry," shouted Tip. He turned to the others. "What are we gonna do? We go on in three minutes."

"We have to cancel," said Sal.

"You don't cancel when you're opening for Green fucking River," said Oscar.

"We can do instrumentals," said Tip.

"Yeah sure," said Sal.

I stepped forward. "Hey, I can sing."

They all turned, looked at me annoyed, then went back to talking.

"I can try to sing," said Oscar.

"Do you know the words?" said Tip.

"No."

I stood back, and sang as loud as I could:
"Gonna come, a come, a come to you
depression hits
all, all the way through-hoo."
They turned, shocked.

"I told you," I said. "I have your demo. I know every song."

"We can't go on stage with you," said Oscar. "You haven't rehearsed with us. This is a band problem."

"Alright," I said, turning to walk off. "I'll be by the equipment after you've worked this out."

Polychrome emerged late, and we moved the band's equipment to the stage. I went back to Ann. She was leaning against the wall and rolled into me. We were kissing as they walked on stage. The band tore into it without introduction. It sounded better than their demo. It was music unlike any I'd ever heard; music of discontent, driving and noisy. There were no vocals, just instruments. It was like punk, but a twist of metal mixed with needless rage. I pulled Ann into the mosh pit.

I'd never heard this song before, but I knew this music. It was like punching your way out of a drug-induced cocoon, like the day I quit taking Ritalin. Around we went, swirling, thrashing, reveling in our aggression.

Then the song stopped. The guitar player stepped up to the mic. "Our singer is out in the van, passed out," he said as the club went silent, "so we're fuckin goin' on without him."

The crowd booed.

"Hey, come on," said Oscar, "only a dick shoots up before a gig."

The crowd started to chant, "Henry, Henry, Henry."

"We're going to play some instrumentals," said Oscar.

The crowd continued chanting. Tip walked over and whispered into Oscar's ear.

"Alright," said Oscar, "calm down. We got a new roadie today who claims he can sing our songs." The crowd started to boo. "In fact, he's so new, I don't remember his name. He's around here somewhere. He's got a mashed-up face and is wearing a jacket with Loser painted on the back."

Ann looked at me, shocked. I climbed on stage as the crowd went silent. Tip and Oscar surrounded me. "You know our demo, right?"

"Every song."

"That's three," said Tip. "In order to get paid, we need to do one more. Do you know Master of Puppets?"

"I don't do metal," I said.

"How about Stranglehold?"

"The Nuge? Get real."

"Well, what do you know?"

"How about We got the Neutron Bomb?" I said.

"The Weirdos?" Tip and Oscar looked at each other and grinned. "We do that song every set. Let's do it now."

I stepped up to the mic and looked at the audience, each person curious, wondering what this small-town fuck in the Loser jacket was going to sound like. Though every eye was on me, I wasn't nervous, and for the first time in my life, I did not feel shy. I heard drumsticks: click, click, click, click... Then power at my back.

All the years of my parents guiding me, telling me how to dress, keeping me from music and television, ramming the bible down my throat; teachers drilling me to the right when every inch of me wanted to go left; the books with jumbled letters; Steve Hannity shoving me into a locker; Cher and her father who destroyed her; Bone for taking his own life; the pills... the ones that had the CIBA/34 engraved on buffered tablets. It all came out as I screamed into that microphone, pulling out every bit of rage that had been hiding within the nuclear membranes of my smallest cells.

Anger!

I felt it, the air sizzling around me, that convergence of energies. I knew the entire world would listen, and they would never forget me. I knew then that I wasn't made to excel in math. I wasn't born to read or score in academics. I wasn't created to be an indentured servant, putting in forty-plus on the line, barely making enough to get by. And I knew that at this moment I had met my destiny. I would no longer be a victim because it felt too good to be angry.

284

This moment was perfect; nothing could be added, nothing taken.

Good to be angry.

Angry...

GET THE MESSAGE OUT!

Canadian poet **Simon Occulis** was born Brandon Pitts in Los Angeles, California. Shaped by teenage years spent in Richland, Washington, epicenter of America's cold war offensive where his high school logo was an image of the Mushroom Cloud over Nagasaki, his art evolved into a unique assessment of our times.

After immigrating to Canada, Occulis rose as an influential force in Toronto's Gadist literary movement, being cited as an "Emerging Voice" by the Diaspora Dialogues in 2011.

Backed by electrifying poetry recitals in Canada, the United States, and Europe, **Occulis'** three poetry books, written as Brandon Pitts: *Pressure to Sing, Tender in Age of Fury,* and *In the Company of Crows,* received both popular and critical acclaim. Each book enjoys a cult following and has gone into multiple pressings.

The Gospel of Now is the debut of **Occulis** and the first of a series of projects under this new artistic identity.

Occulis now lives in Montreal.

ACKNOWLEDGEMENTS

There is no such thing as a work of art that is conceived by one mind, birthed from an isolated talent. There are always contributions from others.

A special thanks to Essie Diamond for editing this novel and her essential critiques. Essie's involvement was the turning point in this project. Without her, the manuscript would be in the recycling bin.

And to Jennifer Hosein for reading the rough draft and proofreading the final. Jennifer is a great artist and poet. Check her out.

A thank you to photographer Charles Peterson for allowing me to be inspired by his picture of the Tad/Nirvana show at the University of Washington Ballroom in Seattle. The painting that graces the cover owes a debt to his work. I am told by my brother who attended the show that the stage diver is a guy named Doug the Slug.

I based this novel on my short story, "The BC Crib," published by Bookland Press in their anthology, *Canadian Voices Vol. 2* (2010), and the short story, *Privilege*, published by Conceit Magazine, in their anthology of short fiction, *The Bracelet Charm* (2009).

I want to thank my brother Curtis Pitts (Sub Pop Employee of the Month) because I used Milk Bone, the name of the zine that he published in the late 80s. He and his friends were a big inspiration for this story. He was an immense help getting this book off the ground. There is no better brother than Curtis.

To all the other DIYers who grew up in Richland in the 80s, who made their own demo tapes, had gigs in basements and parties. You know who you are. Thanks for the inspiration.

A thank you to Jehov Hernandez who served as a muse for the initial idea, and Joe Torres, who talked me through some ideas when I was struggling. Joe remembers those days. Also, a special thanks to Miriam Morin for allowing me to interview her to gain crucial insight that helped shape the tone of this book.

The bands mentioned in this novel are real, except Polychrome. I owe a special shout out to the local Richland band, Diddley Squat, whom I describe in the chapters, "A-Street" and "Mikultra." These guys were as much a part of the pre-grunge scene as their Seattle counterparts.

I'd like to give special thanks to James T. Ferris X, singer of the Eastern Washington band, Moral Crux, whose lyrics I quote to the songs: "Law and Order" and "Is There Life Before Death?" Moral Crux was a big inspiration for the ethos of this novel. Buy their records!

I also quote lyrics from the following songs:

Weirdos' "We Got the Neutron Bomb."

Pink Floyd's, "Breathe," along with song titles from "The Dark Side of the Moon."

The Vandal's, "The Legend of Pat Brown"

The Germs', "Lexicon Devil"

Foreigner's, "I Want To Know What Love Is."

Green River's, "Ten-thousand Things"

Thank you to Matt Goody who sat in his office at Mosaic Press, demanding I hand over the shitty first draft so he could give me valuable guidance. Matt, I couldn't have done it without you!

Thank you to Howard Astor of Mosaic Press for believing in me as a literary talent and offering me much needed support and assurance in my time of self-doubt.

Also, a thank you to early advocates of the original Deacon Jones sagas, (the two short stories that took place in Richland), Jasmine D'Costa and Perry Terrel of Conceit Magazine.

I want to thank early beta readers of this work who suffered through subpar drafts; Iddie Forka, Topaz Amber Dawn, IF the Poet, Stedmond Pardy and my mother, who was honest and drove me to make it better.

An extra special thanks to my wife Bexie who read multiple drafts of this book and pushed me to excel, demanding that I raise the bar. Bexie, I've grown so much as an artist thanks to your brutal honesty and constructive insights. Your really are an art consumer par excellence.

Most of all, if you lived in Richland back then; if you were there, you are all one big culmination of the characters and situations in this story. Thank you!

Though there was some exaggeration, most of the situations, names of streets, and sites around Richland and Hanford are real. And those that are fictitious, like the Bockscar Cafe, are based on real places that have since taken down their pictures celebrating the Fat Man bomb and Japanese annihilation. And yes, there really were Atomic Marbles in the gum-ball machines at the Science Center, and Richland High still has a mushroom cloud for a mascot.

I wish I could've mentioned the Atomic Ale Brewpub in Richland, but they weren't around in those days. But hey, I wrote my short story, the BC Crib while drinking their Plutonium Porter at the bar, getting dollar discounts because it was the anniversary of the Manhattan Project.

And last but not least, if you think I've been talking about you; the names, characters, and situations in this book are fictitious. I'm all about writing bullshit to protect the guilty.

Blessings and love,
Yours,
Occulis — 2am, le Plateau, Montreal, December 2021

Statement from the author

Being a teenager in a Manhattan Project town forms the foundation of my art. When you grow up in a community where the people are proud that they made the plutonium for the Nagasaki and Trinity Test bombs, you can't get away from it. Social commentary's going into the mix.

I created the Gospel of Now, along with the companion artworks, to document that surreal space of living in an isolated Manhattan Project town at the zenith of the Cold War, and its under-documented contribution, along with other rural Washington State communities, to the Seattle cultural explosion of the 90s.

The illustrations for the Gospel of Now were created using woodcut prints, inspired by the work of Paul Gauguin and the German Expressionist Die Brücke. The wood gives my lines a medieval quality to contrast with the technological achievements of the atomic age. I also used this method to pay homage to the DIY zines of the 1980s who used primitive self-taught graphic techniques. The original Milk Bone zine carved its logo into a rubber erasure to use as a stamp.

For the cover and companion paintings used for promotion, I made the oil paint using the pre-industrial technique of grinding powdered pigment into linseed oil by hand.

Using pre-industrial art supplies and methods enabled me to contrast the collective hope and pride of the community that created the plutonium for the first atomic bomb with the current reality, a community dedicated to the environmental cleanup of the Hanford Site, and its resilient ability to reinvent itself and reconcile its past.